I0587193

SENSING TRUTH

Susan C. Daffron

A Jennings & O'Shea Novel

Book 3

Published by Magic Fur Press
An imprint of Logical Expressions, Inc.
P.O. Box 383
Ponderay, ID 83852

This is a work of fiction. All names, characters, places, and events are either the product of the author's imagination or are used fictitiously. Any resemblance to actual persons, living or dead, business organizations, events, or locales is purely coincidental.

Sensing Truth

Copyright © 2017 by Susan C. Daffron
All rights reserved.

No part of this book may be reproduced, transmitted, or distributed in any printed or electronic form without the prior written permission of both the copyright owner and the publisher.

ISBN: 978-1-61038-052-2 (paperback)
       978-1-61038-053-9 (EPUB)

Like all of my books, *Sensing Truth* is dedicated to
my husband James Byrd,
my best friend and biggest supporter.
Thanks for everything!

<u>Books by Susan C. Daffron</u>
The Alpine Grove Romantic Comedies
Chez Stinky

Fuzzy Logic

The Art of Wag

Snow Furries

Bark to the Future

Howl at the Loon

The Good, the Bad, and the Pugly

The Treasure of the Hairy Cadre

The Luck of the Paw

Daydream Retriever

The Hound of Music

The Jennings & O'Shea Mysteries
Sensing Trouble

Sensing Secrets

Sensing Truth

Chapter 1

Undercover

I had a normal life once. But that life is over. In fact, I can safely say that 1997 has been the most bizarre year of my thirty-three on this planet. First, I thought I'd lost my mind. Then I thought I'd lost my mother. After I found Mom, I had a better idea of what was wrong with me. I learned that I may not be crazy, but whatever *is* wrong with me has made my life considerably more complicated.

I was sitting at a table across from Riley O'Shea. When we met, I thought he might be my stepbrother because we thought our parents had gotten married without telling us. As it turns out, they didn't marry, so we're not even distantly related. Now I'm not entirely sure what Riley is. Definitely a friend. And now more like a friend with considerable benefits. But even the best of friends don't always agree, and Riley was irritated with me. His response wasn't unusual, particularly when he became obstinate.

With my most sympathetic frownie face, I said, "I told you, you wouldn't like the idea. But you know why I'm suggesting it, don't you?"

"I know," he grumbled.

"No one is going to believe that someone as thin as you are doesn't have a serious medical problem."

1

"I get it." Riley stood up and grabbed my plate from the table. "But I still can't believe you want me to do this, and I definitely don't have to like it."

"You know it makes sense."

He stomped over to the kitchen and dropped the plates into the sink with more force than was probably necessary. His fluffy dog Zelda followed him like a white shadow, hoping that some crumb or morsel of food might miraculously leap off one of the plates into her mouth. With a glance down at the dog, he turned to face me, leaned on the sink, and crossed his arms. "Meg, I'm serious. I *really* don't want to shave my head."

"Do you have any other ideas? We need disguises. All the people who have been chasing us know you as the skinny dude with the hot Mustang and the long hair."

"I put Shelby in storage. Wasn't giving up my car enough?"

"I know it was difficult because you love that car, but the problem is you still look like you. Glasses might be a good idea too."

"My eyesight is fine. I don't need or want glasses. This idea keeps getting worse all the time." He pointed at me. "So what's your disguise supposed to be? All that red hair of yours stands out too, you know. If I have to shave my head, you have to cut your hair."

I tugged at a long strand of my auburn locks. "But I don't look good with short hair."

"Worse than I'll look with *no* hair?"

He had me there. "I suppose I could trim it a little."

"They had that henna stuff in different colors. If you cut your hair and dye it, no one will recognize you. Maybe you can get some geeky glasses and those heavy black clodhopper shoes. Then you'd be like a more well endowed version of that real estate office assistant we met in Seattle. You can be a pseudo-goth Pacific Northwest urban dweller."

"You mean that woman who looked like a black-and-white photograph? Yuck. The monochrome motif doesn't work for me. I'd resemble a walking zombie, and even in the Northwest that's not considered attractive."

"Disguises were your idea."

"I've been bombed, attacked, and threatened more in the last few weeks than I have been in my entire life. You can't argue with the fact that we need to lay low."

Riley sat down at the table, scrubbed his face with his palms, and dropped his hands with a thump. "It's so cold and damp here, my head is going to freeze."

"You can buy a hat. We need to think up some new names too. I was thinking maybe you could be Ryan, so I'd be less likely to screw it up."

Riley grinned. "Since you tend to keep me amused, you can be Maggie Mae."

"You're hilarious, but I refuse to be named after a Rod Stewart song." I pointed at him. "Plus, hello? Like Meg, Maggie is a nickname for Margaret."

"Too bad, I kinda liked it. If you can't handle inspiration from Rod the Bod, how about Mandy by Barry Manilow?"

I pondered the lyrics of the song. "That's incredibly sappy, but oddly appropriate. I guess I can live with Mandy."

Riley got up, walked around the table, and leaned down to give me a quick kiss. "You're more of a gooey romantic than you let on, Mandy."

I reached out and grabbed his hand before he walked off. "Yo, Ryan, this story works for you. You just had chemotherapy and you want to do something good with your life, in case the chemo doesn't take. So you decided to go volunteer with this environmental group."

"I'm a tree-hugger with cancer. How uplifting." He squeezed my hand. "So what's your story, Mandy?"

"We're a couple, and I came with you to the retreat." I smiled. "I don't want to change that part. We've been through so much together that I can't pretend we're random acquaintances. I'm not that good an actress."

"It would be difficult." He let go of my hand and returned to the kitchen. "But you'll have to come up with more of a back story for Mandy to make it believable."

"I'm working on it." I followed him. Zelda wasn't the only one hoping for more food. Riley was an amazing cook, and I was still hungry. "Have you figured out what to do about transportation? Ryan and Mandy can't drive into this retreat in a rental car that has your real name all over the paperwork."

"I scanned through the local classifieds. What do you think about a Bronco?"

"I assume you don't mean an unruly horse. Is that an automobile?"

"There's a guy selling a 1977 Ford Bronco not too far from here."

"You do realize that means nothing to me. What does it look like?"

"It's a four-by-four. The good news is that it should be good in the mud around here. The bad news is that this one might not actually run. The ad says "as is" and that it's been sitting in the guy's yard for a while, so he might be willing to sell it for parts."

"Parts? As in pieces? Given the amount of rain, it's probably rusted into a pile of twisted metal. If, by some miracle it's still whole, we'd need a chain saw to extract it from the vegetation."

"Maybe, but old Broncos are cool."

"I'll take your word for it. If Ryan is the kind of guy who would drive a twenty-year-old Bronco, it works for me."

"If I can get it to run, Zelda would love it. We could get to hiking trails that we've never been able to access before."

"That would be after we come up with disguises, infiltrate this mysterious retreat, figure out what's wrong with our senses, determine why Enviro Freedom wants our parents to do research for them, and then understand the connection between Enviro Freedom, Archetypal Online Systems, and Hector's band of creeps. Oh, and after that, we need to find some way to convince people to stop spewing the harmful radiation that's making our lives miserable."

"I suppose we do have a few things we have to deal with first."

"Just a few."

～

As it turns out, going undercover is more complicated than you might expect. It's not like there's a manual or classes you can take that explain what you need to do. But one thing's for sure—you can't go around using your own identification. Sooner or later, someone asks for your driver's license and your cover is blown. So our first task was to figure out how to obtain or create new IDs. Riley seemed convinced that he could make something passable, but I wasn't quite so optimistic.

Our rental car also could be traced back to Riley, so we needed to return it sooner rather than later. Buying everything with cash to avoid detection of our whereabouts was going to be a pain, but I didn't see any other way to get us completely off the radar. Any decent PI could track us by following our trail of credit-card usage, but one advantage of holing up at a secret retreat is that your shopping options are limited.

After breakfast, we brought Zelda with us in the rental car to find a store where we could buy lamination supplies. I still didn't like this idea at all and expressed my concerns to Riley.

He scratched at the stubble on his scruffy chin and sighed. "Meg, would you stop worrying. We're not going to get caught."

"What else do people laminate *other* than fake IDs? Don't you think buying this stuff is going to raise a few eyebrows?"

"People laminate all kinds of stuff. No one will notice." Riley hit the turn signal. "But first, I want to check out this Bronco."

"We can't look at a car before you have your fake ID. Riley O'Shea needs to disappear, not go out and get a new car."

"When you're buying a junker, no one checks your ID. Sellers are usually so thrilled to be rid of it, they take the cash and wave goodbye."

"But you haven't cut off your hair yet either. We need to get clippers."

"Although I'm eagerly anticipating my impending baldness, that's going to have to wait until after I check out our new ride."

"But if you buy it, your name will be on the title!"

"Relax." Riley glanced away from the road to grin at me. "I have a plan."

Sometimes I didn't like Riley's plans, but he was driving, so there wasn't much I could do. I silently watched the drizzle outside the windows as we wound down the rural roads. We turned onto a one-lane gravel road that deteriorated into a patchwork of muddy potholes. Riley attempted to swerve around them with only limited success.

The front wheel slammed into a deep crater, and he mumbled "Sorry."

"The rental car folks are going to be thrilled. We need to return this poor car before you kill it. Good thing they don't know what you did to your last car."

Riley raised his eyebrows. "I can't believe you're bringing that up. I sacrificed Shelby's paint job to save your bacon."

"*Your* bacon was involved too, as I recall."

He parked in a grassy area and an elderly German shepherd who had been sleeping on the front porch stood up, woofed twice, and having successfully completed his guard-dog duties, returned to a horizontal state to continue his nap.

From behind us, Zelda growled at the canine insults and Riley shushed her. "Zee, you need to keep an eye on the car. We'll be fine."

I leaned over to Riley and grabbed his arm before he could get out. "This place looks like it's out of the movie *Deliverance*. No car is worth this."

He shook his arm free. "Calm down, Meg. Jeez, what has gotten into you?"

A very old, very round man opened the screen door and stood on the porch. The shepherd looked up at his master and thumped his tail a few times. The man waved and shouted at us, "You here about the Bronco?"

Riley affirmed that was our mission, and the man said, "I'm Bob and that lazy dog over there is Frank." He gestured his hand toward a field and said, "Follow me. The rig is back behind the chicken coop, next to the Farmall."

I whispered to Riley, "What's a Farmall?"

"An old tractor."

"Great."

We dutifully followed Bob, and Frank followed us, the dog's tail swaying back and forth through the drizzle. The chickens fluttered around in excitement as we walked by, and I smiled. Considering the size of the flock, I guessed Bob probably ate a lot of omelets.

Next to an extremely rusty tractor that once might have been red, sat an olive green SUV that was presumably a rather ancient Ford Bronco. At one time, the roof may have been white, but at this point, a patina of green covered the entire vehicle so it was like we were viewing it through a green camera filter.

I bent to peer at the interior through the grimy window and jumped back when a spider crawled up the inside. I covered my hand over my mouth to muffle my girly shriek, but was only partially successful.

Riley glanced at me and raised his eyebrows in a silent rebuke. He turned to Bob. "Would you pop the hood for me?"

Bob yanked on the driver's-side door a few times, and the door creaked open with a reluctant grinding of metal on metal. Riley lifted the hood and began poking at mysterious things in the engine. He looked around the hood at Bob. "Could you start it?"

Bob looked a little worried about that concept, but pulled a key out of his pocket and got into the Bronco. "It might take a coupla tries to get her going."

A couple of tries turned out to be approximately seven hundred. Riley advised Bob on a few nuances of starting technique, and the Bronco finally stuttered to life with a great belching noise. I stepped away from it, worried that the novelty of operation might lead to something worse, like an explosion.

Bob got out and stood next to Riley. They both stared at the engine, which was making horrible noises akin to whale sounds crossed with cats in heat. Riley reached into the engine, and one of the worst screeching noises subsided. Bob shouted, "Dang! How'd you do that?"

After Bob shut down the wheezing, sputtering engine, Riley walked around the Bronco, sat in the driver's seat for a while, played with knobs and shifters, and riffled through some garbage littering the interior. Then he crawled underneath the thing. Frank sniffed at Riley's sneakers, and I tried not to cringe at the soggy nastiness that might be lurking under the vehicle. Drenched bugs, oily snakes, manure? Gross.

The cloying drizzle was relentless, and I was getting cold. After the foray underneath the car, Riley returned to his examination of the engine. I nudged his arm to get his attention and widened my eyes in an unspoken "Are you done yet?" encouragement to wrap up this process. I wanted to leave and return to our errands.

Riley pointed at the box in the rear cargo area of the Bronco. "So, Bob, does it come with those extra parts?"

"Yeah, you can have 'em. I replaced some stuff, but it was years ago, and I don't remember what those things do anymore." He looked puzzled for a moment. "Waitaminute. I gotta check through the box to make sure there aren't no tractor parts in there first. I might need those."

I said, "We'll discuss the pros and cons while you do that."

I pulled Riley away from the vehicle and hissed, "You aren't serious about buying this hunk of junk, are you?"

He leaned down so Bob wouldn't overhear. "Meg, this is a great deal. It's mostly just dirty. The frame isn't bent that I can tell, so it hasn't been in a wreck. The engine is in better shape than I expected. It's a 302 V-8 and with a little work and customization, it could have some serious horsepower."

"Unbelievable." I shook my head. "I don't want to touch it."

"Sorry, Mandy, but this is your new ride."

Riley turned away from me and walked over to Bob, who was crouched down next to the box, sorting through his rusty pile of parts. "So the ad said five hundred."

Bob stood up and stroked the vehicle lovingly. "Yep, she's cherry."

Riley leaned against the Bronco and ran his finger through the slimy greenish film coating on the roof. "You and I both know it's got some problems, so how about two-fifty?"

"I dunno. I did a lot of work on her."

"I'm guessing that was a long time ago, wasn't it?" Riley gestured toward the pasture and vast forest beyond it. "Sitting in a field like this isn't doing this Bronco any good. I'll take it off your hands for two-fifty, assuming the title is clean."

"I had her in the barn up until last week. I dug her out so people could check her out."

"I see." Riley folded his hands in front of him. "What about the title?"

"I bought her new twenty years ago, so the title's in my name." Bob set a greasy part back into the box. "I gotta find it though."

"C'mon, Bob. I need the title. And a couple of quarts of oil if you have it."

"You got cash?"

Riley pulled out his wallet and waved it. "Right here."

"You got a deal!" Bob put out his hand. "So wait, what's your name?"

Riley shook Bob's hand. "Tim."

"Well Tim, looks like you got yerself a Bronco. I'll be right back with that title."

Riley and I watched as he scuttled past the chicken coop to the house. I leaned inside to inspect the interior again. It didn't even have a backseat. And to my dismay, a family of rodents appeared to have set up a homestead on the floor of the passenger side.

I backed away and looked up at Riley. "When you want to be, you're quite the negotiator. I can't believe you talked him down by half. Or maybe I can. If you can get this hunk of crap out of the yard, it will be a miracle. You didn't even take it for a test drive!"

"You didn't see Shelby when I bought her."

Riley's cherry–red, classic Mustang was utterly gorgeous because he'd spent years restoring it. I knew how much it had pained him to give up his car and put it in storage. "The Mustang looked like *this*?"

"Worse, in some ways. Although I will say, Shelby hadn't been sitting in a field, so she didn't have mice."

I shuddered. "Ugh. Give me the keys to the rental. There's no way I'm getting into that thing until you clean it out. I'll follow you with Zelda in the rental car in case our new ride doesn't make it."

"That's not a bad idea."

∼

Riley managed to limp the Bronco back to the condo where we were staying near Glacier, Washington, but the drive took a while. The antique rust-bucket stalled a total of fourteen times. I know because I counted. Zelda seemed confused by my need to stop the rental car and wait while Riley struggled to get the vehicle back in motion.

The condo was located in a beautiful setting situated along the Nooksack River. It also happened to be strategically located not too far from the secret retreat that we planned to infiltrate.

I let Zelda out and walked over to examine the Bronco. Riley was already looking at the engine. Because he was likely to be doing a lot of that, I decided I should try to be supportive. Unfortunately, I tend to have trouble hiding my feelings. I pointed at the grimy engine. "Your new Bronco seems to need to nap at regular intervals."

"The carburetor needs a complete overhaul." He pointed at something filthy. "That needs to be replaced too."

"This doesn't come as a shock to me. Are you going to name it?"

He wriggled something that might have been important, but looked like a hose to me. "I suppose."

"It's green. How about the Green Machine?"

Riley disconnected a clamp, pulled out the hose thingie, and shook something fuzzy, yet revolting, out of it. He glanced at me. "What?"

"You're quite focused when you're in gear head mode."

"I need to get this to run well enough to make it to the retreat."

"It's raining and we still need to go shopping." I pointed at Zelda. "And your dog needs a walk."

"I need to check a couple of things before we go. We'll need to stop by an auto-parts store." He unscrewed something, pulled off the top, and dumped more detritus out of the bottom. "Mice moved into the air-filter compartment. It needs a new air filter too."

"Eww. How many rodents are inhabiting this thing? How about Frankenstein?"

"What?"

"The *name*. If you're going to fix this doom buggy, you need a name. You named the Mustang Shelby. What are you naming this...*thing*? Old hag?"

"Very funny."

"It's green. How about the Hulk?"

"That doesn't work if I decide to paint it a different color."

"Given the way it behaves on the road, I vote for Lurch."

Riley finally looked at me and laughed. "All right, that one's funny."

Zelda tugged on her leash and I said, "Since we've settled this burning question, Zee and I will leave you and Lurch alone for a few minutes. Have fun."

After Zelda and I returned from our walk, Riley was willing to tear himself away from Lurch, and we went to do our errands. By the time we returned, I was starving. When I'm hungry, I can become surly, a fact that was not lost on everyone else in our condo. Zelda retreated to the bedroom, and Riley went back out into the rain to install some of his new automotive parts.

I got some crackers for a snack, which lured Zelda back out from the bedroom. I threw a Goldfish at her, which she snatched from the air. "So Zee, I guess I have to face the whole hair problem, don't I?"

I reached for the plastic container of henna on the table. I had used henna before to dye my hair red, which I liked. Going to "dark brown sable" wasn't appealing, but I'd vetoed Persian black deep ebony. That was far too depressing and the color might never fade out, so I'd have to shave my head like Riley. Yeah, he'd find that way too amusing. No way.

I chomped a few more Goldfish as I morosely read over the instructions a few times, trying to muster a tiny bit of enthusiasm about becoming a brunette. I reached for another cracker but the bag was empty. I'm a stress eater, and I should know better than to sit down with a bag of crackers when I'm contemplating a distressing hair adventure.

Riley walked into the room and Zelda ran to greet him. He washed his hands at the sink and sat down at the table across from me. "What happened to you?"

"Goldfish and dark brown henna."

"Not a tasty combination. So I guess you're getting ready to deal with your hair."

"I'm going to look awful."

"As I might have mentioned, this was *your* idea."

"I know. We have to do it. But how about if I cut your hair first?" I got up and walked over to his chair. I gently pulled the elastic off his ponytail and slowly ran my fingers through his long, dark brown wavy hair. "I'm going to miss your hair."

"Not as much as I am. If you cut off all my hair and then wimp out by leaving yours alone, I won't forgive you. *Ever.*"

I ran a finger back from his temple, around his ear, and down the nape of his neck. "I would never do that."

He reached for my hand, pulled it off his neck, and kissed my palm. "Sure, you would. I see what you're doing here and distracting me isn't going to work."

"It was worth a try." I bent to give him a kiss. "Okay, I'm going to suck it up and be brave now. We *have* to do this. I'll get the scissors."

Zelda followed us into the bathroom and we stood in front of the mirror. I stripped off my shirt and handed the scissors to Riley. "To show good faith, I'll go first."

Riley took the scissors and met my eyes in the mirror. He held his hand up perpendicular to my hair near my chin. "Here?"

I nodded and closed my eyes. "Do it."

As the snipping noise from the scissors got closer to my ear, I squeezed my eyes shut more firmly, as if that might help. Tendrils of hair floated over and onto my bare skin and I tried not to flinch at the tickly sensations.

The noise of the scissors stopped, and I felt Riley kiss my ear. He whispered, "It's cute."

I opened my eyes and tried not to gasp. I hadn't seen that much of my neck in years. My neck seemed longer than I remembered, and my collarbones looked oddly enormous.

Riley smiled. "See, it's not so bad. And now you have less hair to henna."

"I don't look like me anymore."

"Wasn't that the point?" He handed me the scissors. "Now you get your revenge."

I looked down at my hair on the floor, then at the mirror again. "I guess it could be worse. At least you cut it straight."

"Your job will be simpler," Riley said as he walked out of the bathroom. He returned with a chair, removed his t-shirt, and sat down. "Let's get this over with."

I ran two fingers down his hair, creating a line to cut, and held up the scissors. Until recently, I hadn't known how soft and silky Riley's hair was. The dark strands slipped through my fingers and I let go. He swiveled to look at me. "What are you doing back there?"

I slowly set the scissors on the counter and faced Riley. "I'm no good at this!"

Riley pulled me into his lap and put his arms around me. "You don't have to become the world's greatest hairdresser. Shave my head and be done with it."

"No, I mean, going undercover. I'm a terrible liar. You know that. I think these environmentalists are up to no good. We have reasons to believe they might be blowing things up. What if we get our parents in trouble?"

"It will be fine. We just have to get our disguises nailed down. Then we need to figure out what to do about Zelda."

At the mention of her name, Zelda wagged her fluffy tail.

I reached down to stroke the dog's head. "Do? What do you mean *do?*"

"We can't show up there with her. Haven't you thought about this? Ryan the cancer survivor can't walk into this place with a dog. Zee is pretty distinctive. She also tried to take a bite out of a couple of Hector's men, so it's not like they'd forget her."

"Well, Hector and his creeps won't be there." The truth was I hadn't thought about how Zelda would relate to our story. I'd assumed she'd be with us. In fact, I hadn't thought through this whole sneaking-into-the-retreat idea well at all. I'd suggested it and forged ahead without considering the ramifications, which is so typical of me. Now that it was happening, I felt like crying. "What are you saying? We can't just…I mean, it's *Zelda.*"

"I have an idea, but it's going to be tricky because we have no way to contact our parents first."

"I hope it's better than the Bronco idea."

Riley gave me one of his fixed deadpan stares. "It's along the same lines. While you were in the rental car agitating to leave, I had Bob sign over the title to the Bronco. But I gave him my dad's name. I showed him my driver's license and covered up my first name with my thumb."

"Okay, I'm impressed." I smiled. "That was sneaky. But what does it have to do with Zee?"

"We need to go down to the river and access the retreat the back way over the rocks, like we did before. Then we wait around for our parents to come by on their daily walk and give Zee to Dad. He can say she's a stray and take her in.

No environmentalist worth his compassionate salt is going to turn away a poor stray dog."

"Zee is a much better gift for your dad than a rusty old piece of junk like Lurch. Wait until he finds out he's the proud owner of a barely running old Bronco." I gave Riley the biggest, hardest hug I could. "But thank goodness one of us is still thinking. I think my brain has left the station."

"I've been, uh, wondering what's going on with you. There have been a lot of changes with us lately. Are you having second thoughts?"

I waved my hands, "No, nothing like that. Not at all. Being together—us, I mean—that's good. Better than good. Great, actually."

"Then what's bothering you?"

"I'm worried about spending time with my mother."

"Why? You lived with her for years. We've talked about her dozens of times and you kept saying how much you missed her."

"I did. I *do*. But we don't always get along. I keep remembering what it was like when I was a teenager." I looked into Riley's eyes. "You were the perfect kid, weren't you? Never gave your dad any trouble, right?"

Riley pursed his lips and shrugged slightly. "I suppose. We spent a lot of time building stuff and goofing around with all his equipment in the garage."

"I thought so."

"I'm getting the impression you weren't quite as laid back." He chuckled. "Why does this not surprise me?"

"I got in a lot of trouble."

"Like the great homecoming-queen exposé you wrote?"

"Believe me, my electrifying 'Stuffed ballot boxes and stuffed bras' article was only the beginning. My mom and I fought all the time, except when I was giving her the silent treatment. How am I going to cope with being around her and acting like she and I haven't spent *years* arguing with each other?"

"That was a long time ago. Maybe you and your mother can work out some of this old stuff while we're there." He pointed at the scissors. "So can we get this over with? My baldness awaits."

I ran my fingers back from his temples through his long hair again and gave him a kiss. "Goodbye, lovely soft hair. Grow back soon."

Chapter 2

Visual Acuity

When I opened my eyes the next morning, I was curled up in a warm, snuggly embrace with Riley. He had a way of intertwining his long arms and legs around me that was comforting, and I was enjoying the benefits aspect of the evolution of our friendship. When I first met Riley and we ended up traveling together, he mentioned that he could sleep better with me around because I smelled good to his super sniffer.

At the time, it seemed peculiar, but I wasn't one to talk, given my own oddities. Then more recently, Riley figured out how to isolate the scents of hormones, which I found embarrassing because he often could tell my emotional state. Worse, he could also tell if I was attracted to someone.

Now that we were not only sleeping in the same room, but also in the same bed, I discovered that having my pheromones reveal to Riley what I liked and didn't like had some definite advantages. He also pointed out that sex releases oxytocin, the bonding hormone that makes people feel closer both emotionally and physically. Far be it from me to argue with science. Our relationship had evolved in an extremely pleasurable way.

Because I'd spent so much time with Riley, I found the dramatic change in his appearance startling. After I'd run the clippers around on his head, I'd pointed out that he was going to need to be a little more diligent about shaving. He professed to hate the activity, but shaving once in a while whenever he got around to it wasn't going to work anymore. Now that he was completely clean-shaven and almost bald, Riley looked about fifteen years younger than he actually was, which made me feel creepy in a Mrs. Robinson kind of way. Wasn't I too young to be a cougar?

My sleepy ruminations must have been psychically loud because Riley woke up. I rolled over and looked into his eyes. At least his eyes were still the same. Still dark, dark brown and expressive, with thick eyelashes women would kill for.

He smiled at me. "I'm glad you didn't shriek at the sight of me."

I kissed him. "Hey, you're still you. That's all that matters. Your hair will grow back eventually."

"Well, Erin finally got her wish in spades."

I wasn't too excited about the mention of his ex-girlfriend, but the woman had nagged Riley mercilessly about cutting his long hair. I ran my palm across the fuzz on his scalp. "You look like you've been drafted into the military. Want me to take a picture for her?"

"Thanks, but no thanks." He kissed me more enthusiastically. "But if you want to distract me from the fact that my head is cold, that could be fun."

"Tempting, but Mandy and Ryan have to go to their eye appointments this morning."

Riley did a few creative things that made me wish I'd scheduled the appointments later in the day, but I finally gained some willpower and extracted myself from bed. "We're going to be late."

After hustling through Zelda's walk and breakfast, we went out to the mall to visit the eyeglass emporium. Although I'd felt like an idiot asking, it turns out you can buy glasses even if your vision is fine. When I called, the receptionist encouraged me to make an appointment and I'd reluctantly agreed.

My eyesight seemed okay, but getting your eyes checked regularly is one of those things responsible people do as they get older. I couldn't remember the last time I'd had my eyes examined, so my status as a responsible person was in jeopardy. In other words, the receptionist talked me into it. Riley remained less than thrilled about the idea of wearing glasses, but seemed to have resigned himself to it because glasses were part of the disguise.

Maybe it's my test phobia coming into play, but something about getting my eyes examined makes me anxious. Am I a failure if I can't read the teeny-weeny letters on the bottom row? Am I actually inventing the fact that the letter is an E and not an F or can I truly see it?

Riley's appointment was first, so I perused frames while he was in with the optometrist. Although a few of the designs were okay, with my new short brown hair, many of the glasses gave me an unfortunate resemblance to Velma on Scooby Doo. Somehow in less than twenty-four hours, I'd managed to go from Daphne the red-haired ingénue to Velma the nerd in the ugly sweater. This realization didn't make me feel pretty.

Riley came out of the exam room and his eyes were even darker than usual because his pupils were dilated. I hustled into the room to avoid him because he also seemed to be extremely cranky.

The eye doctor was a balding man with round wire-framed glasses that gave him an owlish appearance. It was comforting that the man doing the exam wore glasses himself. Someone with perfect eyesight wouldn't be as sympathetic to my test anxieties.

We went through the typical drill of reading off letters and it turned out all my worries were for naught. I breezed through the various exams. It was so easy that I don't know why I had been nervous. Why did I always get myself into a state about stuff like this?

When we were done, the doctor was silent. My worries returned, and I smiled weakly. "Is everything okay?"

He looked at his clipboard, then at me. "I don't know what to say. You have the best eyesight I've ever measured in my fifteen years as an optometrist. I thought maybe I did something wrong, but I ran the test twice. Then I randomized the letters again in case you might have memorized a chart. I can't figure out how you can see so well."

"Then I guess I don't need glasses."

"Far from it. Your eyes are perfect. Better than perfect. Whatever you're doing, keep doing it."

I thanked the doctor, left the exam room, and conferred with the frame saleswoman about glasses with no prescription. Riley and I tried on a lot of frames and modeled them for each other. After staring at my reflection in the mirror for ages, I gave up and embraced my new geeky Velma look. Ugh.

After I vetoed several options, Riley finally settled on some simple wire frames that weren't too bad, although somehow they made him look even younger still. People were going to think I was dating a remarkably tall twelve-year-old. Eww.

Because neither of us needed prescription lenses, we were able to take our fake glasses and leave.

On the walk back to the car, Riley still seemed irritated about something.

I asked, "What's with you?"

"My eyes aren't perfect anymore. It's yet another part of me that's falling apart. Maybe it's from doing so much driving."

"Do you need prescription glasses? Why didn't you say something?"

"It's so slight it wasn't worth waiting for glasses. The doctor said if it gets worse, I could get reading glasses at the drug store. But my eyes aren't twenty-twenty anymore, which means I'm getting old."

I took his arm and patted it. "You're not old. In fact, you're looking younger every day."

Riley laughed. "From the tone of your voice, I'm thinking this isn't a compliment, Mandy."

"Of course it is, Ryan. We've been together for six months, and right after we met, you were diagnosed with cancer and went through chemo treatments. I've stood by you through thick and thin."

Riley stopped walking and looked at down at me. "That's not far from the truth. Well, except the cancer part. But you were there when I was in the hospital. It was all a mess with Erin showing up, and I probably didn't say anything to you then. But you took care of Zee and I hope you know how much I appreciated that…and everything else."

I stood on my tiptoes and kissed him. "Yeah, I know."

~

We stopped by a print shop so Riley could make some color copies, and on the drive back to the condo I explained how the doctor had been confused during my eye exam. "The doctor kept saying he thought he messed up the test somehow."

Riley readjusted his glasses. "I doubt it. We know you have, for lack of a better word, *special* vision. Most people don't see a colorful aura around people. I know I don't."

"It doesn't seem particularly special to me. I see what I see. Now that I think about it, I suppose I might be able to see better than I used to, but it's been so gradual I figured it might be because I wasn't spending so much time sitting in front of a computer screen writing anymore."

"You can tell when something is bothering me just by looking at me. No one else can do that."

"That's not a big mystery. It's because I *know* you." I removed my Velma specs and fiddled with the earpiece, which was hitting my ear in the wrong place. Ouch.

"All right, if you say so. Have you figured out what color your own aura is?"

"What?"

"We determined that you see an aura around people like us who have special abilities. You told me my aura is teal blue. We spent an hour looking at ourselves in the mirror to select these awful glasses. I've never asked you before, but what color do you see around yourself?"

"Um. Well, I'm not sure. I was looking at the glasses." The truth was I hadn't thought much about it. I closed my eyes and considered what I'd seen in my reflection in the mirror at the eye doctor's office. "I think...uh, I don't know.

Well, maybe. I guess I might be purple. A light purple, like the color of lilacs."

"Cool. Maybe you can use those powerful peepers to help me mock up the fake IDs."

"I can't believe we're supposed to be from North Dakota. Why there of all places? What if someone asks about it? I've never even been near North Dakota."

"Neither has anyone else. They won't ask. If they do, say the winters are bad."

"Maybe I'll take my laptop to the cabin and read a few fun facts about North Dakota online so I don't end up sounding like an idiot." The condo complex where we were staying had no phones in the units and exactly one online connection in the attic of an ancient wooden recreation building. This lack of communication with the outside world might be great for those who came to the area to get away from it all, but for me it was a pain.

"You need to do that later. After we get back, we need go for our hike and hand Zee over to Dad. He said he and Ellen go for their walk after lunch, so we should have enough time to get over there."

"I don't understand how you can be so calm about giving her up." I turned to look over my shoulder at Zelda, who was keeping vigil in the back seat, watching the scenery go by. I reached my hand back to pet her soft fur. "Oh, Zee, I'm gonna cry, I just know it."

Zelda thumped her tail a few times, seemingly unfazed by the notion of having a new owner. At least one of us was going to be a grownup about this transfer. I needed to keep telling myself that it was only temporary and that Riley's father had taken care of Zelda before.

"It's one night, Meg. Tomorrow we return this rental car, drive to the retreat in the Bronco, and see if we can get the environmentalists to let us volunteer."

"I guess I can handle one night, but you still need to hose out Lurch. That thing is disgusting, and I'm not touching it until you make sure it's no longer a biohazard."

"Yeah, yeah. Remember, you're going to have to use all your persuasive skills to get us in there because I'm not good at that."

"Just make sure you have your story straight, Ryan, and I'll take care of the rest." I crossed my arms across my chest. Although I talked a good game, I was more than a little anxious about getting us into the retreat. Most nonprofits embraced new volunteers because free labor is priced right. But most nonprofits also weren't as secretive as Enviro Freedom, so I wasn't sure they'd be up for uninvited guests.

After lunch, we headed out to find the trail to the retreat again. Riley slowly drove down the muddy rural road. This time we weren't being chased and we knew where we were going, so it was a much more leisurely ride. Even though Riley was being stoic, I was sure he secretly was as distressed as I was about having to say goodbye to Zelda, so he wasn't eager to reach the trailhead.

Zelda seemed to pick up on our somber mood and was curled up in the back seat, getting jostled by the bumps as Riley navigated through the potholes. Once we got to the point that the road was impassible for the rental car, Riley pulled over and we got out. As we strolled in the direction of the river, the sound of the rushing water grew louder. The trail followed along the riverbank and required a fair amount of bushwhacking through oversized forms of plant life. All the rain had made the vegetation vigorously happy, and it was difficult to work our way down the trail to the fence.

The huge stockade fence dead-ended into a massive pile of boulders at the river's edge. As we had before, we clambered over the rocks to the other side. With the exception of the fact that it wasn't pouring, the inside of the retreat grounds looked the same as it had the last time we'd been there a few days earlier. But it felt different.

I reached for Riley's hand, and we started walking along the river toward a covered picnic pavilion where we'd talked to our parents before.

I stopped and he turned to look at me. I pulled his hand to tug him closer to me and grinned. "This is where you made your move."

"True."

"Was it planned? Did you decide, hey, after I've dragged Meg through the woods and over the rocks, I'm going to kiss her silly?"

"Jeez, I don't know. Do you really have to interrogate me about *that*?"

"I'm trying to gain insight into how your mind works. Do men plan out these things or are they spontaneous?"

"I have a feeling this is a trick question and there's a 'right' answer here. Unfortunately, I'm not sure what it is. What do you want me to say?"

"It's not a trick question. What were you thinking?"

"That you looked cold and I wanted to kiss you, so I did." He spread his arms wide and raised his eyebrows. "Is that what you wanted to hear?"

"Spontaneous is good." I stepped forward and put my arms around his neck. "I like spontaneity, but I was thinking..."

Before I could finish, Riley wrapped his arms around me and kissed me like he had before, which is to say, *extremely* well, so I forgot whatever it was that I was going to say.

Zelda barked and we jumped apart. I looked down at the dog, who was wagging her tail and focusing her attention on the people walking toward us. I looked up at Riley with a smile. "Have you noticed that every time we make out, our parents show up? We could have saved a lot of money on gas and motel rooms if you'd made your move earlier."

Riley laughed. "I don't think that would have worked, but I guess we'll never know, will we?"

We walked toward our parents, with Zelda leaping around exuberantly, apparently thrilled to see her buddy Tim O'Shea again. Maybe leaving her here wouldn't be so bad after all.

I hugged my mother. "Hi, Mom. It's good to see you again."

"Your new haircut is cute, dear," she replied. "I didn't know you wore glasses."

Tim studied Riley. "I guess you're going for a different look."

"Bald, nearsighted cancer patient," Riley replied. "It's part of our disguise. We're here to give you Zelda and explain our cover story to you. Tomorrow you have to pretend you've never laid eyes on us before."

We walked to the pavilion, sat down, and our parents listened patiently as Riley and I went over our plan. While

I talked, I also stroked the fur on Zelda's head, trying to get in a few more moments of furry affection before we left her.

Finally, it was time to say goodbye, and Riley took off Zelda's collar and leash. He pulled a rope out of the pocket of his raincoat, looped it around the dog's neck, and handed the end to his father. "Pretend you found this rope on your walk. If you don't have some way to hang on to her, she might run after us and actually run away. We don't want that."

I squeaked, "Please take good care of her."

Tim looked solemn and crouched down in front of Zelda. "You're coming with me, Zee. It's like when you stayed with me those times Riley went on business trips. Remember that?"

Zelda offered a tentative wag, and I reached down to pet her. "We'll see you tomorrow."

Riley ruffled her ears and said, "You be good, Zee," and gave her a hand signal. Zelda got up and sat next to Tim.

We all hugged goodbye and I watched as our parents continued their walk accompanied by Zelda, who turned her head to look back at us a couple of times.

Riley stuffed the collar and leash into his coat pocket, took off his glasses, and pressed the heels of his palms to his eyes. "Jeez, these glasses drive me nuts."

After he put his glasses back on, I took his hand. "Like you said, we'll see Zelda tomorrow."

"I know. We need to go pack up and get ready to infiltrate."

"She'll be fine, Riley."

He didn't respond to my comment, but he pulled me into his arms, hugged me hard, and said, "Let's get out of here."

~

After we got back to the condo, Riley grabbed a bucket, filled it with soapy water, and went outside to tackle the nasty Lurch-cleaning project. He was gone for hours removing God knows what from Lurch's interior, and when he came back inside, he was completely filthy.

I'd been lounging on the sofa reading a novel to distract myself from the lack of canine companionship. I set my book aside. "I'm guessing the Bronco looks better than you do."

"It's better, but we should be glad the retreat isn't far away. There's only so much I could do. I think the transmission may be terminal."

"Good thing you have Triple A."

He shrugged, "Riley has Triple A, but Ryan doesn't. Not being me is going to take some getting used to, and I'm trying not to think about it. Right now, I need a shower."

I got up and walked to stand in front of him. "Want help?"

He grinned and held out a hand to me. "Who knows what might be crawling on me by now? You can help me wash off the creepy crawlies."

"Don't gross me out or I'll change my mind."

After Riley was clean and well scrubbed, he made dinner. Both of us were in a much better mood after slippery shower fun, but something still felt off about the evening because our canine copilot wasn't around begging for food.

We packed our stuff and went over our background stories for probably the ninety-fifth time. Tomorrow was the moment of truth. We had to talk our way into the retreat. Although I tried not to reveal my doubts to Riley, I kept thinking, "What if they say no? Then what will we do? What if we have to leave the area without Zelda?" Even the idea made my heart hurt. We *had* to get in. We just had to.

The next morning, we loaded up Lurch with our stuff and checked out of our cute little condo by the river. I followed Riley to Bellingham in the rental car, and Lurch stalled out only three times on the way. It was an improvement from the fourteen times it crapped out on its last excursion, so Riley was making progress on the automotive front. Although whatever Riley had done to Lurch had helped, I wondered if anyone at the retreat would actually be dumb enough to believe we'd driven that heap all the way from North Dakota.

After we said goodbye to the rental, I got into the Bronco. The seats were torn and the floor had no carpet or floor mats. The bottom of the vehicle was bare exposed metal with a thick coating of rust. I was glad to see the mouse nest was gone, but I didn't want to end up with my feet dragging through the floor onto the highway à la Fred Flintstone.

I looked at Riley. "Are you sure Lurch is safe? I'm a little scared to ride in this thing."

"We don't have far to go, and I think it will make it. Probably." He turned the key in the ignition, and the vehicle wheezed and tried to stall out before settling into an uncertain rumble. With a pat on the steering wheel, Riley said, "C'mon Lurch. Only a little farther and then I promise I'll fix you up."

It was a slow trip back to Glacier because we had to stop multiple times to let Lurch rest while Riley fiddled with things under the hood. It wasn't like we were on a timetable, but I was antsy about getting to the retreat and beginning our infiltration. I wanted to see Mom and Zelda far more than I wanted to sit on the side of the road waiting around in this grimy machine.

After Riley got back into the car and started it again for what felt like the hundredth time, I lost it. "We're *never* going to get there at this rate! Why did you buy this horrible piece of crap? I want to be able to drive more than three hundred feet before the engine dies."

I went on like that for probably five minutes, until I ran out of nasty things to say about Lurch. The fact is that arguing with someone who isn't arguing back kind of takes the wind out of your sails. I was behaving like a shrew—or worse—like Riley's ex-girlfriend.

At my silence, Riley glanced at me. "Are you done?"

"Yes."

"I understand that you're upset, but I'd appreciate it if you wouldn't take it out on me."

"I know. I'll be shutting up now."

"Maybe you could think about what you're going to say to these people at the retreat."

"That's *all* I have been thinking about."

Riley reached over to take my hand. "It will be all right, Meg. You're the one who has no trouble talking to anybody."

"But what if I've lost my touch? I feel like it's been forever since I was a reporter."

"You just went on a tirade about an old Bronco. It's not like you've lost your voice or something."

"Very funny."

"All I'm saying is stop freaking out. It's not helping."

"Okay, I get it. I'm sorry."

We left the highway and made our way down a muddy dirt road toward the river. Our theory was that the retreat had to be down this road somewhere. We hadn't taken the rental car all the way to the end because the road was too rough for the poor little vehicle to handle. After one of the unscheduled stall-out stops, Riley managed to get Lurch into four-wheel drive, and we resumed our journey, heading deeper into the dense forest.

The road finally dead-ended at a large gate, and Lurch stalled out with an air of finality. I looked at Riley. "How does anyone get in here?"

"There's an intercom. Go tell them we want to go inside."

"And they're going to welcome us with open arms? Give me a break. I don't think so. What am I supposed to say?"

"You'll think of something."

I got out and walked to the intercom. I pressed the button and said, "I'd like to come inside, please."

A garbled voice came from the speaker and I think it said, "What?" Or maybe "Who are you?"

The audio was worse than one of those derelict clown speakers at a fast-food drive-through. But that gave me an idea. "My name is mumphegic. Let me in, please."

"What?" a voice from the speaker squawked.

"My name is mumphegic! I'm here to see olesmurf."

I turned to look back at Riley, who mimed "Now what?" I shook my head and then jumped when the huge metal gate creaked on its wheels and began rolling off to one side. I raised my arms in a "touchdown" maneuver and ran back to Lurch.

"What did you say?" Riley asked as I got in.

"Nothing you'd understand."

He shrugged and we pulled through the gate. After all the planning and worry, we were in at last!

~

We drove down the long driveway to a clearing and parked in front of a large wooden building that was surrounded by an array of tiny A-frame cabins and other larger outbuildings. Most of the buildings were old and in the process of being refurbished. People were busy hammering and painting. Everyone seemed terribly industrious.

We walked into the large building where a short woman with wild, curly red hair was talking on the phone. I raised my eyebrows at Riley and whispered, "Well, it looks like *somebody* gets to use the telephone."

He didn't respond, but I could see, "Shut up, Meg" in his eyes, so I went for my most professional serious reporter face. Time to pretend that I was attending a press conference, preferably with a speaker I didn't consider a complete idiot.

I stood politely in front of the desk, waiting for the woman to complete her call. She glanced at us in surprise, the fact that we were new here apparently sinking in. I could only assume visitors were not a common occurrence at a secret retreat.

Riley stood with his hands clasped in front of him, staring down at the woman, who now looked decidedly uncomfortable. She ended her phone call, which was clearly not business-related.

I cleared my throat and smiled politely. "My name is Amanda Ingalls and this is my fiancé Ryan McCarthy. A friend of mine told us that you need volunteers, so we are offering our services."

"We don't need volunteers." She looked down as she tidied some papers on the desk, and then looked back up at me. "How did you find this place?"

"My friend Rachel said that you had a retreat. We drove here from North Dakota." I quickly grabbed Riley's hand, and in my best fake choked-up voice continued, "Ryan has been…sick and we want to help."

She gave me a stern look. "You do realize we don't have medical facilities here."

I wiped a fake tear from my eye. "I know that! We want to do something to help the planet before it's too late. Something *meaningful* to help Mother Earth. Can't you understand that?"

I sniffed a few times for emphasis, laying it on thick. But then an agonizing pain pounded my temple and I slapped my hands to both sides of my head, crumpling to the floor. The pain was excruciating, and as I looked around, I felt as if I were enveloped in a blue mist while someone screamed nearby. I turned and looked up at Riley, who had an alarmed expression on his face. I heard myself squeak, "Help," before everything went black.

When I opened my eyes again, Riley had his arms around me. We were both on the floor and he was pushing my hair back from my temple. "Wake up. Please don't do this now."

At the desperation in his voice, I struggled to sit up. The receptionist was leaning over us and I smiled weakly. "I'm sorry. I guess I didn't take my medication this morning."

The woman gave me the same horrified look that I'd seen many times before. When I'd had my spectacular vision at the newspaper office, most of the people I worked with had shared that expression. Watching someone act like she's lost her mind tends to distress people. You'd think I'd be getting used to the reaction by now.

Riley said, "Can you stand up?" and I nodded. Upon closer inspection, I realized he looked like he might throw up. I'd seen him plenty sick before, but not at the point of actually vomiting on me. I gripped his arm. "Are you okay?"

He gave me a slight head shake to indicate that he wasn't, but said, "I'm fine."

Having seen quite enough of my meltdown, Ms. Redhead was ready for us to get out. She said, "Like I said, we don't need volunteers, so please leave. This is private property."

"Wait! We have skills." I cast about, trying to shake off the gray of my hallucination hangover and think of what I could do. "I can write press releases. Ads to promote your cause. Flyers and marketing materials. I'm a great writer!"

She crossed her arms across her chest. "We don't do that."

I pointed at Riley, who was looking less indisposed now. "Rile...I mean, Ryan has amazing mechanical skills. He can fix anything. Even cars that don't run."

Unmoved by my endorsement, Ms. Redhead pointed toward the exit. "We have a mechanic. Please leave."

Riley grasped my hand more tightly, and I knew he was silently communicating that I was flailing. I glanced at him and the panicked look in his eyes seemed to say, "Do something!"

I kept talking and thinking up reasons why Mandy and Ryan were the best volunteers the environmental world had ever known, but Ms. Redhead wasn't having any of it. Finally, she said, "We are a peaceful community, but I'm going to call someone and have you forcibly removed if you don't leave right now."

I stopped talking, not sure what to do, when a striking woman strode into the room. She had long legs, a commanding presence, and a stunning mane of black hair that flowed down to her thighs. A shiny heart-shaped black pendant hung from a thick silver chain around her neck and rested on the deep burgundy blouse she was wearing. The deep red color looked amazing with her hair. On my best day, I never had a prayer of looking as sleek as this woman. In a stern voice, she said, "Bonnie, get on the phone. We need to find someone to help with the cooking immediately."

I piped up, "Ryan is a fantastic cook. He's the best! We'd be happy to help you. We just got here and want to volunteer."

The tall woman looked down her aquiline nose at me. "Who are you?"

"I'm Amanda Ingalls, but everyone calls me Mandy. And this is my fiancé, Ryan. We've traveled such a long way to get here."

She gave Riley the once-over. "Can you cook? You don't look like…a food-oriented person."

He nodded. "I've gone through treatment, and they say I'm in remission. But I do have some cooking experience."

Bonnie raised her hand as if she were in grade school, in an effort to get the tall woman's attention, "But, Ms. Soloman, I don't think…"

With a dismissive wave, Ms. Soloman ignored Bonnie and continued to focus her attention on Riley. "You can chop vegetables, right? Chef Maurice is shorthanded because

Bruce said he'd peeled his last potato and walked out. No one has seen him since this morning."

Riley asserted he was a veggie-slicing machine and Ms. Soloman turned her attention to me. "What can you do?"

"What do you need?" I asked.

"Our gardener's arthritis is acting up. Are you willing to get your hands dirty?"

I held out my palms toward her. "These hands want to help in absolutely any way possible. We are committed to making a contribution."

The woman swished her gorgeous long hair behind her shoulder and held out her hand to shake mine. "My name is Shannon Soloman. Welcome. We have a cabin where you can stay, but it's not in good repair at the moment. As part of your volunteer work, you can help restore it."

"That's fine," I said. "Ryan is good at fixing things. Give us tools, and we'll work hard. I promise."

"Bonnie, take them to number six." She pointed at us. "Drop off your things and then get to the kitchen. I'll have George meet you there in fifteen minutes to show you the garden."

Although she was clearly irritated that Shannon had completely ignored her, Bonnie silently led us through the maze of buildings to cabin number six, which as the name suggested, was the sixth cabin in a row of tiny A-frames. She pointed at the small wooden structure and said, "This is it. The bathroom is down that way past the maintenance shed. The dining hall is over there. Shannon will expect you to be there ASAP, so you might want to hurry."

We thanked Bonnie and went inside. Riley peered around the door at Bonnie's retreating form, and then closed it behind him. He grabbed me in a hug and then looked into my face. "Are you really all right? What happened back there? You started screaming."

"I don't know. It was like the worst headache I've ever had. Then it just stopped."

"That's similar to what happened to me. All of a sudden, the scents from all the perfumes, soaps, cleaning chemicals, and who knows what else assaulted me. It practically knocked me down."

"I noticed. Thanks for not barfing on me."

Riley laughed and gave me a kiss. "It was touch-and-go there for a minute. We need to find Dad and find out what they're doing. We've been staying in this area for a week, and had no problems until we arrived here."

"Whatever it was, it was unbelievably painful. It's going to be tough to avoid being discovered if I start screaming regularly. Part of the reason I wanted to come to this place was to get *away* from radiation. Wouldn't our parents have mentioned that little detail?"

"You'd think so. In the meantime, let's get our stuff and move in."

I looked around the tiny room, which had a bare wooden floor and blank walls. The only furniture was two cots and a bookshelf. The austere room made a monk's quarters seem opulent. "There's no bathroom here."

"No electricity either."

"So this is basically a wooden tent? You know how I feel about camping."

"I think you're going to have to get over it." He pointed at a dark area on the floor. "I'm pretty sure the wooden tent leaks."

"That's great. Just great."

~

We returned to Lurch and Riley drove back to the cabin. We unloaded, threw all our junk on the cots, and ran off to the dining hall to meet Maurice, the chef with the unfortunate staffing problem.

When we walked in, the huge seating area was empty, but noise was coming from the kitchen. We swished through the two swinging doors and found a huge man hacking at something meaty with a knife. I could practically feel Riley's vegetarian sensibilities recoiling from the bloody mess.

I walked up and introduced myself and Riley to the man, who said his name was Maurice. He didn't look like a Maurice or a chef, but I persevered. "Shannon Soloman said you need kitchen help, and Ryan has cooking experience."

He jabbed the massive blade into the hunk of meat and wiped his hands on his apron. "I need help with prep. That weenie Charles bailed on me. I don't know where he got off to, but from what he said, I don't think he's coming back."

"Do you mean he left the facility?" I asked.

"Sometimes we get a runner. Not everyone is cut out to stay here." He pointed at Riley. "You sure you know about food? Because I need help right now."

"Yes, although I'm better with vegetables," Riley said.

"Great! See that bin of spuds? You can peel them."

I didn't envy Riley's task of peeling what had to be fifty pounds of potatoes. We all turned as a portly man in overalls entered through the swinging doors. He was mostly bald with a ring of white hair and an equally white beard.

Maurice said, "Yo, George. You got my weeds?"

"They're herbs, you old fool," George retorted as he passed a bucket of what did look like weeds to me over to the chef.

"Don't be such a cantankerous old fart, George. You and I both know you can't have beef bourguignon without thyme and parsley."

George stopped in front of me. "Shannon said you know about gardening."

"Yes, that's me." I didn't know a blessed thing about plants, but George wasn't aware of that fact yet.

He gestured toward the door. "Follow me."

Riley suppressed a smile at the "help me" look I gave him as I said, "I guess I'll see you later."

I followed George outside, and he looked me up and down. "You don't strike me as the outdoorsy type."

That was an understatement, although I was a little surprised it was so obvious. "I love being outside in nature. That's why we want to volunteer here."

"Well, farming isn't particularly glamorous, but we all gotta eat. That means today we're weeding. In a place like this with so much rain, we got weeds that wanna take over everything. Our poor little seedlings can't get a breath of air or nutrients unless we give them a little help."

I'd never had a garden and wouldn't know a weed from a seedling if it walked up to me and said hello. "I'm sure the plants are different here, so you'll need to show me what you want me to yank out."

George patiently explained that the little plants with the dark green rounded leaves were zucchini plants and they needed to stay. Everything else needed to be pulled. The task was daunting because the row of zukes looked like a lawn with only a few feeble seedlings poking up out of the grassland. After I pulled out the weeds, I was supposed to put mulch around the tiny plants to keep the weeds from coming back.

He then went on a long, complicated discussion of the pros and cons of mulch, which I mostly tuned out until he started talking about slugs. I was not a fan of slugs, and the idea that the mulch might harbor them didn't make me happy.

According to George, "picking slugs" could end up being one of my future duties. The idea that Slug Removal Associate might be my volunteer job title made me cringe. Gross. You know your career trajectory is not headed in the right direction when your job description goes from ace reporter to slug remover. Well, unless you're a farmer, I suppose.

George was the most dedicated gardener I'd ever met. He'd found his passion, and it was growing organic food. Sadly, I didn't share his enthusiasm. I liked eating, but the process of getting it to the plate was considerably less interesting to me.

After hours of weeding, I staggered back to our wooden tent, shoved our suitcases off the cot, and collapsed flat on my stomach. Every muscle in my body was experiencing some degree of pain or stress, and I was asleep within moments.

I stirred and groaned at the sound of the front door opening. I rolled over and found Riley crouched down next to the cot, smiling at me.

He raised his eyebrows. "What happened to you? Are you all right?"

"Gardening is harsh. I had no idea there were so many weeds in the world. I'm not cut out for this level of backbreaking labor."

Riley stood up and went to sit on the other cot. "I peeled potatoes and found out that Maurice's name is actually Marvin. He told them he studied at some French culinary school, but the truth is he read a Julia Child cookbook."

I struggled into a sitting position. "So I guess we're not the only liars here at the retreat."

"Nope. Maurice needed a job and a place to stay. He says a lot of other people here have similar stories. Something happened in their lives and they met someone who told them about this place."

"I learned that George is a man of the land. He loves farming and growing things. It's like he's a gardening guru surrounded by plants that worship him and have no choice but to grow big and strong."

"I have to return to deal with dinner prep, but Maurice gave me an hour or so to unpack."

"Have you seen our parents or Zelda?"

"Nope. Just peeled a lot of spuds and watched people wander by."

I got up and rummaged through my suitcase for clean clothes. "I need a shower in the worst way."

"I'll say. You don't smell too good."

I yanked off my stinky shirt and threw it at him. "Shut up. It's only going to get worse. According to George, tomorrow we side-dress the zukes."

"What does that mean?"

"Fertilizer. And because we're all organic here, fertilizer means goat poop. It's pelletized, which means it's not as hot as other forms of, well, manure. The good news is that George claims that it stinks less than the chicken poop, which is another possible fertilizer."

"There are chickens?"

"Lots of them. Our friendly neighborhood rooster doesn't necessarily crow at dawn either. The poor thing is completely confused, so he sometimes crows in the middle of the night, which irritates the residents of our little community."

Riley handed my shirt back to me. "I guess I'll find out what egg recipes Julia Child included in *Mastering the Art of French Cooking*."

"French cooking includes croissants. Chocolate croissants are to die for. I can't remember the last time I had one. Are you going to learn how to make those?"

"I doubt it. All the spuds are for beef stew, which I have no plans to eat."

"Maybe you can make your own special side dish of rabbit food."

"I'll figure something out." Riley yanked some clothes out of his suitcase and held up a t-shirt. "We have no closet and no dresser. Unpacking is more fun when you have a place to unpack into. Are we supposed to stack our clothes on this rickety bookshelf?"

"Laundry is another question. Do you suppose they have machines somewhere? Being assigned to the garden is going to significantly increase my need to do laundry."

"If your clothes smell like a chicken coop, we'll need to hang them outside. I refuse to live in this tiny room with your manure-infested wardrobe."

I gave him a two-handed settle-down gesture. "I know. After I've taken a shower, I'll ask around."

"We need to figure out where our parents are and get some answers." He gestured at the tiny space. "I mean, I wasn't expecting luxurious accommodations, but after listening to you scream, feeling sick myself, and peeling potatoes all day, I figure things can only get better from here."

"We can only hope."

Chapter 3

Being Subtle

Although I'd never gone camping myself, I'd heard stories that cemented my opinion about the activity. I resolved never to consider going on any type of vacation that involved roughing it at a crowded campground. The communal bathroom at the retreat was much like descriptions I'd heard of rustic campground bathrooms with mildewed and cracked concrete. Which made me wonder if this place had been a campground before it became a retreat. If it had been, why didn't the locals we'd met at the brewery down the road know about this place? Or maybe they did know about it and thought it was defunct, which might explain why our wooden tent wasn't in the greatest shape.

I pondered these mysteries as I washed my hair under the feeble trickle that passed for a shower. Water pressure seemed to be another amenity that wasn't plentiful here. Maybe cutting my hair hadn't been such a bad idea after all.

Even with limited water, I felt a thousand times better after my shower and was ready to deal with the sea of new faces at dinner. Two other people had been working in the garden with me, but they'd been several rows over and George hadn't introduced us. The garden was huge, and I'd barely weeded half of one row that stretched out for what seemed like miles. My weeding performance probably hadn't been impressive, but it *was* my first day, after all.

49

I went to the dining hall and zeroed in on Riley, who was already seated at a table, poking at a plate full of greens. I sat next to him and gave him a kiss on the cheek. "Look, it's a person I know."

"You smell better."

"Thanks for noticing. That bathroom is disgusting, but the water mostly works."

Riley gestured toward a long table where people were serving food buffet style. "I'm pleased to say that prep cooks don't have to serve. Your feast awaits. Pay special attention to those fine potatoes."

I grabbed a plate and stood in line with many other people. Maybe it was my imagination, but most of them looked tired. Had they been weeding all day too? I passed the plate to the server, who placed some rolls on it along with a bowl of the beef stew. I thanked him and returned to sit next to Riley.

I scanned the room. "Have you seen our parents?"

"I've been watching the door, but they haven't shown up yet."

"Does everyone eat together? Is this the only dining area?"

"I think so, but I don't know for sure." Riley speared a leaf and studied it. "This lettuce is fantastic."

"Only you could get excited about lettuce."

"I think your friend George may be on to something as far as organic gardening. This is delicious."

I dropped the roll I was holding back onto the plate and looked at him incredulously. "I think that's the first time you've ever said anything positive about any food. *Ever.*"

"It's excellent."

"I'll tell George. Even though he doesn't know what a picky eater you are, he'll still be pleased."

"I'm not picky."

I stared at him for a moment, marveling at the absurdity of the statement, until a movement out of the corner of my eye caught my attention. I wanted to leap up and shriek, "Mom!" but I nudged Riley with my elbow instead. "Mom's here."

He turned to look and I jabbed him more forcefully this time. "Be subtle. We don't know them, remember?"

Riley pulled off his glasses and rubbed at the lenses with his shirt while scanning the room. "Dad's over there in line."

"It's impossible to miss us. We're sitting here all by ourselves like the loser new kids in school. Maybe they'll take pity on us and sit here."

"Believe me, nobody ever takes pity on the losers. Social misfits hang out along the perimeter with the other outcasts and geeks."

It turned out he was right. Our parents wandered over to a crowded table on the other side of the room and sat down with people they seemed to know well. I took a bite of my stew. The potatoes were extremely good. Maybe they'd been grown here too in one of the rows of plants I hadn't weeded yet. I'd undoubtedly find out soon enough.

I found myself irritated at the sound of my mother's laughter. "I hate awkward dining situations like this where you don't know anyone. It's like attending a wedding reception for a couple you barely know. Should we mingle and make small talk?"

"This may come as a shock, but I'm not much of a mingler."

"So now what? We need to talk to our parents. Should I go spill some stew on my mother and pretend it's an accident?"

Riley put his hand on mine. "Be patient. We don't have to talk to them this second, and we don't want to say anything in front of, well, anybody. Relax and eat your potatoes."

I jammed my fork into the stew, annoyed that he was right again. I wasn't used to acting like a shy person. It wasn't in my nature. "Fine. Maybe if we sit here long enough, they'll notice their offspring have arrived."

We ate slowly and were the last people left in the room, except for the folks at the cool table, hanging out with our parents. At last, they all moved to get up and Tim glanced at us. I could see him start with recognition and tug at my mother's sleeve. I hoped no one else noticed his surprise. Way to play it cool, Dad. Oh well.

Tim crossed the room toward us while my mother chatted up the other people at the table until they finally left. We were alone in the dining hall. Or I hoped we were alone. I whispered to Riley, "Are there still people in the kitchen cleaning up?"

"Probably. Don't say anything suspicious, all right?"

"I wouldn't do that."

"Yes, you would."

I stuck out my tongue at him, which he ignored. He then stepped around me so he could say hello to Tim.

I smiled at Tim and said, "We're new here. I'm Mandy and this is Ryan."

Tim obviously wasn't much of an actor, but he said stiffly. "I'm pleased to meet you."

My mother joined our little group, and we went through the introduction charade with her.

I said, "So what do people do after dinner? I'm guessing people go to bed early."

"We usually sit at home, have some tea, and read in front of the fireplace," my mother said.

My jaw dropped. "You have electricity?"

Riley said, "And a fireplace?"

"Our place is real nice," Tim added. "The decor is a little frilly, but I got used to it."

"*Frilly?*" I said in a high-pitched voice. "You have *frills?*"

Tim shrugged. "Well, you know, lace on the curtains… that kind of thing."

"We have absolutely no frills whatsoever," I said. "Our place is utterly frill-free."

"I'd settle for a dresser," Riley mumbled.

Apparently having clued into the fact that we were staying in the low-rent district, my mother said in her most polite voice, "Would you like to come over for some tea? We'd love to get to know you better."

"Absolutely! That would be wonderful. We don't know anyone and I miss our friends," I replied.

Mom gave us directions to their bungalow, which sounded adorable. We said our goodbyes and agreed to meet in an hour. Our parents were staying on the opposite side of the grounds, about as far away from our tiny A-frame as you could get.

Riley held my hand as we strolled back to wooden tent number six. "I thought you were going to lose it there for a minute."

"I was pissed. I mean, they have *electricity*! What kind of place *is* this? How come they have all the comforts of home, and we're practically camping out? It's not fair!"

"No one ever said life was fair, Mandy."

"I hate it when you say that. Life *should* be fair."

~

After we stopped by the tent and did a little more unpacking, we strolled to our parents' place. It was a gorgeous evening, and I finally started to relax. The air was fragrant with the scent of pine needles that had been warmed by the afternoon sun. It was late, but we were so far north that sunlight still filtered through the trees and I could hear the distant sounds of the rushing river. If we had to infiltrate a secret retreat, at least it was located in a beautiful area.

We knocked on the door of the cottage and heard a dog bark. I knew that bark and grinned at Riley, who squeezed my hand. Once inside, I got to do what I'd wanted to do since I'd arrived, which was hug my mother and pet Zelda's soft fur.

Riley barely made it in the door before Zelda was all over him. The dog was ecstatic to see her absolute favorite human in the universe. He sat down on the floor in front of the door so Zelda could crawl into his lap. She waggled with glee, and he hugged her ruff. Although Zee liked me, I didn't compare to Riley. Once she was done loving him up, she finally let me say hello and give her some affection too.

Riley stood up, brushed off some dog hair, and we hugged our parents. Mom led me into the living room, which truly did have frilly curtains. A tea tray was set up on the coffee table in front of a stone fireplace. No wonder they didn't want to leave this place. I didn't either.

Mom poured a cup of tea and handed it to me. "How was your first day?"

"Long." I replied. "I'm assigned to the garden."

"Isn't George wonderful? I could talk to him for hours. His knowledge of the natural world is astonishing," Mom said.

"Weeding gives you lots of time to think. Maybe that's why he's so philosophical." I sipped my tea. "Speaking of thinking, Riley and I have about a thousand questions."

Zelda was leaning on Riley, attached to him like canine Velcro. He stopped petting her for a moment to add, "The most important question is about radiation. A few minutes after we arrived here, something happened. I felt awful and Meg had a headache, but it went away. I never considered the possibility we'd be affected here because this retreat is located in the middle of nowhere."

"Unfortunately, Bonnie was there when I screamed." I said. "So within the first five minutes we were here, one person already thinks we're bizarre. She kept telling us to leave."

"Why did you scream?" my mother asked.

"She does that sometimes," Riley said. "It tends to alarm people. Including me. You'd think I'd be used to it, but I'm not."

"The headache was agonizing, and it was like there was too much pain for my brain to even think up a good vision," I said.

Tim set his teacup back on the coffee table. "I think that might have been my fault. Sorry about that."

"What were you *doing*?" I demanded.

"I was experimenting with testing some EM shielding. I thought it worked, but maybe not."

"You need to revisit your data, Dad." Riley said. "You were *way* off."

I reached over to pet Zelda. "I thought Riley was going blow chunks all over me."

Riley raised his eyebrows at me but didn't respond. He turned to Tim, "I could help you analyze what's happening. Maybe there's something else going on that you haven't taken into account."

"That's another question I have." I interrupted. "If I'm working in the garden all day every day, how am I going to find out anything? Do people here ever get time off?"

"I haven't thought about it because I've been so involved in my work," Mom said. Tim nodded his agreement.

This was typical Mom behavior. When I was a teenager, I'd resented all the time she spent on her classes and homework to get her PhD. And when she wasn't doing that, she was off earning a living. Later as an adult, intellectually, I understood I wasn't being fair because she'd supported me without any help from my deadbeat father.

But knowing she'd been a struggling single mother didn't take away from my childish complaint that I always came second after Mom's intellectual pursuits. And then when she did pay attention to me, I felt like I was a bug under a microscope, which made me uncomfortable and embarrassed. No kid wants to be psychoanalyzed by her *mother*. Yeesh.

"Maybe there's a weeding schedule. When he let me leave, I was too tired to ask George. He did say I needed to come back tomorrow." I slouched down on the sofa. "He wants to see if the slugs are out. Maybe I'll ask for a day off to recover."

Mom laughed. "That reminds me of when we went to that fancy French restaurant and ordered escargot. You made quite a scene once you found out what it was."

"I did not." I crossed my arms. "Asking the waiter for a menu item that does not come in a shell was perfectly reasonable."

"Not the way you did it, honey."

"By the way, Mom, I think I told you that when we were in Alpine Grove I saw your kitchen table at your old house. Why isn't it here?" I asked.

"That was when Meg wanted to break into your house," Riley added.

I glared at him. "I didn't do anything. The owner showed up and let us in."

Mom said, "The table didn't fit in the dining room space in this house. I thought they put it in a shed behind our lab here."

"What about that photograph of me? The black-and-white one grandpa took when I was a little kid. It sat in the dining room for years," I said. "I found it with the table. The owner's kid said that some guy with black hair gave it to him when the kid helped move the table back into the house."

Mom gave me an odd look I couldn't decipher, and Tim seemed to sense that this was not a topic Mom wanted to explore further. He turned to Riley and said, "Did you get Shelby into storage okay?"

"Yes, it was fine." Riley grinned at him. "And I got a Bronco—a seventy-seven Ranger with a hard-top and a 302."

Tim leaned forward. "You could bump up the horsepower with a stroker kit."

"I know! I thought of that too. It's got a lot of potential." Riley said.

"Potential that's been carefully camouflaged under a thick layer of dirt and rust," I added.

Riley turned to me. "Meg has no vision."

"Bring the Bronco the next time you come over," Tim said. "I can't wait to check her out."

The conversation between Riley and Tim devolved into a geeky automotive discussion about Lurch, and my mother rolled her eyes in a way I saw in the mirror regularly.

She moved to sit closer to me. "As you could probably tell, I was surprised to find out that you're involved with Tim's son. Now I'm curious about something."

When my mother became curious about my life, she usually asked questions I didn't want to answer. I tried not to sigh. "About what?"

"I was wondering how your special abilities affect your sex life."

"I, um, I haven't had visions during sex, Mom." My mind wandered. Now I had something new to fret about. Riley had enough to worry about when dealing with me without that too.

"I was thinking that the visions are coming from your subconscious, and the mind is a powerful aphrodisiac. Have your fantasies been affected?"

Wow. I so didn't want to venture into this conversational minefield. "I, uh, haven't put much thought into it."

"Well, I assume you do fantasize about Riley, don't you?"

At the sound of his name, Riley glanced at us. I felt the heat rising on my cheeks. Thanks to his overly sensitive sense of smell, Riley knew I'd done plenty of fantasizing about Lars, the gorgeous former clown and real estate agent. But about Riley, not so much, probably because he was usually only about two feet away. "I, well, sure."

My mother picked up her teacup, took a sip, and peered over the rim at me. "The science of human attraction intrigues me. The reasons why one person is attracted to a certain person and not another is not completely understood. How did you end up together?"

"I told you. We were on the road together for weeks, looking for you."

"You mean platonically? How interesting."

It wasn't *interesting*. This was my life, not a science project. "I didn't think about…um…it was, I don't know. Well, at the time, Riley had a girlfriend. But that's his business."

"What changed?"

"They broke up and then later things evolved I guess." I glanced at Riley, who didn't seem to be listening. He was not a big fan of sharing personal information, but what was I supposed to do?

My mother set her teacup down. "So it sounds like you were friends first and it evolved into a romantic relationship."

"Yes."

"I see."

Mom had this way of staring at me without speaking that caused me to involuntarily blurt out whatever I was thinking. It was like she was silently willing me to confess my secrets, and it worked every single time.

I tried waiting her out and as the silence lengthened, I failed again, gesturing helplessly with my hands. "I don't know what you want me to say. We were standing along the river and it was raining and then Riley looked down at me and there was something in his eyes. The way he looked at me, it was like my heart stopped for a second. We'd been through so much together. And then he kissed me, and everything was completely different. I was so happy and confused. All I knew was I wanted him to kiss me all the time and never stop."

I frowned at my outburst and shrieked to myself, "*Shut up, Meg!*"

Mom picked up her teacup from the table and took a sip, looking thoughtful. "That's fascinating. Often sexual attraction comes first. So you weren't attracted on a physical level initially? Do you think that has affected your sexual compatibility?"

"Mom, why are you asking me this? Ask Riley if you want to know!"

Riley looked over at me and raised his eyebrows. I smiled weakly at him and turned back to my mother. "Maybe we could talk more tomorrow. It's getting late, and I have a lot of weeds to pull in the morning."

I moved to go, and Zelda leaped up, following Riley and me to the door. We hugged our parents goodbye and told Zee to behave. Outside, the feel of the fresh moist air on my overheated cheeks was refreshing, and I inhaled deeply, relieved to be away from my mother.

Riley took my hand, "What happened back there?"

"Didn't you hear? I was being grilled about my sex life."

"Hmm, so what you're saying is that you felt uncomfortable being interrogated about personal topics. How ironic."

"She wasn't only asking about me. She was talking about *our* sex life. With each other, which I know you would not want me talking about."

"Probably not, but it's still ironic." Riley said.

"No, it's not. I wanted to scream at her to make her stop. I *knew* being around my mother would be a problem."

"You didn't scream, which I view as a win," he said, swinging our hands between us. "Dad can't wait to get a look at Lurch's engine, so I need to bring the Bronco over tomorrow."

"Do you ever talk about anything other than cars with your father?"

"Electronics."

"I mean something personal. Now he knows about our sensory problems, but you went for months without telling him. You thought you were going to die and never even brought it up."

"He knew I wasn't feeling well."

"Did he attribute it to your heart problem?"

"He doesn't know about that."

I stopped to look at him. "You can't be serious. It's genetic. How could you *not* tell him? What if he has the same problem?"

"I know he doesn't. After he met Ellen, he said she talked him into having a physical. He had a stress test and was kidding around about how at least he wouldn't have a heart attack, trying to keep up with a younger woman."

"Does he know you might drop dead?"

"Anyone could drop dead anytime. What's this all about?" Riley leaned down closer to me. "Let's not forget you didn't tell your mother about your visions."

"I was about to. And I already told you we don't communicate well, so I figured it would be better to tell her in person."

"She's incredibly smart. I can see why my Dad fell for her. I don't see why you're making such a big deal out of your conversation tonight."

"You wouldn't understand because you never talk about anything personal with your dad."

"I do too."

"Sorry, but machines and radio frequencies aren't personal. My mother has this way of digging into my psyche. It's hard to explain, but if I tell her I'm worried or stressed about something, I end up feeling worse about it after she sinks her claws into it. When I was a teenager, I stopped talking to her entirely."

"That's depressing."

"You know more than anyone how much I love my mother, but sometimes I felt like I was one of her upper-level psych-research projects, not her daughter."

Riley stopped, put his arms around me, and gave me a kiss. "I'm sorry. Maybe spending more time with her now as an adult will help."

"Maybe."

～

After walking from our parent's bungalow to our wooden tent, we pushed the two cots together to make one larger bed we could share. Thanks to all the stress of subterfuge, exercise, and my teenage hang-ups, I was physically and mentally exhausted. I curled up with Riley and passed out almost immediately.

When I woke up, I was ready to face another day of infiltration. My mother wasn't the only one who was good at asking questions. Today I was going to get out, meet people, and find out what was going on here.

Every organization has some type of hierarchy. Clearly, Riley and I were in the dungeon when it came to the communal pecking order, but we needed to know more about the people at the top. What was their vision for Enviro Freedom? What was the point of the group's existence? What did the people running the show want from it? I was determined to find out.

Riley and I strolled over to the dining hall to get breakfast. The sky was overcast and it was threatening to rain again. Our one day of glorious sunshine was over, and I swatted at a mosquito that was buzzing around me. The insect life was reveling in the humid weather.

Riley said he was off the hook for the breakfast and lunch chopping and peeling activities. His task was dinner prep, which started right after lunch, so he had mornings free. That meant that after we had breakfast he would be able to walk Zelda and hang out with his father. I confess that I was more than a little jealous because I missed Zelda.

George had been vague about when I was supposed to work, so I was less sure than Riley was about what I was supposed to do and when. In the absence of information, I made the bold assumption that I didn't have to work until after breakfast. A girl has to eat, after all.

Part of the reason Riley didn't have to work breakfast prep was because there wasn't much to the meal. It was what motels refer to as a continental breakfast, which sounds elaborate, but is generally only cold cereal, toast, and pastries. Because it wasn't an official sit-down affair, we watched as people wandered in, grabbed some food, ate, and then went off to deal with whatever it was they did all day.

Although I didn't say anything, I was happy to see that Riley was still eating like a relatively normal person. He'd eaten dinner and now was consuming toast and juice, which for him was a veritable pig-out. The last thing we needed was for his health to fall apart again. We had enough problems.

After breakfast, I gave Riley a goodbye kiss and walked to the garden area. While we were eating it had drizzled, and the clouds remained heavy with moisture. The evergreens around the gardens were sprouting new needles, and the bright green tips on the boughs contrasted with the darkness of the gray sky. I swatted at a mosquito and belatedly realized I had no insect repellent.

As the swarm around me grew more insistent, it was clear I was going to be eaten alive before I even made it to the garden. The combination of sunshine and rain seemed to have awakened the energy of every flying, biting insect in the forest. I increased my pace and hustled through the gate into the garden area.

George stood up and waved. "I was wondering if you were going to come back or not. Sometimes people don't."

I scurried up to him, trying to outrun the swarm. "What time am I supposed to be here?"

"We usually start early to beat the bugs and the heat. Then we take a break in the middle of the day."

"I didn't beat the bugs. Do you have any bug spray?" I was flailing around, swatting at bugs like I was possessed. "Please, I'm dying here!"

George pulled a bottle out of his gardening apron and handed it to me. "Here you go. It's a nontoxic lotion, but the skeeters don't like the smell."

I wouldn't have cared if it was napalm, if it made the bugs go away. I frantically rubbed the lotion over my arms. "Thank you so much!"

I finally relaxed when I saw a six-legged creature deterred from landing on me. I started to hand the bottle back to George, but he suggested I keep it. I thanked him and asked, "What time in the morning am I supposed to be here?"

"Five is good. We farmers need to get out early."

My jaw dropped. Five in the *morning*? Was he kidding? No wonder I'd never considered farming as a career option. I made an effort to compose myself, as if the idea weren't horrifying. "That's definitely early."

"I usually work for a couple hours, go over to grab a little breakfast, then come back. Around noon, we take a break for lunch. After that, I go take a nap, and then return for a couple hours in the afternoon. It's good to pace yourself."

He wasn't wrong about that. Yesterday, I thought I was going to die after only a few hours of weeding. But I was either a little old or a little young to be taking naps, wasn't I? "I'm sorry I was late today. Should I continue weeding the zukes?"

George gave me some direction on my upcoming weeding tasks, and I was left alone with my soggy plants. Yanking vegetation was a little easier this morning thanks to the damp soil, but it was a cold and dreary affair. I did end up meeting a few of my fellow gardeners though, so I had a little more camaraderie as we methodically tugged our way down the long rows.

Griffin was a lanky guy probably ten years younger than I was, with a long blonde ponytail and beard. He seemed to spend most of his time manning the wheelbarrow, dragging straw, manure, weeds, and rocks around the garden. Jane had a short pixie haircut that was almost completely obscured by her gigantic straw hat. She told me that she had worked her own garden for years, but met George and wanted to learn about farming.

Jane was fast friends with another garden helper named Felicia, who shared her passion for flowers and plants. Felicia wore her light auburn hair in a thick braid that fell down her back, giving me a major case of hair envy. The woman was way into gardening, and she claimed she didn't want to forget anything George told her. She carried a little notebook with her, and as George explained something, she busily jotted notes about the task.

As we worked, it quickly became clear that I was the only person with zero gardening experience and knowledge of plants. Everyone else knew what was going on and hung on George's every word. I kept my questions to a minimum, content to let Felicia record his wisdom. Even though I was clueless about farming, I did enjoy listening to him talk about nature. He had a slow, patient way of speaking that was soothing.

Rarely had I met anyone who seemed so comfortable with who he was and his place in the world. Growing food was what George wanted to do with his life, and he was pleased that he had the opportunity to do it in this vast expanse of fertile land. We should all be so lucky. I spent a lot of personal brainpower trying to figure out what I was going to do with the rest of my life. The idea of being completely content was a foreign concept.

It was worse because I'd thought I'd discovered what I wanted to do. What I thought I was *destined* to do. When I was a reporter, it had been a huge part of my identity. Since my special abilities had destroyed what I used to think of as my life, I'd lost that confidence in who I was. I missed that sense of self that George obviously had.

I was spacing out, getting into the zen of weeding, when Felicia said something interesting. I perked up a little and subtly moved closer to get more details. She and Jane were discussing the Founder's upcoming visit.

When they paused in their chatting, I asked, "Who is the Founder?"

Felicia's eyes widened, "Why, the founder of Enviro Freedom, of course."

"You know—Ralston Landecker," Jane added. "He's the reason we're all here."

I made a feeble effort to cover my gaffe. "Oh sure, okay. I never heard him addressed as the Founder before." Ugh. My comment was lame, but the two women continued talking about the Founder in reverent tones, so maybe they didn't notice.

Rather than say anything else that might reveal my ignorance, I opted to shut up and quietly eavesdrop. From their conversation, the impression I got was that the rumor mill was working overtime about the Founder's impending visit. He was reportedly distressed at the lack of progress we were making here at the retreat. The word was that he was disappointed in our lack of commitment to the cause.

The humidity was oppressive, and my skin was coated with a noxious combination of sweat, drizzle, dirt, and mosquito repellent. We all broke for the midday respite, and as I walked back to my tiny abode, I considered what I'd heard. The Founder seemed like quite an interesting fellow. Mixed in with quite a bit of New Age mumbo jumbo and editorializing from Felicia, it sounded like the Founder actually channeled some otherworldly being. That was a little bizarre.

The voices or being or whatever it was seemed to be on a timetable and wanted to learn more about the research being done. Did critters in other dimensions have deadlines? The whole thing sounded nuts, and I wanted to find out more about this Founder guy. But first, I wanted to wash my face. Yuck.

The afternoon weeding passed uneventfully and Felicia and Jane had moved on to a different project on the other side of the garden, so I didn't learn anything. I did rummage around the woodshed and found a set of gardening gloves that fit better, so at least my hands were happier.

The rest of me was considerably less happy when I encountered quite possibly the largest black bug I'd ever seen. With a high-pitched shriek, I leaped up, shook my hands like I was dog paddling, and yanked off my gloves.

George meandered over and I pointed at the enormous bug staring up at us and wiggling its long antennae. "That thing was crawling on me!"

He bent over, picked it up, and held it up to his eyes. "Mmm, could be a ground beetle. Or leaf beetle. Hard to tell for sure."

"It was *crawling* on me. Does it bite? It looks like something from a prehistoric era!"

"I doubt he'd bite, although I can't say for sure. It's hard to know if he's one of the ones that eats my plants or not. They look pretty similar. All these beetles are tough to tell apart, so I let them be."

His comment sounded suspiciously like a Beatles song, but I wasn't going to reference the Fab Four with someone I barely knew. "Could you let it be somewhere else that's far away from me?"

"Sure." He smiled at the bug in his palm, and then looked back at me. "I'm guessing you're not going to be too pleased when you find our resident snake."

"There's a snake?" I looked around me for anything that might be slithering by my feet.

"His name is Leon. He's only a little garter snake, but he eats all kinds of good stuff."

I repressed a shudder as George slowly strolled away, carrying the gigantic insect. The only thing that remained was my raging case of bug paranoia and lingering anxiety that I might meet Leon.

Chapter 4

Adjustments

After my afternoon weeding extravaganza, I took a much-needed shower and felt decent enough to face my fellow human beings at dinner. Somehow on my trips back and forth to the wooden tent I'd missed meeting up with Riley. It was possible our schedules weren't going to overlap at all.

After weeks of seeing him all day every day, I had a pent-up need to talk to him, particularly about everything I'd overheard about the Founder. I rushed to the dining hall and walked in the door. I didn't see our parents, but I did see Riley.

He was sitting next to a petite woman who had shoulder-length wavy hair that was almost exactly the same shade as mine was now. Maybe she was a devotee of dark brown sable henna too. I had to admit that the hair color looked far better on her than it did on me.

Riley was laughing at whatever Ms. Petite and Adorable was saying. I'd never seen him so relaxed with anyone else other than me. It felt strange, and the look on her face made me feel like I'd missed out on some special secret.

I walked up, sat down next to Riley, and put out my hand to the tiny woman. "Hi, I'm Mandy, Ryan's girlfriend. We just got here. I work in the garden. What do you do?"

Ms. Petite and Adorable seemed mildly taken aback by my mini-speech, but said politely, "I'm Veronica, and I do fundraising."

"Interesting. When we arrived, I asked about fundraising because I have a lot of writing experience. But they told us Enviro Freedom doesn't do that type of work."

"Maybe it's because they already have a fundraiser. Me."

I was starting to not like tiny Veronica's perky little attitude. I leaned around Riley toward her. "All I'm saying is that my writing skills are being wasted in the garden."

Riley put his palm on my leg and gave my thigh a gentle squeeze. "Aren't you hungry? Today's delight includes soup that involved a lot of carrots. They're good for your eyes."

I glanced at him and knew what he was getting at. I shoved his hand off my leg. Fine. I'd back off, but come on, I was a professional writer. I'd won awards, and they had me out there in the dirt pulling weeds. "My eyes are fine."

"Try the soup anyway." Riley raised his eyebrows, which I knew meant, "What is your problem?" I could practically hear him saying it in my head.

I got up and went to go stand in line, extremely irritated for no apparent reason. I was probably overtired from hours of weeding. What I wouldn't do for a desk job again.

I glared over my shoulder at Veronica, who now seemed to be sitting even closer to Riley. What was *that* about? Was she flirting with him? She didn't even know him. Was he sniffing out her pheromones? I clutched my plate more tightly and turned back to face the server. "I've heard today's soup is good."

I returned to my spot at the table next to Riley, who seemed to be engrossed in some long-winded tale Veronica was telling about her travels in Montana. I didn't care and focused on ignoring her chirpy voice while I slurped up my soup. Riley was right; it was tasty. I snarfed down the rest of the meal and grabbed a few rolls from the basket. I couldn't stand listening to Veronica for a moment longer. Time to leave.

I nudged Riley, "See you later."

He turned in his chair to look at me. "Where are you going? Aren't we going to go, uh, have tea?"

"I can't face that again tonight. I'm tired." I got up and took a big bite of my roll. I needed to get outside. Maybe all that fresh-air time I was getting among the plants was good for me, after all.

It was unlike me to want to get away from people after an entire day of being by myself in the garden, and I wasn't sure what to think. What was wrong with me? Riley was the one who was always agitating for alone time. Not me. On the other hand, when I was a reporter I wasn't always interviewing people. I also used to spend a lot of time writing or doing research, which is fairly solitary.

The night air felt good, and most of the mosquitoes seemed to have gone home for the evening. Since we'd arrived, I hadn't had a chance to simply explore or even walk down to the river. I knew it was down there somewhere because I could hear it in the distance. Over the past two days, I'd spent so much time running from place to place, I hadn't had any spare time to walk on the paths where our parents liked to take their daily stroll.

I walked in the direction of the river, wishing Zelda were with me, and then realized there was no reason she couldn't go for a walk too. I turned back toward the bungalow where our parents were staying. I knew they weren't in the dining area, so they were probably at home.

I knocked on the door and was greeted by a cacophony of barking. My mother opened the door and smiled. "Meg, this is a surprise. We weren't expecting you until later. Where's Riley?"

"Probably at dinner. I was wondering if I could borrow Zelda."

At the sound of her name, Zelda charged toward me and I crouched down to collect all that soft white fur in my arms. "Hey, Zee! I miss you."

"Do you want to come in? We were about to go over to the dining hall to eat, but we could snack on something here instead, if you like."

"No, please go on to dinner. I want to go for a walk with Zee." At the magic "w" word, Zelda started leaping around, making rrr-ing noises, and waggling her body in a show of enthusiasm for the idea.

"I think she'd like that." Mom removed a leash from the hook. "She's all yours. We'll see you later."

I gave my mother a hug and Zelda and I went outside. "Okay, Zee, I think the trail is over there, but I'm guessing you know better than I do where it goes. Don't get me lost."

Zelda investigated a tree and then moved into what I thought of as her marching trot, forging ahead into the twilight. I followed her on the perimeter trail, which I knew went to the river. I was looking forward to sitting at the picnic table in the covered pavilion and listening to the sound of the rushing river up close.

We walked for a while and I felt some of the stress drain from my body, replaced by a comforting bone-tiredness from all my gardening exertion. At least I'd be in better shape by the time we left here. I'd also know way more about botany than I ever would have expected. I told Zelda about my day, leaving out my girly scream when I met the mega-bug. She didn't need to know about that part.

Zelda stopped short and turned around so she was facing the trail behind us. "What's up, Zee. Did you hear a squirrel?"

The dog suddenly hurled herself forward, pulling the leash out of my hand almost before I realized what was happening. I charged back up the trail after her. So much for my peaceful walk. I yelled, "Zee, you get back here! Zelda, *come*! I mean it!"

I was so focused on the dog that I ran around a bend on the trail and shrieked when I collided with Riley, who appeared out of nowhere. Zelda leaped with joyous abandon, thrilled to see her favorite person. I was less thrilled and shook myself out of his grasp. "What are you doing here?"

"I'm looking for you. Why are you wandering around out here? What is *wrong* with you today?"

"You got to see Zelda today, but I spent all day cooped up with bugs and weeds." I picked up Zelda's leash off the ground. "I wanted to get away from there and take her for a walk."

Riley took the leash from me. "Is it okay if I walk with you?"

"Zee seems to embrace that idea, and I need to tell you what I learned today anyway."

"I want to talk to you about what I found out too, but is something else bothering you?"

"No." At his silence, I waved my hands in exasperation. "Okay, *yes*. This is going to sound pathetic, but I'm having trouble adjusting to my life as Mandy. I thought it would be more interesting. Finding out information. Gathering intel. But today, mostly I dealt with bugs. The real kind, not telephones. I'm talking gigantic, scary bugs."

"I'm happy to say there aren't bugs in the kitchen, but having people ask me about my health is tiresome. Everyone knows someone who has had cancer and they want to tell me about it."

"Is that what you and Veronica were talking about?"

"Among other things. She's very friendly, which probably makes her a good fundraiser."

"With that perky little-girl voice, who could turn her down? It would be like telling a Girl Scout you're not buying her cookies."

"I suppose your voice is a little more acerbic."

I stopped and put my fists on my hips. "*Acerbic?* What's that supposed to mean?"

"Nothing. You're just irritated because she has the job you want."

"They'll never give it to me because I don't look and sound like I jumped off the set of *Peter Pan*."

He grinned. "I don't believe it. You're not only jealous about the job, you're jealous she was talking to *me*, aren't you?"

"I most certainly am not." Was I? Okay, maybe a little.

Riley put his arms around me. "You need to be patient. We're not going to figure out everything overnight."

I returned the hug, rested my cheek on his chest, and my pent-up tension and anxiety began to evaporate. "I didn't see you all day. Will you think I'm a wimp if I say I missed talking to you? After traveling together for so long, it's a shock to my system not having you around all the time."

He pushed a clump of hair behind my ear and kissed my earlobe. "Nope, not wimpy at all. I think it's sweet. Sometime, you're going to have to…"

Whatever he was going to say next was interrupted by a crash that came from somewhere in the darkness on the trail ahead of us. We leaped apart, and Zelda growled. All the fur on her back was standing straight up and she crept forward slowly. Riley pulled her back. "No, Zee. Wait."

A short man with black hair emerged from the trees. It was one of Hector's men who had been chasing us for weeks. I slapped my hand over my mouth to repress a scream.

He said, "Dammit, I think I got lost. Is this the tree-hugger retreat?"

I dropped my hand and demanded, "What are you doing here?" I tried to sound brave and forceful, but it came out more like a squeak.

Riley added, "Don't come any closer or I'll let go of this dog, and you know what she'll do."

"Don't let that animal near me! I need your help. I've been trying to get here for God only knows how long. You have to help me."

Riley and I looked at each other. That certainly was *not* the response I'd expected.

~

After I recovered from my stunned silence, I said, "Why on earth would we help you? You've been chasing us all over the country. And you *attacked* me!" I was pleased to see that I must have broken his nose during our last altercation. It was crooked because I'd slammed his face with a tote bag that held a gigantic romance novel. Served him right.

The man held up his hands in a gesture of surrender. "It wasn't my fault. I had to do that."

"Why?" Riley said. Zelda's growling increased in intensity to emphasize his point. She wasn't too fond of this guy either.

"Settle down for a sec and let me explain. My name is Lester." He gestured toward me, then Riley. "And yeah, I was trying to capture you. So what happened to you guys? I mean, that's a pretty serious haircut you got, dude."

"It's a long story. But you'd better talk fast because Zelda looks like she's in a biting mood." I said.

"Okay, okay. So it's like this. Me and Nick was working for Hector. But it wasn't my idea. Nick was there too and he sometimes had to keep me in line. But then he didn't, and… okay, I'm getting ahead of myself. Anyway, his sister was my wife. So he's my, uh…whatever."

"Brother-in-law." Riley said.

"Yeah, right. Anyway, Hector took Nicole. Just plucked her right off the street. Then he tells me and Nick that if we don't help him, we'll never see her again."

"Keep talking," I said. Unfortunately, this scenario sounded familiar. It wasn't the first time we'd heard about Hector getting in the middle of a family, taking people away, and making threats.

"Nick didn't want nothing to happen to his sister, and I didn't want Hector to do something to her either."

I pointed at Lester. "Hold on. You're saying Nick had a sister named Nicole? I'm not buying this. What kind of parents would name two kids so they both end up being called Nicky? Give me a break."

"I'm serious! They thought it was cute or something. I don't know. And Nicole would slap you if you ever called her Nicky. I found out real quick that you don't *ever* want to call her that."

The tale was absurd enough that I could believe clueless parents might saddle siblings with similar names. I shrugged. "Okay, moving on. Why are you here by yourself? Where did the other guy go? What happened to Nick?"

"If this is some type of trap…" Riley added.

"It's not! I swear. Nick and I had a parting of the ways. He decided he was gonna go back home."

"Why?" I asked.

"Well, it turns out that Nicole ended up starting up a thing with Hector. Once he got into the whole Kiss thing, she fell for him."

"That's ridiculous. He was the worst singer I've ever heard. And I use the term 'singer' lightly. Hector couldn't carry a tune," I said.

"Oh, she didn't listen to him. She had the hots for Gene Simmons ever since I knew her. Once Hector put on those outfits, she was in lust."

I resisted the urge to throw up. Gross. "I guess you weren't in the band?"

"No way. I'm not wearing those plastic outfits. I'd look stupid."

I'd seen the show live and Lester wasn't wrong about that. "So what happened?"

"I found out Hector had been off screwing my wife, and after a show I lost it and kinda roughed Hector up a little. I broke his plastic armor, so he was pissed and pulled a knife on me. He said he was going to chop me up into little pieces, and I decided it was time to go."

"So, if you're here, where is Hector?" Riley asked. "Is he nearby?"

"I sure hope not. He was furious at me and Nick when we lost you the last time. I was sure I saw you go down that road, but then the hot Mustang was gone. I knew you had to be back here somewhere, so I came back. You have to help me."

I waved my hand, "You haven't explained why we would do that. We have absolutely no reason to help you."

"Because I know what's going on. You are the only people that Hector hasn't been able to catch. I'll tell you what he's after if you help me hide. I need to stay away from him, and you want to know what he's doing. So it's like a win-win."

I didn't quite see it that way, but I did like the idea of learning more about what Hector was up to because all we had was supposition and guesses. "You promise you're not going to hurt us in any way?"

"And you promise you absolutely will *not* tell Hector where we are?" Riley added.

"Why would I?" Lester turned his palms toward the sky. "I got nuthin'. Nick took my van. Hector took my phone and my wife. I got nuthin' left. I spent the last of my money taking a bus and then walked from Glacier. It's a long way. I ended up near the river, then there was this big fence and I went around it."

We'd done the same thing, so we knew the route. The story was believable, partly because of the state of his clothes, which were torn and dirty. Somewhere along the way, he'd lost the jacket. Hiking in a suit had to be uncomfortable, and his gray trousers probably couldn't be saved. He must have been rained on and gone through a lot of mud to get here.

I glanced up at Riley, who had a thoughtful expression on his face. I said, "Maybe they'd take him in. George needs more help in the garden. It's vast and weed-infested."

Riley pulled off his glasses and rubbed his eyes. "You aren't seriously considering this, are you?"

"I want the information," I said.

Riley put his glasses back on and shushed Zelda, who continued to growl quietly. "If we do this, you need to not blow our cover, Lester. While we're here, I'm Ryan and she's Mandy."

Lester nodded. "Cute names."

"I'm his girlfriend and we're from North Dakota. The short hair is because he had cancer," I said.

"Whoa, that sucks. I didn't know that. Is that why you went to the hospital?"

"No," Riley snapped. "It's part of the cover story. Pay attention."

I was a little disturbed to learn that Lester knew about Riley's recent stay at Harborview Medical Center in Seattle, but persevered. "We shaved his head so it would look like Ryan went through chemotherapy. It's pretend, okay?"

"Got it."

Riley turned to me. "It's late. What are we going to do? Walk up to Shannon and say we found this guy? Then what?"

"Let's grab our stuff and crash with our, um, friends, Tim and Ellen. He can stay in wooden tent six." I pointed at Lester. "We can deal with him in the morning. I have to be in the garden at five."

Riley grinned. "Five in the morning? You're kidding. *You?*"

"It's not by choice." I turned to Lester. "You will stay in the cabin until I come and get you, understand? You do not under any circumstances say who we truly are."

Lester ran his fingertip across his chest. "Cross my heart."

"In exchange, you can explain what Hector is doing." I turned and grabbed Riley's hand. "Starting right now, on the way to our cabin. You said you ended up with Hector when he captured your wife."

"Yeah, Nicole was having migraines, and the doctor gave her pills that helped. But she was spaced out and dopey all the time because of the drugs. So me, Nick, and her were walking down the street near our house in Chicago to go get a pizza. A van pulls up and some guy grabs her and she's gone."

"That sounds familiar," I said. In Alpine Grove, I'd been grabbed in a similar way by an extremely nasty woman named Helen who worked with Hector.

"Well, me and Nicky, we chased that van, but we were too slow." Lester stumbled on a rock. "Goddamn, I'm so tired I can barely think. Anyhow, we're freakin' out so we go to the pizza joint and call the cops on the pay phone there."

"I'm guessing they weren't helpful," I said.

"They didn't do jack. Hector turned up on my doorstep the next day, and that's when he threatened to hurt Nicole. Nick was staying with me. Neither of us wanted anything to happen to Nicole, and we were sorta in-between jobs anyway. So we figured 'what the heck' and went with him."

"What is Hector after?" Riley said.

"People who can do special stuff. He thought Nicole had special vision, but she had plain old migraines. I don't understand that part too well. But you know that guy Dean that we captured? That guy could hear like nobody's business. It was weird."

"We know about that part," I said. "Where did Hector take these people?"

"To some building in Los Angeles. It was big like a warehouse or something, but I never went inside. Because we lost Dean on the way, Hector was super pissed off by the time we got there."

"Is there anyone you didn't lose?" I asked.

"Lars was a creepy guy who was supposed to get dropped off too, but Hector didn't do it because Lars ended up having a kid with him." Lester stumbled again. "Nice kid, but the whole thing was a pain in the patootie."

"Anyone else?" Riley asked.

"Hector said he'd grabbed some people before. He said he outsourced grabbing to Nick and me, but he was always griping about how we weren't as good as him. He had to run the circus and then the band, so grabbing was our job, but we weren't that great at it."

I decided to ask the question I really wanted to ask. "Why was Hector taking these people?"

"He was hired by some big company. If these people started complaining, some bigwigs were gonna lose a bunch of money. They paid him a mint to get certain people off the streets. I didn't get hardly any money for all that running around we did either. Gas is expensive."

"What was the name of the company?" Riley asked.

"Arche…uh…typical or something like that. It's some Internet business, I guess. Online stuff and cell phones." He waved at the trees. "I lost my damn cell phone, but I probably wouldn't get a signal here anyway."

"Yes, we know, but it's not so bad," I said. "Do you know who Hector was dealing with at Archetypal? Who was his contact?"

"Some guy named Matt. Hector was always saying, 'Matt's gonna be mad' about this or that."

I'd had my suspicions, but now I knew for sure. Matt Eskridge was an executive I knew at Archetypal and was also my ex-boyfriend. I used to be half-kidding when I said he was evil. But as it turned out, he actually was. I didn't think my opinion of Matt could have sunk any further, but knowing he was behind the abduction of people like me took it to a new low.

We arrived at the tent and packed our stuff while Lester went to visit the bathroom to take a much-needed shower. He didn't smell good, and if he touched anything in his current state, Riley would probably never be willing to sleep in our wooden tent again.

Zelda jumped up on the cot and supervised while I threw my stuff into my suitcase. I glanced at Riley, who paused in his packing to say, "So, Matt the Prick strikes again, huh? You can sure pick 'em."

"You do realize that doesn't say anything good about you, right?"

"I suppose, but I like to think that your taste has improved."

"That's what my mother said." I threw a shirt at him. "Shut up and pack. We have to move back in with our parents now."

"I'm guessing they're not going to love this idea."

"No, probably not."

~

While we were dealing with Lester, our parents had been at dinner, and there was no answer when we knocked on the door of their cottage. They probably were still hanging out with the people at the cool table in the dining hall.

I tried the door handle, and it was locked. I picked up my suitcase and threw the strap over my shoulder. "I'm going around the side."

"You're not thinking of breaking into our parents' house, are you?" Riley said as he dropped his suitcase and the cooler on the ground.

I turned around and started around the perimeter of the bungalow. "Mom likes to sleep with the window open."

Riley and Zelda followed me and as I'd predicted, the bedroom window was open. "Hey, Mr. Mechanical Engineer, could you take out the screen? I'm too short."

"I can't believe you want to do this."

"Oh come on, didn't you ever sneak into your house after curfew?"

Riley tugged at the top of the screen. "I'm starting to have a better understanding of why you and your mom fought so much when you were in high school."

"Give me a boost up. I'll crawl inside and unlock the front door."

"This is such a bad idea."

I reached up, put my arms around his neck, and gave him a quick peck on the lips. "Parents have to love you no matter what. Help me up there before the mosquitoes wake up and discover the screen is out."

Riley looked into my eyes for a moment, and then smiled slightly. He tugged my body close to his, wrapped his arms around me, and leaned me backward over his arm into a dip for the classic movie-star lip lock. The intensity of the kiss was so startling that I found myself clinging to him. Partly it was so he wouldn't drop me on the ground, but also because I was shaking and practically giddy from the many wild, delicious sensations.

He released me and pulled me upright again. "If I'm going to get caught breaking curfew, it should be worth it."

"Wow." I attempted to catch my breath as I pulled my shirt back down. "Yeah, you're...okay...wow. Definitely worth it."

"All right, up you go." He seized me around my waist, lifted me up, and chucked me through the window. I landed on the floor with a thud. Maybe it wasn't the most graceful entrance, but I was in. I stood and leaned out the window. "Grab my stuff."

Riley held up the screen. "Get out of the way. Zee and I will be right there."

I let them in and Zelda ran off to the kitchen, probably to see if she'd magically been fed while we were out. Riley and I dropped our stuff next to the sofa and sat down.

I leaned my head back and closed my eyes. "It feels so good to sit down. This has been a long day."

Riley ran his fingertip down the side of my neck. I opened my eyes again, and he smiled at me. "You were supposed to tell me what you learned today."

I sat up straight to look at him. "So were you. And you said I'm going to have to do something, but we were rudely interrupted by Lester the Loser. Is there something I'm supposed to do?"

"Maybe." Riley took off his glasses and set them on the coffee table. "Why don't you tell me what you found out?"

I went through the information I'd gleaned from my fellow gardeners about the mysterious Founder and his impending visit.

When I was done, Riley said. "So he talks to another dimension? That's a little weird. Who is this guy?"

"I don't know much about him other than his name is Ralston Landecker."

Riley rubbed his chin. "That name sounds familiar. I think I've heard it before, but I'm not sure why."

"So what did you find out?"

"Nothing as interesting as you did. The kitchen folks are pretty focused on cooking, but I had a lot of time to chat with Dad this morning."

"Did you talk about anything other than Lurch?"

"I found out that the way they get outside information is through their research assistants. Your mom works with a guy named Sid and Dad works with Patrick. They use a computer with access to various online research databases."

I leaned over, put my hands on either side of Riley's face, and locked my gaze with his. "You are going to find this computer, embrace your inner geek, and hook up my laptop to it so you can download everything. I want access to absolutely everything they know."

He offered a sly smile. "My inner geek might need some convincing."

I dropped my hands and pulled my legs up so I was kneeling on the sofa, facing him. "What kind of convincing?"

He threaded his long fingers into my hair and kissed me. "I'm sure you'll think of something."

I considered quite a few options, but shook my head. "You realize that if I touch you, our parents will walk through the door. I think my mother has some type of radar."

Undeterred, Riley pulled me into his lap and tilted his head, brushing his lips across my cheek and down my neck, sending thrilling shivers down my spine. I gave up on any semblance of propriety, kissed him on the lips, and yanked him down to me, so I could feel his body pressed against mine.

A few minutes later, Zelda stood up and barked, and I fell off the sofa, followed by Riley, who landed more or less on top of me. He scrambled to sit up and I reached under the coffee table for my shirt. As the door opened, I pulled the shirt over my head and nonchalantly ran a palm over my hair. "Hi, Mom."

Our parents stood in the doorway looking down at us. Riley pulled his knees up from under the coffee table and wrapped his arms around them. "Hi, Dad."

"What are you doing here?" my mother asked.

Tim said, "Don't you have your own cabin?"

I tugged at my shirt and looked down. It was on backwards. "Yeah, um, we found someone, and he's staying there."

Riley added, "We were hoping we could stay here tonight."

Mom glanced at me and then my suitcase. "It appears you already have made yourself at home."

"Did I forget to lock the door again?" Tim asked.

Riley and I looked at each other and then nodded in unison. I gave my shirt another tug, and Mom squinted at me with one of those "I know what you were up to" looks that I knew all too well.

My mother waved her hands upward. "Well, get up off the floor, for heaven's sake."

We scrambled to sit politely on the sofa. I crossed my legs like a lady, put my hands on my knees, and tried to look attentive.

Mom said, "What do you mean you *found* someone?"

"When I took Zelda for her walk, we met a man," I said.

Tim and my mother peppered us with questions about Lester, and we had to go through a long explanation of why we would consider helping a guy who had attacked us. Although helping Lester didn't sound particularly wise, he did seem to loathe Hector as much as we did, which scored extra points.

Tired of the parental grilling, I said, "The bottom line is that I want to get more information out of him. He's the only person we've met who knows what Hector is up to."

"Lester was getting a little incoherent, so we grabbed our stuff and let him stay in our cabin," Riley added. "He'd been walking for a long time, and I think he was exhausted."

"We don't have a spare bedroom here, you know," Mom said.

"That's fine," Riley said. "I've got a sleeping bag."

Mom ran out of arguments, and finally she and Tim wished us a good night, gave us hugs, and retired to their bedroom.

Riley and I sat down on the sofa again, and Zelda jumped up next to him. He put his arm around my shoulders. "This will be cozy."

"You're way too tall to fit on this couch. What are we supposed to do?"

"I'm sure you'll think of something."

Recognizing the mischievous glint in Riley's eyes, I reached to unbutton the top button of his shirt. "I did have some ideas, but you have to be quiet."

"I can be quiet if you can."

That was debatable, but I was willing to risk it.

⁓

At the sound of heavy breathing in my ear, I swatted around the side of my head. "Aren't you tired?"

From the other side of me, Riley mumbled. "What?"

The sofa was narrow and the sleeping bag was tangled up so my legs were intertwined with Riley's like we were crocheted together. I managed to turn my head and encountered Zelda's wet black snout in my face. "Zee, ick! Go to sleep."

Zelda licked the tip of my nose and wagged expectantly. I elbowed Riley. "I'm not sure what this dog wants, but she wants something."

He groaned and raised his head to look over me at the dog. "What?"

Zelda wagged again and made a soft rrr-ing noise. I sat up and squinted at the wall clock in the kitchen area behind us. "I have to get up."

"It's dark."

"I know." I rolled off the sofa onto the floor, pushing Zelda out of the way in the process. I collected my clothes and got dressed. "I'll take her out before I collect Lester and introduce him to the garden."

Riley sat up and scrubbed his face with his hands. "I'll go with you, since Zelda seems convinced she needs a walk."

"Maybe she knew I had to get up." I leaned over to hug the dog. "Have you decided you're my personal alarm clock, Zee?"

We tiptoed out of the bungalow and walked into the crisp morning air. The first light of the sun created a thin halo over the trees as we strolled back to our cabin.

I said, "No one should be awake at 4:30. I need caffeine in the worst way."

"The plants won't care that you're sleepy."

"How come you're so alert? I know you couldn't have gotten much sleep."

He put his arm around my shoulder. "Except for that blast of radiation when we first got here, I feel better than I have in months. Dad isn't sure exactly what happened, but he promised he'd try not to do it again."

"Gee, thanks, Dad."

"I can see why he likes it here. Peeling and chopping vegetables is boring, but it gives me time to think."

"I don't suppose you eat any of the veggies, do you?"

"Actually, I do. They're really fresh."

I clasped his hand and gave it a squeeze. "This could be you finally getting healthier."

"Maybe. I'm starting to feel more like me again."

I wished I could say the same thing, but I couldn't. I felt more lost than ever. Although I wasn't dealing with debilitating visions at the moment, I was confused about almost everything in my life.

Six months ago, I'd had moments when I thought I had everything figured out at last. I had money in the bank and was on track to pay off my student loans. I got to go on extravagant trips and dine in swanky restaurants with my gorgeous executive then-boyfriend, and to work at a job that satisfied me both professionally and personally. And then all of it fell apart so completely that I barely knew who I was anymore.

I glanced at Riley, who looked completely content, strolling along with Zelda. He'd apparently forgotten about his glasses and left them on the coffee table. The relationship I had with him was so different from anything I'd experienced that I didn't quite know what to make of it.

Typically, I'd meet a guy, fall head over heels in lust, and be so overwhelmed with the rush of infatuation that I'd do something incredibly dumb. With Matt, the Evil Executive, my stupid move was giving him the benefit of a whole lot of doubts and burning a whole lot of bridges with friends I'd had for a long time. Before Matt, I'd moved in with a guy named Al. Our cohabitation lasted a week before I realized what a huge mistake it was and moved myself right back out. I tended to jump headlong into relationships without thinking, so my dating history was like a sine wave with extreme highs and deep lows.

Everything that had happened with Riley was backwards. When we first met, I didn't fall in lust with him or even like him much. He drove me nuts, and then we effectively moved in together, traveling all over the West. But over time, even though we argued—probably because of our shared weird adversity—we became friends. Now we were more than friends, but I had no idea how he felt about much of anything that was going on between us. Well, anything other than that he liked sex, which duh—what human male doesn't?

It wasn't like we'd rushed into anything, since it had taken months for us to even kiss. But something about being with Riley was comforting in a way I couldn't explain. And being with him wasn't like the unnatural experience I'd had with Lars that had related to his sensory abnormality.

What I felt with Riley was more subtle. I enjoyed simply holding his hand as we walked through the dark forest. It was almost embarrassing because I definitely wasn't the clingy type. But now I was insatiable, always wanting to touch him.

Maybe it was because he'd scraped me up off the floor so many times after my screaming visions. Or it was possible some hormonal science-related chemical thing was going on. Or maybe it was simply proximity. We'd been more or less stuck with one another while we were searching for our parents. But what would happen when we were finally able to leave this retreat? Would Riley and I go our separate ways? Stay together? Part of me desperately wanted clarification, and the other part was afraid to find out.

Riley tugged gently on my hand. "You're awfully quiet. Are you sleepwalking?"

"I'm awake, but I'm cold, and I still want coffee. How am I going to be able to stand getting up and pulling weeds every morning without coffee? This is cruel and unusual. We don't have any way to make coffee in our crappy wooden tent and the dining hall isn't open all night. It stinks."

"Well, that was quite a tirade. I'm remembering why I bought a coffeemaker and dragged it into all those motel rooms."

"Lack of caffeine makes me cranky." I returned to my sulky silence and Riley wisely let me be.

We arrived at the wooden tent and Riley knocked on the door. Zelda rrr-ed at the groan that came from within. We took it as a signal that we should go inside. The door was unlocked, which wasn't surprising because Lester had no possessions to steal.

We walked inside and found Lester spread-eagled on the cot stark naked, which was far, far more of Lester than I wanted to see. Thank goodness the light wasn't good. But the sun was coming up, so I quickly turned around to face the door.

Zelda growled and Riley said, "Get up, Lester. It's time for you to go get a job."

"Dude, keep that dog away from me. And why are you here? It's dark. No one's at work," he said.

"You're wrong about that," I said. "Farmers get up early. Please put your clothes on." The idea of ever sleeping on that cot again made my skin crawl. Yuck.

With a lot of thumping and grumbling, Lester reassembled his wardrobe. I waited until all was quiet and turned to peek. Much to my relief, he was wearing his filthy shirt and suit pants again.

Lester spread his arms wide, "Happy now?"

"Thank you." I made a sweeping game show hostess gesture toward the door. "Let's go. We're going to be late."

"What is this job? Some kind of night shift?" Lester said.

"Weeding." Riley and I said in unison as Lester shut the door behind us.

Lester didn't look pleased, but he waited while I said goodbye to Riley. I hugged him and whispered, "Could you convince your dad to let us stay there? They have that extra room they're using as a study. Maybe we could get a cot from somewhere."

"I doubt they're going to want to do that."

"They have electricity, so I could have coffee in the morning. Please?"

He gave me a quick kiss. "All right, I'll try."

"Try really hard, okay?"

Chapter 5

Similarities

I walked to the garden with Lester and introduced him to George. As I'd hoped, George was such a mellow person that he didn't ask a whole lot of questions about why Lester was there. He took Lester off to a different section of the garden, leaving me alone with my weeds.

The time passed quickly, probably because I was half-asleep. By the time George stopped for breakfast, I was ravenous. If I was this hungry, Lester had to be dying. The night before we'd left him a few of our crackers and other snacks that remained from our travels, but it had probably been a while since the guy had eaten a full meal.

I walked with George and Lester to the dining hall, and Lester said, "I could get used to free food."

George said, "I find it satisfying to see the results of all the hard work we do in the garden."

"Emphasis on work," I said.

At the sound of footsteps running behind us, I turned to look. Felicia was scampering to catch up with us, her braid swinging back and forth behind her. She said breathlessly, "George, did you hear about the Founder?"

He shook his head. Part of my goal today was to learn more about our fearless leader, so I was intrigued. I gave

Felicia my most ingratiating smile. "I didn't hear anything either. What happened?"

"He was communicating with Dwayne, and we have new guidance."

"Who's Dwayne?" I asked.

Felicia flipped her braid behind her shoulder. "Don't you know *anything*? He's the entity the Founder channels from the other side."

Oops. Blurting out questions like that was going to get me in trouble. I needed to shut up and listen. "Right, sorry. I forgot. What did Dwayne say?"

Felicia continued. "Dwayne is upset that our environment and the beings on our planet are being harmed by unseen forces."

"He told the Founder that?" I asked. "How does that work?"

George said in his slow drawl, "As I understand it, channeling is different for different people. Have you heard how the Founder does it, Felicia?"

Felicia admitted that she hadn't, and George continued, "It's said that Dwayne offers advice and information through the Founder's voice while he's in a trance, but I haven't seen it myself."

I'd read about channeling before and piped up, "There was a book that was channeled through a Columbia University psychologist. I went to Columbia, but she was gone by the time I was there."

George glanced at me. "You went to Columbia University? New York City must have been quite an adjustment from North Dakota."

Crap. What was wrong with me? Mandy hadn't gone to grad school, much less Columbia. Why couldn't I shut up for once? "I mean, well, I visited when I took a trip to New York. There's an art museum, and I hear they have a great journalism school." I should know.

Felicia gave me the stink-eye before continuing, "As I was saying, the Founder communicated with Dwayne, and it was a powerful session. I guess Dwayne shared a lot of his wisdom from the other side. He says it's time for us to marshal more followers to combat the threats to our natural world. Actions must be taken to stop the forces that are harming the planet and its creatures."

Lester said, "Wait a second. You're saying this guy talks to dead people? That's like Shirley MacLaine-type whacko stuff. What a load of bull."

I had trouble maintaining a straight face because I was the ultimate cynical skeptic. Lester had said almost exactly what I was thinking, but I said serenely, "We're all here because we believe in helping the environment. The planet needs our help."

"Oh yeah, right. Whatever," he replied as he shoved his way into the dining hall. "Damnation, I could eat a horse."

Riley was sitting at a table on the far side of the room. He smiled at me and Lester, who evidently had forgotten all about Dwayne and the Founder, hustled to the buffet, and was now engrossed in collecting a stack of sugary pastries and putting them on his plate.

I grabbed a piece of toast and some coffee and went to sit next to Riley. I leaned over and whispered in his ear, "I figured you'd be hanging out with dear old dad."

"He and your mom aren't too happy with me, so I decided to wait around here for you."

I chuckled. "It's about time you got to share in some of the parental fun."

"You also seemed upset this morning." Riley nodded at Lester as he settled in across from us. "Hi, Lester. How was work?"

Lester was chewing, but managed to mumble, "Mmmphgh, okay I guess." He chomped his bear claw and held it up, tilting it toward me. "You do this every single day? How can you stand it? Weeding is a drag."

I took a long, heavenly sip from my coffee mug. "It's only my third day."

We all were focusing on eating and enjoying the wonder of caffeine when Shannon marched toward our table, her high heels making sharp tapping noises on the wooden floor. She was impeccably dressed again in another burgundy blouse and the pretty necklace.

I studied her more closely and determined that she wasn't only wearing burgundy. A deep reddish halo surrounded her as well. I gave a tiny gasp of realization, and Riley glanced at me. I was bursting to tell him what I'd seen, but I couldn't. The aura meant Shannon was one of us and she must have a special sensory ability. We needed to find out what it was.

She stopped in front of me and pointed at Lester. "Who is this man?"

Lester stood up, wiped some sugar from his palm onto his pants, and extended his hand. "I'm Lester. Pleased to meet you."

Although Shannon looked disinclined to touch him, she politely shook Lester's hand. "I'm Shannon Soloman. How did you get here?"

"I walked over from the garden. George is real nice." He turned to wave at George, who was sitting with Felicia at another table. "He showed me what's a weed and what's not."

"I'm sure he did," Shannon said. She turned to me and asked, "Do you know this person?"

I rubbed my eyes, startled at how vividly I could see her halo now that I knew it was there. She had to know about the radiation and must have been affected by the accidental blast from Tim's experiment the other day. No wonder she'd been in such a bad mood when we met.

Riley nudged me, "Are you all right?"

"Sorry. Yes, we met Lester last night," I sputtered as I glanced at Riley. He always had a teal blue aura, but I usually ignored it. I turned my head to look around the room. No one else was colorful except for Riley and Shannon. Interesting.

Shannon folded her arms across her chest. "Why didn't anyone tell me about this visitor?"

"It was late," I said.

Lester added, "I was real tired from walking. They let me sleep in their bed."

That sounded utterly repulsive, so I clarified, "Tim and Ellen let us stay with them last night, so Lester could stay in our cabin."

Shannon's eyes narrowed. Did she suspect that we knew Tim and Ellen a little too well? I did look a little like my mom and although Riley apparently took after his mother, if you knew he and Tim were related, you could see how they resembled one another in certain ways. Did Shannon know what was going on? I went for an innocent, harmless expression. "Those two are the sweetest couple. We met them when they were out walking their dog."

Riley said, "I love dogs, so we had to go over and pet it."

Zelda would be offended if she knew Riley had called her an "it," but he had to pretend he didn't know her. I moved into full-bore storytelling-liar mode. "We used to have a dog named Penny, but my parents back in North Dakota are taking care of her now. After Ryan got sick, we had to move to a smaller place and they didn't take dogs. Then, well, we decided to come here and I knew we couldn't travel with her." I widened my eyes. "Penny gets carsick in the *worst* way. But I miss that little dog so much. She's part cocker spaniel, I think. Maybe mixed with German shepherd. I'm not sure, but she has the most beautiful, soulful brown eyes."

Shannon scowled at me. "That's nice, but no one has explained to me why this man is here."

"He's working in the garden," I said.

Lester volunteered, "George was telling me about, uh, ecosystems this morning. I really, really love plants. Oh, and some of the bugs are good, you know. Not all of them are bad, so you shouldn't squish 'em. I heard there's a snake in the garden. That will be so cool if I get to play with a snake."

Shannon shook her head. "I'll talk to George. But there are no more available cabins, so you two need to work something out."

"Lester can stay in our tent—I mean cabin. We moved our stuff out," I said and winced as Riley jabbed me in the ribs with his elbow.

I glared at him. "I'm sure it will be fine."

Riley didn't say anything but his lips tightened. He yanked his glasses off and looked down, pretending to clean them with his shirt. I could tell he was extremely irritated, but too bad. Mom and Dad were just going to have to deal with new roommates.

Shannon left the table and went to confer with George. Riley tugged at my sleeve to get my attention. "Are you done? You probably need to get back to work."

"George is still here talking to Shannon, so I can hang out until he's done."

Riley grabbed my hand and gave it a forceful squeeze. "Let's go wait for him outside, Mandy."

I glared at him, pulled my hand away, and grabbed the mug so I could suck down the last of my coffee. "Whatever you say, *sweetheart*."

We left Lester at the table, bussed our dishes, and I followed Riley outside. I pointed at the dining hall behind us. "I'm guessing there's something you want to say to me alone?"

"Your mom almost lost her mind when I suggested we stay there." He shook his head. "It seems that she is as excited about spending time with you as you are with her."

"It will be okay."

"She said that you are confrontational and fight with her in—and I quote—'a volatile and combative way.' I wasn't quite sure how to respond to that."

"She's got a lot of nerve. I am not combative. Who is she to call *me* volatile?"

Riley leaned toward me. "If the volatile shoe fits…"

"She's completely overreacting. I'm sorry, but she's going to have to cope with my presence because I refuse to bunk with Lester. That's too revolting to contemplate. I think someone is going to need to burn that cot."

"Well, thanks to you, right now I need to smooth things over with Dad before I go to work in the kitchen."

I grabbed his hand with both of mine. "Wait! I need to tell you something."

"It had better be good."

"Shannon has a reddish aura. She's one of us. I'm sure of it."

"I'll ask Dad if he's seen anything odd. She doesn't look sick, and she hasn't screamed."

"That we know about anyway. Maybe she has touch or hearing issues."

"I suppose." He glanced at the dining hall behind me and bent to give me a peck on the cheek. "Here comes George. I'll see what I can find out from Dad."

I threw my arms around his neck and looked him in the eyes. "Oh, come on. That's not a goodbye kiss. We're engaged, so you'll have to do better than that."

He gave me a halfhearted kiss and peeled my arms from his neck. "Being around you and your mother is going to drive me to drink."

"I know you don't drink. Half the time you barely eat."

"Maybe I should start. See you later."

~

My second morning shift passed uneventfully. I pulled a lot of weeds and determined that Felicia was a horticultural suck-up. She followed George around like a lost puppy. I was impressed at his patience and willingness to answer her thousands of questions. What a pest.

During the afternoon weeding event, I ended up in a row near Jane, who, unlike Felicia, wasn't much of a conversationalist. I tried to engage in small talk, but she didn't seem interested, and Griffin moved around too much with his wheelbarrow for me to be able to extract any information from him either.

I was spacing out, my mind wandering aimlessly as I fretted about a lot of things I couldn't do anything about, when a bolt of lightning flashed across the sky, followed by the rumble of thunder. The sky unleashed more thunder, lighting, and a deluge of rain and hail.

George stood up, waved, and shouted. "Let's get out of here! See you tomorrow, unless it keeps raining like this."

I stood up, put my hands on my lower back, and flexed backward before turning and running through the rain to the dining hall. During the time I'd been in Washington State, I'd discovered that when the weather got serious about rain, it got really serious.

I entered the dining hall, stopped, and shook myself like a dog. I was drenched and pulled my sodden shirt away from my body. Maybe Riley had acquired a key to our parents' abode by now. I walked across the dining area to the kitchen and swished through the swinging doors.

Music was blasting and Maurice's gigantic body was hunched over a massive pot on a shiny six-burner commercial stove. He looked up from his stirring and gave me a wolf whistle. "Yo, Ryan! Looks like your girlfriend won a wet t-shirt contest."

Riley turned, set down his knife, and grinned at me.

I gestured toward the door and shouted over the heavy metal. "I need to talk to you!"

Riley waved at Maurice, pointed at me, and followed me out into the dining hall.

I grabbed the bottom of my shirt and twisted it to squeeze some of the water out. "Do you know if anyone is home at our parents' place? If not, do you have a key?"

"They're probably at their lab. I guess you're not up for breaking and entering today?"

"I prefer to embark on criminal activity when it's not pouring. And I'm too short to get into that window by myself, so you have to share in my life of crime."

"Great."

"Have you seen the lab yet?"

"I did, and I met the 'boys,' as our parents call their research assistants. They seem nice enough." He reached into his pocket. "Here's the key to the house."

I moved to take it from him and held onto his hand. "Are you still mad at me?"

"We can talk about it later." He jerked his thumb toward the kitchen. "I have to get back to my vegetables."

It was a long walk through the pouring rain to get to my parents' bungalow, but the thought of being able to partake of private bathroom facilities was a big motivator. As soon as I was inside, I greeted Zelda, grabbed clothes, and went straight for the shower.

Afterward I felt as if every muscle in my body melted, and I collapsed on the sofa with Zelda. We took a little nap on the sleeping bag until the door opened and she launched off the couch. I was relieved to see it was Riley and not our parents.

He came in and sat next to me. "How come you're not at dinner? I figured you'd be hungry."

"I was petting Zelda and she convinced me I needed a nap. Are the 'rents still at the lab?"

"Probably. They said they go to dinner late. Do you want to go over and get something to eat?"

"Did you already eat?"

"No. When you didn't show up first in line at dinner, I wondered what had happened to you."

I slumped back on the sofa. "I'm exhausted and we need to talk. Is there anything here we can snack on?"

"Maybe." Riley got up and Zelda followed him into the kitchen. "If nothing else, I can feed Zee."

While Riley fed the dog and assembled snack food that he deemed acceptable, I relayed everything I'd learned about the Founder and we talked more about how colorful Shannon was to me.

Riley handed me a sandwich and we sat down at the table. I dug in and chewed happily, glad to be able to relax and not pretend to be someone I wasn't. I passed Zelda a chip. "Here's the thing. It's not like I can walk up and say, 'Hey, Shannon, had any bizarre sensory problems lately?' But the fact that she's a specialist explains why they brought our parents here. Shannon probably wants them to figure out how to fix our problem as much as we do."

"That makes sense. The channeling stuff with the Founder is strange though."

"Felicia is a total crystal-hugger. Lester said it was Shirley MacLaine-level weird, which cracked me up."

Riley set down his sandwich and got the soft, faraway look in his eyes that meant he was thinking.

"What?"

"What, what?"

"What are you thinking so hard about?" I held up the sandwich, preparing to take another bite. "Crystal-huggers?"

"Sort of. Crystals are used in radio communications and computer-related stuff. They can be shaped so they vibrate at a specific frequency."

"Frequency, like electromagnetic frequency?"

"Maybe. I don't know if there's any relationship." He waved his hand dismissively. "I'm going nowhere with this line of thought. Never mind."

"Well, if you ask Felicia, she'd tell you that crystals have healing energy. And they align chakras." I smiled. "Hey baby, how are your chakras doing?"

"Very funny."

I polished off my sandwich. "Have you figured out how you're going to download research for me?"

"Why don't we just ask our parents?"

"We can try, but my mom may get weird about it. She never wanted me reading her research. That's part of why I was afraid I was the subject half the time. Otherwise, why would she care?"

"Let's ask them, Meg. They're on our side, remember?"

"If they say no, or don't have access to that room, we need to find out how we can get a key and get at that computer. As far as we know, it's the only thing connected to the outside world. I have no idea what's going on with Archetypal or anything. It's been days since we've read any news, and I'm having withdrawals."

Riley stood up and carried his plate to the kitchen. "All right, fine. But I'll talk to Dad first."

As if they knew we were talking about them, the door opened and Tim and my mother walked in. She set her tote bag down on the hall table and turned to me. "Well, I see you've already made yourself at home in our home...*again*."

I waved. "Hi, Mom. Thanks for letting us crash here."

"Did I have a choice?" she asked. "Shannon came to talk to me today and interrupted what I was working on."

I knew nothing annoyed my mother more than people disturbing her when she was working. That meant she was undoubtedly in a bad mood before she'd even walked in the door. "Riley gave me the key because it started to pour, and I got soaked. I came back here to take a shower. Then I fell asleep."

"That's so like you. I've never seen anyone who needs as much sleep as you do," Mom said. "When you lived at home, I'd sometimes peek in the door of your room to check and make sure you were still alive."

I tried not to grind my teeth at her tone. "I wasn't *always* asleep when I was in my room, you know. I stayed up late doing homework every night."

"Yes, I often wonder how you managed in college without me nagging you to get your work done."

I closed my eyes for a second. Was she actually going to bring that up again? "Gosh, thanks for asking, Mom. I even managed to graduate too. So now are you going to point out that I don't have a PhD?"

"It is a lot of work. I should know. Do we have any food left or did you eat it all?"

"I think I might have left a piece of moldy lettuce in the fridge for you."

My mother whirled around and I could hear her mumble, "Nice attitude. You're welcome," before she stomped into the bedroom and closed the door.

I put my hands out in a helpless gesture and said to Tim, "I'm sorry, but Riley and I needed to talk, and I'm exhausted from gardening and pretending to be Mandy, so we hung out here."

Riley said, "Dad, do you think there are any extra cots anywhere? I was thinking we could sleep in the study, so Meg and I are a little more out of the way."

Tim's expression brightened, and he patted Riley on the back. "Yes, that's a great idea. There's a shed behind the lab that's filled with supplies and extra furniture. Let's drive over there and take a look. I want to see how those modifications to the carburetor worked out anyway."

Riley grabbed the keys to Lurch off the coffee table and grinned at me. "We'll be back in a few. Have fun with your mom."

That was unlikely, particularly if she stayed in the bedroom sulking about my presence.

～

Zelda went with Riley and Tim on their excursion, leaving me alone with my furious mother. I wasn't sure what to do with myself, and didn't want to sit alone in the living room fretting. Because I was desperately hoping that Riley and his father could find something for us to sleep on, I decided I could expedite the process by moving our suitcases into the small study.

I did a little rearranging to clear the space, and stacked a few books neatly on the small desk.

"What are you doing?" my mother demanded from the doorway.

Startled, I knocked the books onto the floor, where they landed with a crash, knocking over an umbrella that was leaning against the wall.

"I'm trying to get our stuff out of the way."

She walked into the room and began picking up books. "I'll do it. You'll get everything out of order."

I didn't say anything, but grabbed my novel and retreated to my spot on the sofa. When Mom was in this type of mood, she became a model of efficiency and it was best to get out of her way.

Mom crashed around in the study while I laid low, read, and mentally begged for Tim and Riley's return. Finally, the door opened and Zelda ran inside. She leaped onto the sofa and leaned into me for some affection. I obliged and ruffled her ears while Tim and Riley dragged a cot across the room and into the study.

My mother gave them instructions and seemed to be in a better mood, having spent some time restoring order to her environment. Yeah, well, she wouldn't be quite as happy when she found out what an unbelievable slob Riley was. Last night we'd crashed on the sofa before he could do much damage, but we were going to need to keep the study door shut at all times from now on.

Having set up the cot to Mom's satisfaction, Riley sat on the sofa next to Zelda, who seemed to know that he was moving in, and was thrilled to have him around again. She rolled onto her back so he could rub her tummy.

Tim sat down in a wooden rocking chair across from us. "Ellen, did the research boys talk to you about the bombings?"

Ever since I'd almost blown up in a rest stop, I've been a little sensitive to discussions related to explosions, and I sat up straight. "Where?"

"Patrick said that a transmission tower outside of Seattle was bombed, but no one was hurt," Ellen said.

"How does he know? Is Enviro Freedom behind it?" I asked.

"Patrick was reading the news on his computer and mentioned it," Tim said.

My mother sat down in the chair across from me. "I know you said your clown friend believed that Enviro Freedom was behind some bombings, but I'm not sure I believe it."

"For the record, Lars isn't a clown anymore, and I do believe him. He had no reason to lie to me, and he was there when the circus trailers were bombed on the highway. Everyone there seemed to think EF was behind that incident, as well as the bombing of some cell towers near Portland and Los Angeles." I turned to Riley, "Hey, back me up here."

"That's what Lars told us," Riley said quietly, reaching over Zelda to put his hand on my arm.

"But there's no proof," Mom said.

I grasped Riley's hand and squeezed it to acknowledge that I knew he wanted me to settle down, but I certainly wasn't going to let my mother's overly rosy opinion of EF go without comment. "I think you're giving the people who run this place too much credit, Mom. Have you heard about the Founder guy? The guy sounds totally off his nut. I mean, he channels some dead guy named Dwayne. How weird is that?"

"You always jump to conclusions. Everyone here has been incredibly supportive of our work, and they seem to be committed to helping people," Mom retorted.

Tim said, "Well, you have to admit the whole Dwayne thing is a little off the wall. Has anyone actually seen the Founder do this?"

"Shannon has," Ellen said.

"Did Riley tell you that Shannon is one of us? She has some sensory abnormality. Do you know what it is?" I asked.

"How would I know? And how do *you* know?" Mom said.

"I told you, I can see auras. Riley's is blue." I said.

"I'm told it's a pretty teal blue color," Riley added.

Mom crossed her arms. "I think that someone who sees colors that no one else can see shouldn't be so quick to dismiss the idea of channeling."

I let go of Riley's hand, stood up, and went to get some water from the kitchen. I would have preferred a flask full of whiskey, but water would have to do. "You have trouble believing most things I say, so why should this be any different?"

Not surprisingly, the conversation went downhill from there as we discussed my various transgressions including, but not limited to, several times when I stayed out too late, lied about staying overnight with a friend when I was really at a teenage party, and not treating my elders with the proper respect while living under their roof. Riley and Tim looked incredibly uncomfortable until Riley took advantage of a break in the argument that lasted long enough for him to suggest that we should retire.

He closed the door behind him and leaned against it. I moved to go around him, and he stopped me. "We need to talk."

"I need to brush my teeth."

"How about if you help me put some sheets on this cot first?" He pulled a bottom sheet off the pile of linens and swished it across the cot. "If we're going to stay here, you and your mother need to work out some type of truce."

I grabbed a corner of the sheet and pulled it across the thin mattress. "I told you we argue. This isn't new news. She's incredibly critical of everything I do."

"Not any more than you are critical of her."

I dropped the sheet. "Hey, whose side are you on?"

"My own. I can't stand listening to you two bicker about things that happened twenty years ago. And my dad hates strife. He'll go out of his way to avoid confrontation."

"My mother certainly doesn't have that problem."

"Neither do you. The problem is that you're so similar to one another."

I yanked the sheet to tuck it in and pulled it out of Riley's hands. "Oops, sorry. I'm absolutely nothing like my mother. Don't give me that look. I'm *not*."

"Yes, you are. You're both opinionated, smart, passionate women. How can you possibly not see that?"

"She's a workaholic who was more interested in science than her own daughter. If I ever have kids, I'm not going to be like her."

"Maybe not, but she knows exactly how to push your buttons."

"Thanks for noticing. Sometimes I can tell by the look in her eye that whatever she's going to say next is going to make me angry."

"I'm sure she feels the same way about you." Riley sat on the cot and stuffed a pillow into a pillowcase. "Here's an idea. What if you don't take the bait? Let her get whatever is bothering her out of her system. Don't respond. Don't say anything."

"I can't do that. What if she's *wrong?* I can't simply say nothing."

"Yes, you can. Or one or both of us is going to have to get out of here. Probably me."

"I can't believe you're actually threatening to leave." I threw my pillow at him. "I'm going to brush my teeth."

Fortunately, no one else was in the bathroom because it totally messes up your dramatic exit when you stalk out of a heated discussion and then have to return because the bathroom is occupied. I forcefully brushed my teeth, spit, and grimaced at myself in the mirror.

I hated it when Riley was right. It infuriated me to admit it, but I was behaving like a spoiled brat. I'd spent months looking for my mother and now I was fighting with her. What was wrong with me?

I washed my face with cold water, hoping that it might wash away my anger with it. I sighed and returned to the study. Riley had tucked himself under the covers and was lying on his back with his arm over his eyes. Zelda was sprawled out across the end of the cot being a furry foot warmer. I smiled at the scene because I had seen it so many times before.

I nudged Zelda's butt out of the way and crawled in next to Riley. "I'm sorry."

He rolled over to look at me. "You need to work this out, Meg. I'm serious. Retreating alone to a desert island is looking better all the time."

"I know." I draped my arm over him and traced the outline of his shoulder blade. "It's not easy for me to let go of an opinion I believe in. But honestly, don't you think the Founder talking to a dead dude named Dwayne is weird?"

"It doesn't matter what I think. I'm not the one arguing with your mom. After you've stated your opinion, saying it more loudly isn't going to change her mind."

"I suppose." I dropped my head, and my short hair fell in front of my face. How did people put up with short hair? It was always in the way.

He tucked my hair back behind my ear. "Your mom is so much like you, and at this point in her life, she's not going to change. You have to accept that because she's the only mother you're ever going to have. When she pushes your buttons, ignore it. Let it go."

At the note of sadness in his voice, I looked into his eyes, remembering that his mother had died when he was a little boy. "I'll try. So how did you get so smart anyway?

"I had three or four thousand miles of driving around with you to figure it out."

Chapter 6

Night Shift

I woke up to the sound of rain pelting the metal roof, rolled over, and whispered to Riley, "Hey, it's pouring out there! That means I'm off the hook for gardening duty."

He shoved me toward the edge of the cot. "The alarm is going to go off in three minutes. Turn it off."

"It's cold."

With a kick and another shove, he said, "It's four twenty-seven. Go!"

I acceded to the request and quickly retreated under the covers. "Since I don't have to work today, we can figure out how to get access to that research computer."

"Later. Go to sleep."

"We need to know about those bombings too. I'm sure EF did it."

"Go to sleep."

"I want to find out what's going on. I know there's something going on. This place isn't just about saving trees. I'm sure of it."

Riley turned over to face me, pulled me to him, and kissed me so I forgot what I was thinking. I mumbled, "Okay, maybe later."

The next time I woke, dim light was peeking around the curtains and I could hear noises from the living room. Zelda was standing at the study door making little rrr-ing sounds.

Riley sat up and rubbed his eyes. "All right, Zee. Hold on a minute."

We got dressed and staggered out into the living room as our parents were preparing to leave for the lab.

I walked to my mother and said, "I'm sorry about last night, Mom."

We hugged, and I added, "Because of the rain, I don't have to work. I was hoping Riley and I could visit your lab. I know he's seen it, but I haven't and I'd like to learn more about what you're working on."

Riley said, "Zelda is getting squirrelly and needs a longer walk. Maybe we could walk over with her later."

"That would be fine," Ellen replied. "Will we see you at breakfast?"

I glanced at the clock, then at Riley. "Maybe. I need coffee first though."

Riley nodded. "Believe me, she does."

After our parents left, Riley took Zelda out, and we had our coffee. It felt decadent to be sitting inside and not crawling around in the dirt, weeding, and worrying about disturbing Leon the snake.

I took a sip of fabulous coffee, feeling much better than I had for a while. I didn't have to deal with manual labor, I was staying in a house with electricity, and I'd apologized to Mom and Riley. Everything was okay again.

I hugged my mug with my palms, enjoying the warmth. "What do you suppose Lester is doing right now?"

Riley glanced over his mug at me. "Do we care?"

"Not really. I hope he doesn't blab about us before we can get the information we need."

"Letting him stay wasn't my idea. I would have been happier if we'd thrown him in the river."

I waved off the comment. "You said your dad doesn't have a key to the room where the computer is. I can't believe they don't do *any* research themselves. Doesn't that seem strange to you?"

"Having your own assistant is great if you have a lot of work to do." He sighed heavily and put down his mug. "My assistant Cheryl did all the research and admin garbage I had to deal with, so I could focus on product development."

"You had an assistant? I can't quite imagine you being a boss."

"I ran a company, Meg. What did you expect?"

"I guess I never think of you that way."

Riley stood up, grabbed my empty mug, and grumbled something unintelligible on his way to the kitchen.

I continued, "Today is our big chance for infiltration. I'm thinking we scope out the scene at the lab with our parents, then, depending on what we learn, I can go back later while you're chopping veggies in the kitchen."

"And do what?"

"Connect to the world. Download information. Get answers and share what we know. I need to post multiple articles to the site. As we've confirmed our suspicions, I've been writing everything up. Well, when we've had electricity, that is. I'm a little behind, but I do have a bunch of notes."

He set the refilled mug down in front of me. "And you're going to do this with all those hacking skills you have? Don't you think they have passwords? How do you think that's going to work out?"

"Good point. We can't involve our parents though. Mom, in particular, thinks Enviro Freedom is all unicorns and rainbows."

"I wouldn't go that far, but I agree you shouldn't involve them in your investigation."

"I won't. But I was hoping you might apply some geek skills."

"Let's check things out at the lab first and then talk about it. Don't go off and do something dumb."

"Excuse me?" I put the mug down. "What's that supposed to mean?"

"All I'm saying is maybe you could think things through before we do anything, all right?" He stood up. "I need a shower."

Okay, maybe Riley was still a little pissed off at me. It wouldn't be the first time I couldn't determine his state of mind. But later he'd get some alone time away from me chopping vegetables, which might even out his mood.

By the time I showered and could stand to face the world, Zelda was making it clear that the human dawdling wasn't acceptable. She ran around the table a few times, barked, and generally made a nuisance of herself.

Riley told Zelda to sit and clipped her leash on her collar.

I pointed at the wagging dog. "What's with Zee?"

"I think our parents weren't giving her enough exercise. And the last couple of days I was hanging out with Dad, trying to get the Bronco to run better, so she only got short walks."

"It shows." I crouched down and petted the soft fur on her head. "Do you miss riding around in the car?"

"Yeah, well, with any luck we'll return to the open road soon."

"What are you talking about?" I grabbed the umbrella and pointed at the door to indicate I was ready to head out. "Are you threatening to leave again? I tried to be nice to Mom this morning. I even apologized."

Riley opened the door and locked it behind us. "I'm not going anywhere at the moment. Don't worry about it."

I mentally shrugged. Something was bothering him, but he obviously didn't want to talk about it, so I decided to be quiet and listen to the rain instead. It was probably the first time since we'd been in Washington that I was enjoying the wet weather. That said more about my laziness than anything else though.

We got to the lab and Tim was solicitous, showing me all of his great toys. I didn't understand what most of them were, but I managed to make appreciative noises at the right times. We toured the room where the sole computer was and met the "boys." Mom's research assistant, Sid, was a soft-spoken twenty-something with light brown hair and a goatee.

Tim's research assistant, Patrick, was older and said that years ago he'd dropped out of college. He wanted to study engineering, but the math almost killed him. After years of working lots of different jobs in construction, he still found the subject interesting and claimed that getting to learn from Tim was the most fun he'd ever had at work.

It was easy to see why Patrick liked working with Tim. Because Tim was a natural teacher, I could easily imagine how Riley got turned on to fixing and building things when he was a little kid. Tim's enthusiasm was infectious and he was great at patiently explaining technical topics without using a bunch of jargon.

Riley and Tim stayed behind for a few minutes, talking to Patrick in his office about subjects so geeky that I lost interest. I followed Mom into her huge office, which had books and papers scattered everywhere. I didn't feel so bad about taking over the study at the house. Work-wise, she had everything she could possibly need here. She was studying something that she termed "captology." The word was made up by a scientist named BJ Fogg, who coined the term from an acronym: Computers As Persuasive Technologies, or CAPT. So captology was the study of how computers could be used to change people's behavior.

Riley and Tim walked into the office as I pointed at a stack of papers on her desk. "So based on your research, you think that the people designing cellular phones are purposely designing them so users will become addicted to them?"

Mom said, "Yes, that's my working theory. I believe they are using specific triggers to increase adoption. That, in combination with peer pressure, will lead to an explosion in usage." She held up a cell phone. "Archetypal is giving these phones away with their calling plans. But cell phones aren't only telephones. They now also include software like games. These applications are designed to tap into deep-seated human needs for acceptance and social approval."

"Why would people play games on their phones?" Riley asked. "With such a tiny screen, that wouldn't be any fun."

"I've been studying game addiction for quite some time, and from what I can see, Archetypal has included every possible psychological component into their built-in games, so people will want to play them. I'm sure the next step will be connecting phones to the Internet, so people can play with friends."

Riley scratched his chin, which, I noted, he'd neglected to shave. He took the phone from my mother and looked at it. "I guess that makes sense. Multi-player gaming is more popular now, but pressing buttons doesn't seem like it would be fun."

Ellen retrieved the phone from him. "I believe that's where the technology is going. If electromagnetic radiation is truly harmful, we could end up with an enormous percentage of the population suffering physical repercussions because they can't break the addiction to their phones. Unlike a computer, a cell phone is easy to carry around. The implications are disturbing."

"I'll say," I said.

Riley added. "I need to look into buying that remote island."

Mom turned to me. "Honey, now that you've settled in a little, we'd still like to run some tests on you and Riley. Tim has found a way to generate the different frequencies of a cellular signal and we'd like to see what happens firsthand. Perhaps we can isolate exactly what is happening."

"That's what I was testing the other day," Tim added.

I glanced at Riley, who didn't seem any more excited about the idea than I was, given our experience with Tim's earlier experiment. But I knew this was part of the deal and said, "That's okay with me, Mom."

Riley said, "I'm fine with it too, if you think it will help. You'll want to make sure no one is around though because sometimes Meg screams."

After thanking our parents for the tour, we walked back to the house in silence. Thinking about what our parents had said was discouraging on many levels. Even Zelda seemed subdued.

I looked up at Riley's face. "What are you thinking about?"

"The same thing you are, I imagine."

"If Mom's right, and she always is, the future is bleak. We need to warn people about what's likely to happen. I need to publish my articles and write more."

"Then you'll be pleased to hear I stole Patrick's keys off his desk."

I stopped and waved my umbrella to the side so I could give him a hug. "You're amazing!"

"I can't believe I'm participating in your life of crime."

"The truth is important. This is people's lives we're talking about. *Our* lives. We have to do this. You know it's for the greater good."

"I hope so."

~

While Riley was off chopping vegetables, I wrote another article about what I'd learned recently. When we returned to the cottage after dinner, I was unfailingly polite to my mother and didn't make a single wave, so the evening passed without incident. Being an adult was difficult, but after the big lecture from Riley, I felt like it was my responsibility to keep the peace.

We retired to our study and Riley set the alarm for midnight. When it rang, Riley silenced it on the first obnoxious bleep. We both lay there for a few minutes, waiting to see if anyone else heard it. Nothing in the house stirred, so I moved to get up.

I rummaged through my suitcase. "We have a problem."

"I'm glad you realize that. Can we go back to sleep now?"

"No, we're still breaking in. But I don't have a black shirt."

"So what?"

"Everyone knows you wear basic black when you're breaking and entering."

Riley gave me an incredulous look. "*That's* what you're worried about?"

"I suppose it's so green here, my teal top might work too. I need camouflage."

He threw a black t-shirt at me. "Here."

I held it up in front of me. The t-shirt said, 'Specter of Hector' in a stylized heavy-metal font designed to look like the Kiss logo. "When did you get this?"

"Lars gave it to me, but it's too small." He grinned. "Consider it my gift to you."

Although Riley had teased me mercilessly about my reaction to the touch sensitivity Lars had, he'd been generous about helping Lars and his son escape to a new life, so it wasn't surprising that Lars had given him a gift. Even an ugly one.

I pulled on the shirt and frowned at Riley. "We'd better not get caught because I don't want anyone to see me wearing this thing. How mortifying."

"We'd better not get caught for any number of reasons." He tugged an old navy blue sweatshirt over his head. "Let's get this over with."

I handed him his glasses and he set them on the desk. "No one is supposed to see us, so I think I can skip the Clark Kent disguise."

I removed my Velma glasses and looked down at Zelda, who was standing and wagging in front of me. "You need to break the bad news to Zee that she's not coming with us."

Riley crouched down and had a heart-to-heart with Zee, expressing his desire for her to be incredibly quiet while we tiptoed out of the house. She didn't look like she was buying it, but we managed to get out without a huge barking incident, so whatever he said must have been convincing enough.

The rain had backed off to a misty, dense fog that made it difficult to see, which worked to our advantage. Although I'm not typically afraid of the dark, the fog muffled the forest sounds, which coupled with the inky blackness of the new moon, made me feel like I was walking through the set of a horror movie.

An owl hooted from nearby tree and I lurched forward, reaching out to clutch Riley's arm. My laptop bag slipped off my shoulder, and I scrambled to pull myself together. This was ridiculous. I wasn't afraid of owls or the dark.

Riley took the laptop bag from me. "Are you all right?"

"This fog is making me a little jittery. You're sure you have the keys, right?"

"That's the seventh time you've asked me. Like you said, all we have to do is walk through the door as if we belong there."

"Nobody belongs there in the middle of the night. We need a Plan B in case someone shows up."

"It would have been helpful to think up a Plan B earlier."

At the lab, Riley unlocked the door and we went inside. It was pitch black, but we'd agreed that flashlights would be too obvious, so we carefully felt our way back to Patrick's office. I tripped over something and went down on my hands and knees, stifling a yelp of pain.

Riley paused and looked behind him at me. "What are you doing?"

"I tripped, so I'll take the low road." I put my hand out in front of me on the floor and it landed on something that felt suspiciously sticky like old gum. "Eww."

"Shh!"

Riley unlocked the door to Patrick's office and I crawled past him. I felt my way to the guest chair and sat down. Riley set my laptop down next to the desk and sat in front of the research computer. He flipped a switch on the side of the box and mumbled something that sounded suspiciously filthy.

"What's wrong," I hissed.

"This thing is a hundred years old."

"I doubt that."

"Computer years are like dog years." He tapped his fingers on the desk. "Jeez, this could take forever."

The computer beeped and there was a loud whirring noise. Riley put his elbow on the desk and rested his chin on it. The machine groaned and then there was a clunk and Riley sat up. "What the…"

I got up and stood behind the chair. "I'm thinking that blue color isn't good."

"No, it's not. It crashed before it even came up. What a piece of garbage." He flipped the power switch again and the computer went through a long complicated string of numbers and wheezed some more. Then the screen went black.

Riley put his face in his palms. "*This* is the connection to the outside world?" He lifted his head and whacked the top of the computer case, which made the computer wheeze again. The screen flickered to life and then went black again. The brief glimpse I got of green text on the black background seemed archaic, even to me.

Riley nudged me. "I didn't think I'd need tools for this project, so I didn't bring anything. Look in the drawers and see if you can find a screwdriver."

I rummaged around and found one of those sets of tiny screwdrivers that come in a plastic case. "Is this what you want?"

He took it and kissed me. "Perfect." I looked on as Riley disconnected everything, unscrewed several screws, and removed the cover from the computer. His actions unleashed a cloud of dust, and we both coughed and leaned over to peer inside. The room was dark, and I had no idea what I was looking at, but I was pretty sure the inside of a computer wasn't supposed to have a layer of gray fuzzy gunk coating the parts.

I moved to touch the gunk, and Riley grabbed my hand. "Don't. Touch the metal case first to discharge any static."

I waved my hands. "On second thought, I don't want to touch whatever that is that's all over, well, everything."

"I'm surprised it even tried to boot up." He leaned closer. "I think something may have died in there. Maybe a mouse."

I backed away. "Gross! That's so incredibly nasty."

"Stay here. I'm going to get some stuff from my dad's workbench."

I peered into the case again. It did seem a little furry inside. A crash and Riley's subsequent cussing came from the other room. It was a good thing the lab wasn't near any other buildings because those were some very bad words.

He returned and handed me an aerosol can. "Hold this for a second."

I held it up close to read the lettering. "Air in a can? Is this a joke? Do people pay money for this?"

"Shh. Give it to me."

I went back to the guest chair and waited while Riley messed with the innards of the decrepit computer while swearing under his breath.

"You've turned into a real potty mouth this evening."

"How does anyone let a computer get to this state? This is disgusting. I have to wonder if my father knows about this. Jeez. Dad would be appalled." Riley picked up the cover, put it back into place, and plugged in the wires. "Here we go."

The computer beeped and whirred but didn't make any groaning or clunking noises, which was promising. Riley smiled as a greenish glow from the monitor washed over his face.

"Hey, check it out. You're green instead of blue."

"Very funny. At least it came up. But I can't fix slow. This is going to take a while." He tapped at the keyboard. "Fortunately, the security features on a relic like this are pathetic."

"So you can get around them?"

"Already done."

"You're such a geek." I stood up, walked behind the chair, and bent to kiss his cheek. "Get me some intel, baby."

Three hours later, we'd done everything we'd set out to do. Riley checked on the news using the old computer and once he'd figured out passwords for getting online, he hooked up my laptop so we could check out his accounts and deal with posting my new articles. Before we'd gone undercover, Riley and I had reason to believe his lawyer was up to no good, so Riley had put some of his money in a new account. If Riley saw that Elmer Flood, aka Mel, accessed the account, it would indicate the lawyer might be embezzling.

Riley also downloaded hundreds of new emails from his server. I had quite a vocal fan base. If this batch of emails was consistent with earlier ones, a lot of my fans were trolls and lunatics, but a few real emails from people who needed help were mixed in with the drek, so I knew I'd have to carefully go through and read them all.

From prior emails, I'd learned that sensory abnormalities came in many flavors. Assuming the people who wrote to me weren't lying, the way a person's senses were affected by radiation varied dramatically. One guy had lost color vision, so he only saw in black and white. Another person's taste was affected, so all he tasted was bitterness. A woman named Jean wrote to me saying she couldn't feel things anymore, which was dangerous. "Imagine what would happen if you set your hand on a hot stove and didn't realize it." Reading the stories in my email never failed to upset me.

We packed everything up and left the building, carefully putting everything back where we found it and locking up behind us. Although I was thrilled we hadn't gotten caught, I was a little worried that I was only going to get an hour of sleep. My mother wasn't wrong about the fact that I needed my sleep.

The fog had dissipated somewhat so it didn't seem quite as creepy outside, but I reached to snag Riley's arm just in case. I gave it a reassuring squeeze. "It will be okay. You'll figure something out."

He shook his head. "This is exactly what I was afraid of, Meg. My lawyer took the bait. Mel stole money from me, which means he can't be trusted."

"At least he doesn't know we're here."

"I thought the whole going undercover thing might have been overkill, but now I'm glad we covered our tracks as much as we did. If Mel knows this place exists, it's only a matter of time before he figures out we're here."

"I suppose posting my articles is a big clue we're still alive. Maybe we shouldn't have done that. But now we also know more about the bombings. Based on what we read online, I think Enviro Freedom is behind them."

"I hate to say it, but you might be right."

~

Somehow Riley managed to keep Zelda from waking up everyone when we returned to the house. We quietly fell into bed, and I was asleep almost as soon as my head hit the pillow. It seemed like only a nanosecond had passed before the horrible alarm bleeped to let me know it was time to go out to the garden and pull more weeds.

I got dressed, gave Riley a goodbye kiss that he slept through, and stumbled off to work. The fog had lifted, but the air was still soggy. The weather was great if you were a mushroom. For the rest of us, it was damp and unpleasant. Did summer ever arrive in this area or did they skip it?

George was standing next to the gate at the garden. I smiled weakly. "Where do I start?"

He gave me a quizzical look. "Are you okay this morning? You're not coming down with something, are you?"

"I'm a little tired."

"Maybe it's because you look different without your glasses."

I put my hand to my face. *Crap*. My Velma glasses were sitting on the desk right where I'd left them at midnight. "It's okay. I can still see well enough to identify the plants."

He walked me to my assigned row and gave me a friendly pat on the shoulder. "Tomorrow, you're off weeding duty. I've got some seedlings to go in."

"Great." I leaned over to survey the vast grasslands that contained a few veggies struggling to avoid getting choked out completely. It would almost be easier to dig everything up and start over. I whacked at the dirt for a while and moved down the row so I was hidden behind a plant with enormous leaves. Upon closer examination, I thought it might be rhubarb. The pink stalks looked different than they did all chopped up in pie. Who would have thought that the plant it came from had such gigantic leaves?

I started awake and found George crouched in front of me. "Mandy, maybe you should go home and take a nap. If you're getting sick, working in all this damp soil isn't going to help. Rhubarb can't be a great pillow either."

I pulled some vegetation out of my hair. "Maybe you're right. If I get some rest, I might be able to fight this off and avoid getting sick."

I returned to the house and convinced Zelda I wasn't a burglar before she completely lost her marbles and barked her head off. I went to the study, stripped out of my damp clothes, and crawled into bed with Riley, who woke up only long enough to grumble about me being cold before enveloping me in his arms and falling back asleep.

Much later, I opened my eyes and found Riley staring into my face. I could hear our parents rustling around in the living room. I widened my eyes meaningfully at Riley. "What?"

"Aren't you supposed to be at work?"

"I was, but I fell asleep in the rhubarb and now George thinks there's something wrong with me."

"There are so many things I could say to that, but I won't." He grabbed my hand and dragged me into a sitting position. "We need to talk to our parents before they leave for breakfast."

We threw on some clothes and hustled into the living room right as my mother was reaching to grab her tote bag next to the door.

Tim smiled at us. "I didn't realize you were still here.

"Meg, what is that in your hair?" my mother asked.

I reached up and pulled out a piece of leaf. "Rhubarb."

Riley said, "Did you want to do that experiment today? Meg sort of got a little time off."

"George thinks I'm sick," I said. At my mother's stern look, I added. "I was just tired, but he thought that with all the damp weather I might be coming down with something and sent me home."

"The fact that you fell asleep on his plants may have played a role in his decision," Riley said with a smile.

"I used to wonder if you had narcolepsy," Mom said.

I took a deep breath, willing myself not to blurt out the incredibly snotty comment I wanted to make, and turned to Tim instead. "If you're ready, we could stop by the lab later this morning for the experiment."

"I need a couple hours to get set up," he replied. "Patrick and Sid go to lunch at about eleven. Why don't you stop by then?"

I gave my mom a hug and said, "See you later."

Riley and I had a relaxing morning and limited our conversation to inconsequential topics. I think we were both consciously avoiding discussing anything too distressing like his lawyer's malfeasance or the upcoming experiment. When you're about to be a guinea pig, it's best to keep things light.

When we arrived at the office, Patrick greeted us and asked if we'd happened to see his keys anywhere. "They're on a key chain that says Miller Lite on it. I can't figure out where they went. I had them yesterday."

Riley shook his head and I agreed that I'd never laid eyes on them. Patrick shrugged. "Well hey, it's always something. Usually I'm fighting with the computer, but today it's working better than it has in months. Maybe Mercury went out of retrograde or something. Guess you gotta be grateful for small favors, right?"

We agreed that was always a fine course of action and walked to Tim's workbench, where he was fussing with mysterious equipment. I dug my fingernails into my palms. This experiment was unlikely to be fun.

Tim said, "This is a signal generator. It's usually used for testing receivers and other types of communications equipment."

That meant nothing to me, but I nodded politely. "Like radios?"

"Yes, it covers a wide range and is used in all kinds of different applications like cellular, audio, and video broadcasting," Tim said.

Riley said, "So are you going to try to narrow and isolate the signal to determine exactly what's affecting us?"

"Exactly! I mocked up two tiny fake cellular towers. The cellular bands cover a fairly wide spectrum, so by using this I'll be able narrow it down to determine the precise frequency or frequency range that's the problem." Tim grinned and looked so much like Riley I couldn't help but smile. What a nerdy pair.

I reached for Riley's hand. "So I guess we stand here?"

He looked down at me and gave my palm a reassuring squeeze. "Don't look so nervous. At least we're in a controlled environment for a change."

Tim futzed with various dials and switches on his equipment while we stood there waiting. My feet were getting tired, and I was starting to think longingly about lunch. Nothing was happening. Was this experiment going to work?

I glanced across the lab. My mother was leaning over a desk, riffling through a big stack of papers. Probably more research. A red light flowed through the window, casting a pretty glow around Mom. Uh-oh, that couldn't be real. Suddenly, a sharp pain ripped through my temple, and Shannon walked into the lab. I looked around for Riley, but he wasn't there. I yelled for him and when I turned back, Lester was next to Shannon, talking to her. They were surrounded by a red glow and she was clutching the big black pendant that she always wore, stroking it with her fingers. Whatever Lester was saying couldn't possibly be good for us and I yelled for Riley again. There wasn't any blue anywhere. Where had he gone?

I shook my head and opened my eyes. My mother was staring into my face intently. "Meg, are you okay? Oh honey, you scared the life out of me."

I sat up and looked around my mother. Riley was lying on the floor next to me, and Tim was kneeling on the other side of him.

"Riley!" I shoved my mother aside and crawled to him. "Riley, you have to wake up!"

Kneeling next to him, I pressed my ear to his chest. His heart was still beating. I don't know CPR or first aid, but I looked into his face, took a deep breath, and then blew it into his mouth. He shuddered, opened his eyes, and rubbed his upper arm. "Ow."

I collapsed on top of his chest in relief. "Thank God you're okay."

He pushed me off him and I sat up. "What happened? I was afraid it was the not-so-good side effect."

Tim and my mother both started talking at the same time and I waved at them. "Riley, please tell us what happened."

"I guess I was nervous and then you started screaming. All the scents were hitting me at once and I was trying to keep you from landing on the floor. I must have held my breath and my heart started racing. Then I don't know." He ran his palm across the fuzz on his scalp. "I guess I passed out again."

Mom said, "I was terrified when you both collapsed to the floor."

"What do you mean passed out *again?*" Tim said. "I thought you said that the radiation affected your sense of smell."

"This is something else," I said.

"I probably should have mentioned this before Dad, but I have a genetic heart problem called Wolff–Parkinson–White syndrome. I've known about it for a while."

Tim asked about a thousand questions about the syndrome, which Riley had found out about only recently. He'd had lots of medical tests and learned that his heart rhythm looked different than most people's on an EKG.

"I found out about it because the last time he passed out, someone called an ambulance." I said.

Riley stood up, "Calm down, Dad. It's no big deal."

Tim's face had a gray cast, as if he were physically ill. "I could have killed you."

"No, you wouldn't have. This isn't related to the sensory problem or radiation at all," Riley said. "In fact, there's a surgery to fix it, but I haven't gotten around to that yet."

I said, "We've been busy, and we're hoping that some of the less good side effects of the syndrome don't happen."

"This is only the second time in my life I've ever had any symptom of this problem," Riley said.

Mom said in her most placating voice, "Maybe we should go to lunch now. I think we all need a little time to relax."

My hands were still shaking, and I was dealing with the gray cast of my hallucination hangover. I put my hand on Riley's arm. "Mom's right."

Tim seemed to relax a little. "Yeah, I need to write down some numbers. You go ahead. I'll catch up."

Mom patted his shoulder. "I'll save you a seat."

Riley and I followed her out of the lab, and I looked back at Tim who had crumpled into a chair, hunched over a notebook. He wasn't writing, just sitting and staring at the paper.

Having thought Riley had died once before, I understood exactly how he felt.

Chapter 7

Misunderstandings

A t lunch, we sat at a table away from everyone else, so I was able to describe my vision to our parents and Riley.

My mother listened intently until I was finished and then asked Riley, "How many of Meg's visions have you witnessed?"

"I'm not sure. Maybe ten?" He turned to me. "What do you think?"

I thought back over the time we'd been traveling together. Riley had been around for almost every vision since we'd met. "It could be ten. There were a couple you didn't see, like when I was back at my apartment in Maryland and the one when I tried to run into traffic."

"I only saw the end of that one, which was plenty."

Mom said, "You were screaming Riley's name, and I wondered if that was significant."

"Maybe," I said. "It's possible I knew something was wrong. I don't know."

I glanced over at Shannon, who was sitting at a table with Bonnie, the receptionist. Shannon was fondling her necklace like she had been in my vision. Was there something special about the stone?

Riley was half-heartedly poking at a salad. He still looked a little thrashed from the experiment, and I leaned over to whisper to him. "You said something about crystals the other day."

"Yeah, why?"

"They use them in electronics because they vibrate or something, right?"

"Yes."

I discreetly tilted my fork toward Shannon. "Do you think her necklace does something? Maybe it's some kind of special crystal."

"Have you been spending time weeding next to that New Agey woman again?"

"Felicia didn't talk to me when I got to the garden and later I was asleep."

"Because you're the narcolepsy queen."

"Very funny." Clearly, Riley was returning to normal. "Getting back to my point, what if that crystal detects or transmits something? Is that possible?"

Mom leaned forward. "What are you two whispering about over there?"

Shannon turned and walked toward our table, and I shook my head at my mother. "I'll tell you later."

Shannon sauntered up to our table and gave us an ingratiating smile. "I thought I'd check and see how you are handling the living arrangements. I know it's close quarters, but I've expedited repairs to cabin five, so you should be able to move out soon."

I'd seen cabin five, and it was even worse than number six. I volunteered, "There's no hurry."

Mom gave me a swift yet stern glare before flashing a brilliant smile at Shannon. "We so appreciate your consideration. It has been a bit crowded, but because we have different schedules, it's been workable."

Shannon sat down and I made an effort to blank my expression, hoping she might not notice how distressed I was to have her sitting right next to me. Something about her nagged at me, and I suspected she knew my name wasn't Mandy.

I tried not to look guilty of fabricating my identity and pointed at her necklace. "Your pendant is gorgeous. Is it onyx?"

Shannon seemed surprised by my question and reached up to fondle the smooth black heart-shaped stone. "No, it's not a precious or even semi-precious stone. Even though it's not valuable, it has sentimental value because it was a gift from a friend."

Riley said, "What type of stone is it?"

"You've probably never heard of it. It's a crystal from Russia called shungite. Like I said, it's not valuable."

"I absolutely love the necklace," I said. "Do you know where your friend bought it?"

"No, he never mentioned it." Shannon glanced toward the table where Bonnie was sitting, then back at my mother and Tim. "If you could tidy up the lab a bit, we'd appreciate it."

"Of course," Mom said.

"The Founder is visiting this week and will want to speak with you about your progress," Shannon continued.

Tim said, "I thought he wasn't coming until August. Wasn't he traveling?"

"Yes, he has some concerns about some information he's read online and wants to see how things are going here."

I had a feeling I knew, but I asked anyway, "What has he read? The gossip in the garden is that he's upset at the lack of progress."

My mother gasped slightly at my comment and attempted to placate Shannon, "I'm sure he'll be pleased with our research. I know I've made great strides."

"Me too," Tim volunteered a bit lamely. I suspected he was still recovering from the unexpectedly traumatic turn today's research had taken.

"I haven't seen a newspaper since we've been here. Did something happen?" I asked.

"I talked to the Founder last night." Shannon said. "Someone is spreading rumors about our organization and he was quite upset when he read the lies. I looked into it and agree that it's damaging to our cause."

"That's terrible! Who would do that?" I said as innocently as possible. "What's so wrong with wanting to save the planet?"

"I don't know, but some of the information in the article is suspicious." Shannon replied with a stern look.

"In what way?" Riley said.

"Some points that were made indicate..." Shannon said, and then stood up abruptly. "I'm sorry, but need to go. Bonnie is signaling that I have a phone call from the Founder."

After she left, Riley looked at me. "I'm thinking our time here may be running out."

Mom said, "What did you do, Meg?"

"Nothing!" I replied. "Why does everyone always assume I did something?"

"Leaving won't be so bad." Riley took off his glasses and fiddled with the earpieces. "These stupid things hurt my ears."

"We can't leave before I get a look at this Founder guy," I said. "I'd love to see him channel Dwayne too."

Lester stomped up to the table, and at first I didn't recognize him because he was outfitted in a pair of stained overalls. I had to believe the new duds were inherited from George because the pant legs were way too long. Even though he'd rolled up the cuffs, the denim was still dragging on the floor. I stifled a giggle. The guy was dressed like Mr. Green Jeans on Captain Kangaroo.

He sat down next to me. "Where were you today? I had to weed your whole row!"

"George let me go home because I wasn't feeling well," I said.

"You look fine now. You'd better come back because I didn't sign up to do your work. This blows. I'm gonna tell George who you really are," Lester said as he shook his fist at my face.

I leaned forward to get right up into his face. "Then I'll tell him who *you* are. Wouldn't they be interested to know that before you were a gardener, you went around kidnapping people for a living? Oh, and you might have an incredibly nasty guy after you who'd like to see you hurt or dead."

"You wouldn't do that," he said. "And I wouldn't say that was my job description exactly."

"Then what would you say it was *exactly*?" Riley asked.

"Never mind. It's not like I have it on a resume or nothing." Lester stood up. "I'm just saying you better get back out to the garden."

"Don't get your panties in a twist. I'm feeling much better now. I'll be there in a few minutes," I said.

Having said his piece, Lester stormed off in a huff. Unfortunately, it's hard to pull off a good storming when you're wearing oversized overalls. It was a miracle he didn't trip all over himself and fall flat on his face.

Riley stood up and leaned to give me a peck on the lips. "See you later. Dad said the parts he ordered for the Bronco should arrive tomorrow, so I'm going to go do some stuff to get it ready before I begin my chopping."

My parents followed Riley back to the lab and I found myself sitting alone at the table, wishing I didn't have to go back to my row of weeds. The sad fact was I couldn't think of any excuse not to, and Lester was likely to become even more of a problem if I ditched again, so I needed to suck it up and go to the garden.

With a sigh, I pushed myself upright and reluctantly returned to work. There was a time when I couldn't wait to go to work. Every day was a new day, rich with exciting stories to be told.

Working as a reporter didn't usually involve slugs or snakes either. Well, not literally anyway.

$\sim$

My afternoon stint in the garden gave me lots of time to think. Not that it did me much good. My thoughts went in circles, and I came to no useful conclusions about what I should do next as far as investigating.

After dinner, Riley ran off to be with Lurch again. From the sounds of it, he and his dad had spent pretty much every moment they weren't working at their official jobs trying to turn Lurch into a functional machine. Yeah, good luck with that.

I took the opportunity to retire to the study and sift through the mountain of email that Riley had downloaded from the server to my laptop. Although I couldn't send replies without a connection, I could read emails and delete the considerable quantity of spam and missives from nuts who needed to get a life.

I was on the cot with Zelda draped over my feet. Her quiet nasally snoring was interrupted when my mother tapped on the door. "Do you have a minute, honey?"

"Sure." I shut the laptop lid. "I'm just reading some stuff."

She sat in the chair at the desk and pulled a pen out of a cup, twirling it in her hands. "There's something I wanted to ask you about while Riley isn't here."

I set the laptop aside, and Zelda put her muzzle on my lap to take advantage of the warm spot. "It's not about my sex life again, is it? Because Riley really, *really* hates sharing personal stuff, and um, sex involves him too, you know."

"No, no, not at all. It's about the photo you mentioned." Mom clicked the pen a few times. "You said you found a photo in Alpine Grove that your grandfather took of you."

"It was on the kitchen table in your rental house. Maybe you know the picture. I was a little kid, and it was of me and Buster. I don't think I've seen a black-and-white photo of me like that one before."

Mom nodded. "I'd put it away, but I found it again when I was moved to Alpine Grove."

"It had Lars's business card inside the frame. The whole thing was strange, but it led to us finding Lars in a sort of roundabout way, so that was good."

"Someone must have stolen the photo along with the table when our belongings were brought here. But I don't know who or why." Mom shook her head. "It's been bothering me."

I grinned. "Well, now you know how I've felt for months about pretty much everything in my life. All I know is that Grandpa must have taken that photo because no one else used black-and-white film. Is he still alive?"

"I have no idea."

"This is probably something I should have asked a long time ago, but what about Dad?" I said more slowly, "I mean I know he walked out on you, but I don't know any of the details. You wouldn't ever talk about it."

"Oh honey, I didn't want to burden you with it. The fact that you didn't seem to remember what happened seemed like a blessing."

"What *did* happen?"

"He almost burned down the house. After he returned from Vietnam, well, you know he wasn't the same."

"Even though I was little, I understood that something bad had happened to him."

"He became an alcoholic and drug user. One night when I had to work late, I came home and there was a kitchen fire. You were asleep in a chair in the living room, and he'd passed out on the sofa while heating up some food for you."

This story sounded alarmingly like one of my visions. "This might sound off-the-wall, but I'm guessing you were screaming at him from the dining room."

"We were yelling and shouting at each other and, well, thank God the fire department showed up when they did. I wanted to kill him. I actually had a knife in my hand, and he ran out of the house. I never saw him again."

I got up and gave her a hug. "I'm so sorry, Mom. Why didn't you ever tell me?"

"I didn't want you to hate him as much as I did. Knowing nothing seemed better than knowing what actually happened. Maybe I was wrong." She patted my hand. "I didn't know you saw so much of the fire."

"Neither did I. Maybe I blocked out most of it, but I saw the whole thing in a vision."

"That's interesting. Perhaps your conscious mind was protecting you."

"My visions aren't as considerate. I stopped asking about Dad after I decided that a guy who would leave you to raise a child by yourself wasn't worth knowing. I managed to date a lot of men who also weren't worth knowing. There are a lot of creeps in the world."

"Well, Riley certainly seems devoted to you."

Devoted? That was an unusual word choice. I sat back down on the cot and stroked Zelda's head. "I don't know if Riley would say that, but we've been through a lot together."

"He obviously cares about you deeply."

"Well, I care about him too." Even though I had no idea what he was thinking half the time.

Suddenly Zelda jolted from her doze and leaped off the bed, barking at the front door. Riley and Tim came in, and Zelda ran in circles to celebrate their arrival. Mom and I followed Zee out of the study.

Tim greeted Mom and proclaimed, "We made big progress. The Bronco is ready for all the new stuff we got. Tomorrow's the big day. It's going to be great."

Riley was covered in motor oil and seemed considerably less enthusiastic. I tugged at the front of his t-shirt. "What happened to you? You look like you crawled inside Lurch and drowned in a pool of 10W-40."

"I had a little problem with the transmission." He walked by me toward the study. "I need a shower."

I didn't particularly want to know the details of Lurch's big day but followed Riley into the study, closing the door behind us. "Hey, are you okay?"

He grabbed some clothes. "Fine."

"Normally, you like working on Lurch. Did something happen?"

"Nothing beyond the transmission disaster. But I fixed it." He motioned toward the door. "Did you need something?"

I stepped aside. "Are you sure you're okay? Did something happen with your dad?"

"I'm fine, other than that I need a shower."

"There weren't any lingering effects from the experiment, were there?"

"No, I'm fine. What is this about? I'm covered in ancient gear oil, and I want to take a shower." He opened the door and left the room. I sat down on the cot. For someone who was fine, he certainly had acted pretty pissed off from the moment he'd walked in the house.

I returned to the cot and my laptop. When Riley opened the door, Zelda rushed to the cot and jumped up to return to her sleep spot on my feet. I shut the laptop, put it on the desk, and crawled under the covers.

Riley joined me and I curled up next to him, glad for the warmth. He stroked my hair for a while, and I could practically feel him brooding about something. Finally, I sat up and looked at his face. "You have got to tell me what's bothering you because I know something is."

"Go to sleep. You have to get up early, so Lester doesn't lose his marbles again about weeding your row."

"Is this the thing you want me to do? You said that there's something I have to do and now I think you're pissed off that I didn't do…whatever it is that you never told me."

"That's convoluted. You never forget anything, do you?"

"So what is it?"

"Jeez, go to sleep, Meg." He gave me a quick kiss and rolled over. "Your plants await."

Riley had a stubborn streak and if he didn't want to tell me what was on his mind, he wasn't going to, so I complied and fell into a deep sleep. The next morning, I tiptoed out of bed to the garden without any more insight into what was going on with him.

~

The next few days were a blur because of the Founder's impending visit. The retreat rumor mill was going full bore with stories about the man. According to Felicity, the Founder was outraged about the "leak" from within our little community. She spoke of him in whispered reverent tones that made me wonder about her mental stability.

Fortunately, the level of religious zeal around the garden was mitigated by George's even temper and methodical work ethic. I planted probably ten thousand tiny seedlings. As it turned out, I was good at the task because of my small fingers. Lester was booted off seedling duty after he trashed a flat of kale starts. I could tell he was trying George's patience, but to be fair, if you weren't careful, it was easy to break the fragile stems of baby plants. After the Great Kale Fail, George handed Lester a shovel and pointed him toward an untouched area of the garden that needed to be tilled.

I was glad to be out in the garden because rumors also circulated about Shannon. The gossip-mongers reported that she was on a rampage, inspecting everything. The sound of hammering and industrious activity filled the air. Even Mom and Tim seemed stressed about the upcoming visit.

I barely saw Riley who was spending every available moment he wasn't in the kitchen working on Lurch. He claimed he was eating, but if he was, he wasn't eating with me. At night, he returned to the cottage, took a shower, and we went to sleep. Every day, I had silly garden stories or anecdotes I wanted to share with him, but he fell asleep before I could finish talking. He was acting strangely and stubbornly refused to admit anything was wrong. Even my mother noticed that he seemed oddly quiet. I wasn't sure what to do. Usually if I waited long enough, Riley would talk to me after he'd had some time to think. But sheesh, how much time did he need?

The Founder was scheduled to arrive Friday morning, so Thursday afternoon in the garden was a little frantic. I was planting for all I was worth because George was on a mission to have no empty rows and no weeds. In a garden that size, those were herculean goals. Fortunately, the weather had held through the week, so we'd made great progress.

I was working to get 720 beet seedlings into the ground when shouting came from the far end of the garden. I couldn't hear what he was saying, but Lester was gesturing wildly at something on the other side of the fence. Maybe he was scaring away a deer. I hoped it wasn't a bear.

I kept my head down, focusing on my weeding as George strolled down one of the long rows toward Lester. Part of me felt bad for saddling George with such a jerk, but Lester did provide some raw muscle, which was needed, so it wasn't all bad.

George increased his pace and then started to run. I'd never seen George move faster than an amble, so I stood up. What was going on? That wasn't a deer on the other side of the fence. It was a man. The guy was attempting to climb over the fence to get to Lester, which probably wasn't going to end well. The welded wire was enough to keep out deer, but probably wasn't up to supporting the weight of such a tall man.

My jaw dropped as a few synapses in my brain connected and I recognized the tall man. Although he wasn't wearing a suit anymore, I could tell it was Lester's partner in crime, who I now knew was his brother-in-law. Crap. That guy knew who I really was. I needed to tell Riley. Now.

I turned, ran to the gate and out of the garden. Behind me, Felicia said, "Hey, what about the beets?"

I ran to the dining hall, through the doors, and into the kitchen. Heavy-metal music was blasting, and Riley was standing at a counter chopping a massive pile of green peppers. I ran up and slapped my palms on the stainless steel surface to get his attention. Startled, he looked up, and I jerked my thumb toward the door and made the charades "talking" symbol with my hand.

Riley followed me into the dining hall and I flopped forward, putting my hands on my knees, completely out of breath. I was not a runner. Or a jogger, hiker, or any other type of athlete. He bent down to look at me and asked, "What's going on?"

I pointed back toward the door. "Suit guy. Brother-in-law. Lester."

"What?"

I stood up. "Lester's brother-in-law! Whatever his name is…Nick! Hector's other evil creep who chased us. Nick is *here*."

"Where?"

"In the garden. He was trying to climb the fence to get to Lester. I left before he could see me." I reached up to put my arms around Riley's neck and looked into his eyes. "He knows who we are."

Riley pulled my arms off his neck. "True, but assuming Lester wasn't lying, Nick isn't after us anymore. He might want to hide out like Lester did."

"Okay, but…he's bound to say something. Even if he says nothing more than, 'Hi, Meg,' we're screwed."

"Lester said Nick went home. What's he doing here?"

I widened my eyes. "How would I know? But for some reason, he's angry at Lester. Or they're angry at each other. I don't want to know."

"We need to find out." Riley sat in one of the chairs, pulled off his glasses, and pinched the bridge of his nose with his fingertips. "Jeez, I hate this. All right, I guess we're going to have to talk to him."

"When I ran away, George was on his way to investigate what was happening. I couldn't hear what they were saying."

"I can't leave until Maurice gets back. He went to get some cans of tomato sauce from the shed."

I took a deep breath. "I'll do it. Running away was an automatic reaction, but probably not the right one. Definitely not the brave one. George probably wonders what happened to me."

"If you wait a couple minutes, I'll go with you."

I sat down in the chair across from him and wiggled my foot. "How long is this going to take?"

"I don't usually time Maurice's trips to the shed." He stood up. "In the meantime, I've got a lot more green peppers to chop."

"Right." I was sick and tired of Riley's attitude toward me lately. He'd been acting like I had some type of contagious disease. Fine. I stood and gave him a wave. "I'll let you know what happens. Or if I don't turn up tonight, you might ask around."

He grabbed my arm, "Wait, don't go. Can't you wait a couple minutes?"

"No. I'm done waiting for you. I'll go chat with Lester and Nick." I turned around and walked through the dining hall and out the door. Part of me knew I was being stupid, but the other part was too pissed off to care. Maybe it was about time I got caught.

When I returned to the garden, George seemed to have defused the situation. He had his arms crossed and was standing between Nick and Lester, who were silently glaring at each other. I resettled my Velma glasses on my nose. Maybe Nick wouldn't recognize me with brown hair and glasses, but unfortunately, people only seemed to fall for the old glasses ploy in comic books.

Lester noticed my approach and pointed at me. "You! We need to talk to you. Right now."

I smiled and tried to appear nonthreatening and innocent. "Sure. What's up?"

Lester moved away from George and started toward the gate. "Nick, get over here."

"You guys aren't going to get into it again are you?" George dropped his arms. "Mandy, are you going to be okay?"

I waved merrily "I'm fine. So Lester, it looks like Nick has stopped by for a visit."

Lester stomped up to me. "You aren't gonna believe this one. My darling Nicole apparently got a clue and left that scumbag Hector."

I gripped Lester's arm and steered him around, so we were facing away from George. I hissed, "What is Nick doing here?"

"The dumb fool thought Nicole would be here," Lester said as Nick came up alongside me. "Mandy, meet my moron brother-in-law."

"Stop calling me that!" Nick said.

"You didn't answer my question. Why is he here?" I demanded.

Nick said, "When I got home, Hector was waiting for me because Nicole ran out on him. Hector claims she's looking for Lester and wants to get back together."

"That'll be a cold day in…" Lester mumbled.

I waved at him to be quiet. "Continue. Then what happened?"

"Hector beat me up, but I kept telling him I didn't know where Lester was because I didn't. Anyway, Hector finally believes me, but says we'll get 'payback' because he told Matt that Lester is in hiding. Matt's pissed off because he don't want people like us running around who know what's going on."

"That still doesn't explain why you're here." I said.

"After Hector left, I figured I was a sitting duck in Chicago. So I hit the road back to the Northwest because Lester said he was after you." Nick shrugged. "It took me a while to find this stupid place."

Lester looked at Nick and then at me. "Now you know why I call him a moron."

"Stop calling me that!" Nick said.

Riley ran up to us and Nick said, "Hey, do I know you? You look familiar."

"It's the skinny guy, but he got a bad haircut," Lester said, then gestured back and forth between Riley and Nick. "Ryan, meet Nick, the moron."

"Stop calling me that!" Nick protested.

"Why should he?" I interrupted. "I mean, what were you thinking? Only a moron would lead everyone who happens to be after us right *to* us."

Riley said, "I didn't get the whole story, but that does sound pretty stupid."

"It is," I said. "We've got a big problem."

～

I turned to Lester and Nick. "You guys go hide in Lester's cabin for the time being. Figure out where you're going and then go."

Lester said, "But I don't want to leave. There's free food here. All you can eat!"

"Get over it. You need to get out of here. *Now!*" Riley said as he took my hand and pulled me away from them. "I need to talk to you."

"Well, that would be a nice change of pace." I shook my hand out of his because he was practically dragging me toward the cottage. "Are you finally going to tell me what's bothering you?"

He stopped to face me. "I'm leaving, Meg. I was planning to go this weekend, but thanks to Nick's arrival, I think I should move up my schedule."

"What? I'm not ready to leave. We need to get a look at this Founder guy tomorrow."

"That's fine because I'm planning to go alone. Well, except for Zelda. She's coming with me."

"*What?*" I shook my head as if I were dizzy. "I don't understand. What happened?"

"Lester's moron brother-in-law showed up."

"You just said you had already planned to leave before he arrived. Why didn't you talk to me about this?" I gestured back toward the garden. "Those idiots aren't the real reason."

"I'm sorry, but I can't do this anymore. You're the altruistic one wanting to find the truth and help other people like us. I need to return to being Riley, confront Mel, get my money back, and disappear for good this time."

"What about your father? What about *me?*"

He reached to take my hand again and started walking. "Maybe you could stop yelling at me in front of half the compound."

I stomped along beside him in furious silence until we reached the cottage. As he unlocked the door, I said sadly, "I don't understand why you won't talk to me."

We went inside and Zelda greeted us in her typically enthusiastic way. Even all that canine joy wasn't enough to change my mood. My stomach was tied up in knots, and I couldn't decide whether I was going to yell or cry. At this point, it was looking like both.

Riley bent to pet the wiggly dog. "Settle down, Zee."

Zelda and I followed him into the study. "What are you doing?"

"Packing."

"Is this why you've been spending so much time working on Lurch? Does that hunk of junk actually run now?"

He stopped ramming shirts into the suitcase and looked at me. "Yes. I do have a few skills, you know."

"What's that supposed to mean?" I threw up my hands in exasperation. "It's like you had a conversation with me that I missed."

Riley sat on the cot and leaned forward to rest his elbows on his knees. "I told you. I need to go back to my real life."

"It's only a little while longer. Being Ryan isn't so bad. You get to spend lots of time with your dad geeking out on electronics and car stuff." I sat down next to him, leaned my head on his shoulder, and batted my eyelashes playfully. "And you get to have an adorable fiancée."

He moved over so I wasn't touching him, "I can't handle faking it anymore. I'm tired of trying."

"It's not that hard. I mean, Ryan isn't that different in a lot of ways. Sure, chopping vegetables may not be as intellectually stimulating as designing techy stuff, but weeding all day isn't particularly thrilling for me either."

Riley stood up, grabbed another shirt that was lying on a chair, and stuffed it in his suitcase. "I don't want to talk about this anymore, Meg."

"Well, I do. I'm not letting you off the hook this time." I stood up and grabbed his arm away from the suitcase. "You're not leaving here without giving me a decent reason. Not after you made me fall in love with you. I deserve an answer."

"I can't *make* you do anything." He looked up. "Wait. What did you say?"

What had I said? My vulnerable little heart was beating rapidly and I'd said it without thinking, but it was true. "I love you. I'm not sure why I couldn't say it before, but I do."

Riley sat down on the cot, pulled me into his lap, and wrapped his arms around me. He leaned to nuzzle my neck and said, "I'm not sure how it happened, but I love you too."

I moved my head to look in his eyes. "At the risk of sounding cranky at a moment like this, you have a bizarre way of showing it."

"You made some comments that sounded so much like Erin that I figured history was repeating itself."

"Sometimes I speak without thinking. You should know that all too well. What did I say?"

"Probably nothing that you'd remember. A few off-hand remarks that made me feel like you didn't respect me or even care about me at all. I decided there was no way I was falling for another woman who would never love me back. Not *again*." He caressed my cheek. "I kept thinking you'd say something about how you felt, but you didn't."

"I'm sorry. As you know, my experience with romantic relationships isn't the greatest." I kissed him. "But you never said anything either. How is it that we can talk about anything except how we feel about each other?"

"I don't know. But it's why I was planning to leave this weekend. Spending time with you was becoming way too difficult."

"And now?"

He ran a finger around the collar of my t-shirt, pulling it away from my chest. "Now, I think you're wearing way too many clothes."

I leaped on top of him, bouncing Zelda over so that she almost fell off the cot. She daintily hopped to the floor and settled into a spot in the corner, since the humans were obviously going to hog up all the space on the cot.

Later, I was lying curled up alongside Riley when the front door opened and closed. The low tones of our parents' voices came from the living room, and Zelda stood by the study door giving us an accusing glare.

I peered at the clock. "I think we missed dinner."

Riley propped himself up on his elbows. "Zelda did too. I guess I should do something about that."

I pushed him back down to the bed and leaned over to kiss him. "Just so we're clear, I don't want you to go anywhere. Not without me."

He grinned. "If and when it's time to bail out of this place, we'll go together."

"Good. I'm glad we cleared that up." I placed my palm on his chest and felt his heartbeat. "One more thing. When this is over, will you look into getting that heart procedure done? I know you think it won't happen, but that sudden death side effect still bothers me."

"It's called cardiac ablation, and yes I will." He put his hands on both sides of my neck and kissed me. "We can talk about that some other time. Right now, we need to talk to Dad and your mom about the mess with Nick and Lester."

"And feed Zelda. Look at her. She's sitting there giving you the evil eye."

I moved to get up and Riley reached out to stop me. "Meg?"

"Yes?" I interlaced my fingers with his. "Did you need something else? Because our parents are right on the other side of that door, you know."

"I know. I just want to say thanks for making me talk to you."

"I can't *make* you do anything, but you're welcome."

"I love you."

I wrapped my arms around him for one more hug. "I love you too."

Channeling

I was pulling on my jeans when there was a tap on the study door and Mom said, "Meg? Are you in there?"

"I'll be right out."

Riley was yanking on a t-shirt and I gave him a hurry-up motion. He silently mouthed, "Working on it."

Once he was fully clothed I went to open the door, but he put his hand on mine on the doorknob. I looked up and he reached over with both hands to run his fingers through my hair like a comb. He whispered, "It's sticking out everywhere."

I ran my hands across the top of my hair and tried to smooth it down. I raised my eyebrows in query. "Better?"

He shrugged. "It'll have to do."

I opened the door and Zelda launched through it, making a beeline for the kitchen. My mother and Tim were sitting at the table drinking tea.

"We missed you at dinner," Mom said.

I was starving, but set my food fixation aside for the moment. "We had a little run-in with someone we know."

"It's the other guy who was chasing us," Riley added on his way to the kitchen. "He wanted to find Lester. We asked them to leave and then thought it might be a good idea to hang out here until they're gone."

Tim said, "I hate to tell you, but Lester and Nick sat with us at dinner."

"I was afraid that might happen." I slumped down into the chair next to my mother. "Lester likes the free meals."

"That guy can sure power it down." Tim said. "But the good news is that neither of them said anything about you. They didn't say much to us either. Mostly they argued about someone named Nicole. The only thing I found out is that Nick is staying with Lester in his cabin."

Accompanied by his much happier dog, Riley returned from the kitchen and sat down next to his father. "Dad, there's a good chance Meg and I might have to leave soon. Nick may have inadvertently led other people here. If they find us, it won't be good."

"I want to be here when the Founder arrives tomorrow though." I said. "I'm determined to get a look at that guy."

"Honey, there's something else I wanted to mention." Mom said. "We were chatting with Shannon and Tim mentioned that he'd done a couple of experiments involving electromagnetic frequencies. She said we absolutely shouldn't run any tests while the Founder is visiting."

"That's interesting. Do you think he's affected? And wait a minute—she should have been affected like we were. Was she?" I asked.

"She didn't say," Mom replied. "I couldn't tell if she knew Tim had been experimenting, but she was adamant that he not do anything while the Founder is here."

"Why am I wearing these?" Riley removed his glasses and set them aside. "Maybe you were wrong about Shannon, Meg."

I took off my glasses and set them next to Riley's. "It's not like I understand my visions most of the time, but so far, everyone who shows up in them and has an aura has some sensory problem."

Tim said, "I'm working on shielding, but if you guys leave, I won't be able to test it. I mean, even though I isolated the frequency, I'm not sure exactly what causes your, uh, unique reactions. I mean, I could block that frequency entirely, but there's something else going on that I haven't figured out."

"If you've isolated the frequency, can't we just tell the companies not to transmit it from their evil towers?" I asked.

Riley said, "The use of frequency ranges is regulated by the Federal Communications Commission. Archetypal wouldn't listen to us, although they might pay attention to the FCC. But we could be dead before the Feds get around to changing anything."

"I suppose you're right about that. Well, maybe Lester and Nick will leave quietly and avoid ratting us out." I said.

Riley made a skeptical face. "I wouldn't count on it. The longer they stay, the higher the risk. Even if they don't do say anything on purpose, those two are a few screws short of a hardware store."

Mom smiled. "So you're saying they're not the brightest bulbs on the Christmas tree?"

"Having spent time with them, I can tell you they're a few fries short of a Happy Meal," I said.

"Or a few neutrons short of an isotope," Tim said with a chuckle.

I opened my arms in an inclusive gesture. "Okay, so we all understand the problem we have here. It's possible that

Riley and I will have to bail out quickly. If that happens, remember, it's nothing personal."

Mom put her arm around me. "Thanks, honey. I've enjoyed spending time with you."

"Me too, Mom."

Mom and Tim retired to their room, and because Riley knows what I'm like when I'm not fed on a regular basis, he wisely scrounged up some food for us. He also mentioned *he* was hungry, which was something I couldn't remember him ever saying before. It was a little startling to have him behave so normally about food.

The next morning in the dark, I donned my grubby clothes and stumbled over to the garden for my morning shift. George met me at the gate and handed me a flat of 72 seedlings that needed to go into the ground.

I took the tray and looked down at the delicate little plants. "What are they?"

"Kale. They go into the row at the far end near the shed. Lester turned over the soil yesterday, so it should be ready."

"Have you seen him this morning?"

"No. After Nick showed up, he left early. Felicia, Jane, and Griffin stayed a little late to help out."

"I'm sorry I had to leave early. Ryan had a situation, and it was kind of an emergency."

"Is something wrong?"

I shook my head so hard I made the tiny kales wiggle in their tray. "No, no, everything's fine. We had a misunderstanding."

"Well, we all get to quit early today to listen to the Founder, so whatever you can get done this morning will have to do." He made a sweeping gesture toward the long rows of plants. "Farming is like that. You do what you can and hope Mother Nature takes care of the rest."

I walked to my designated location near the shed and settled into power-planting mode. I'd developed my own personal planting routine, so I didn't have to think too hard about each tiny plant anymore. I could let my mind wander and listen to the birds wake up and begin singing as the sun rose. The garden was a peaceful place, and every once in a while I got an insight into why George loved it so.

Lester and Nick didn't show up for the morning shift, and I was hoping they'd disappeared like we'd asked. At noon, I walked with my fellow gardeners to the dining hall, and we filed inside to meet the great Founder. Felicia was aflutter to the point that I thought the poor woman might have some type of seizure or breakdown. The Founder hadn't arrived yet, but maybe she thought he could read minds because she was chanting, "I love you! I dream about you!" in the hope that he'd hear her passionate rantings. Her behavior was akin to Beatles fans when the Fab Four arrived in the United States, complete with tears and squeaky wails of adoration. She'd probably faint dead away once the guy finally showed up.

The Founder attracted a large crowd. I played a little game with myself, trying to remember the names of various attendees. There were a bunch of people I didn't know, but I could name Kristine, Lois, Brooke, John, Anita, Howard, Jennifer, Kristi, Andrea, Patrick, Karl, Rebecca, Bryan, Julie, and Jason. Not all of my brain cells had completely mildewed out in the soggy garden. Sadly, Lester and Nick were also in attendance, presumably after more free food. Oh well.

I finally spotted Riley standing out of the way against the wall at the far side of the dining hall. I hustled over, relieved to be away from Felicia's mooning. As I approached, I met his gaze and the look in his eyes filled me with a delicious warmth.

He smiled, "Welcome to the big event. Our fearless leader is about to bestow his presence upon us."

At the sound of applause, I turned around to face the front of the room and leaned back against Riley. He wrapped an arm around me and bent to graze his lips down my neck to my collarbone.

At the resulting tinglies shooting down my spine, I placed my palm on his forearm, "You're not paying attention."

Riley seemed more interested in my neck than the Founder's arrival, but Bonnie set up a microphone, and it made a horrible screeching noise that quelled his amorous activities. He whispered, "I bet Dwayne didn't appreciate that."

I giggled. "You're not taking this seriously."

A hush fell over the room as a man walked out. He had black hair parted on the side so a lock of hair swished across his forehead. His eyes were dark, and with his bulky build and broad shoulders, he reminded me of James Garner in *The Rockford Files* on TV. Maybe I'd watched too many reruns, but the Founder had the same sardonic I've-got-a-secret smile that I remembered from the show.

I looked away from him, closed my eyes for a moment, and opened them again. It wasn't my imagination. The guy had a sage green aura surrounding him.

He walked up to the microphone and raised his hands toward the sky. "Welcome, my children!"

Everyone in the room cheered, and I turned to look up at Riley to see his response. He just raised his eyebrows at me. People were way into this stuff. It was like a Bible-thumping tent revival.

The Founder continued, "You all know how I've worked to provide a good life for you here. A pure life with clean water, nourishment, honest labor, and a warm place for you to sleep at night. Dwayne has helped me, but maybe you need to hear him too. Sometimes I think you all should hear what I hear, so you understand a bit of what I go through to help you. Dwayne is the spirit that speaks to me and energizes me."

Feeling uncomfortable, I reached to take Riley's hand in mine. Something was oddly compelling about the Founder's voice, and it was easy to see why people listened. This whole thing was beyond strange, heading down the road to scary, and I squeezed his palm in a silent request for reassurance. What had we gotten ourselves into?

The Founder's voice boomed. "Dwayne! Speak through me. Share with my children what I hear in my head, so that everyone in this room may understand."

In a deeper, slower voice, he said, "This is Dwayne. I call to you all to hear my voice. I have never seen anything like this before. Never! People are taking the law and perverting it. They are destroying our planet in pursuit of their own greed and need for power. Life will not be worth living without the trees, the air, the water. People are dying. People are sick.

"We're losing the battle for our divine right to live our lives in a pure landscape that's not polluted with harmful substances. Some of these perils can't even be seen. Many will die. The damage will be done unless you step forward. It is up to us to make a stand!"

The Founder slumped and staggered forward a step before returning to an upright posture. He went on in his original voice, "I can't separate myself from Dwayne, and he understands your troubles. We have both always borne your difficulties on our shoulders. We provide you with a home and I'm not going to change that. Not now and not ever. I am committed to your well-being and keeping you safe. I look out upon you. I see all of your lovely healthy faces, warmed by the sun, nourished by beautiful organic food.

"For months, I've tried to shield you from the evil that is happening out in the world, but now I see that I can't do that any longer. Now we must lay down our lives to protest what is happening to our planet. Protest the criminal activities of those people who care only for themselves and knowingly are poisoning you. You know who those people are.

"They are the people who you ran from in the cities. The people you left to come here and enjoy a peaceful wholesome life. The technology that you left is a killer. People are dying. Silently. Slowly. Evil forces are destroying the air, the water. Your very lives depend on stopping this travesty. I implore you to rise up with me. Are you with me?"

The room exploded in noise as everyone cheered, clapped, and stomped their feet. I looked around and the only ones who looked composed were George and our parents. Mom had her classic squinty expression of disapproval that had historically often been directed at me.

Everyone else was making noise and jumping up, expressing their support, as the Founder chanted "Rise up! You must rise up!"

Riley squeezed my hand again and I leaned my head back against his chest, closing my eyes. How had I not realized this before? Not only was the Founder one of us, but he'd managed to brainwash all of these people. If the Founder asked them to do anything, they'd do it with no questions asked.

~

After the big speech, the Founder followed Shannon out of the room. Everyone else milled around while the food was brought out for lunch. Riley and I settled in at a table with our parents.

My mother leaned over toward me, "Meg, you were right. The Founder is a lunatic."

"Haven't you heard him speak before?" I asked. "Everyone else seemed completely into what he was saying."

"Many of the people have been here for a long time. Some came with him when he set up this place, but he was off traveling by the time we arrived," Mom said. "Most of our information has been third-hand through Shannon. We got to know her because the cottage where we're staying was originally hers."

"Well, that explains all the frills," I retorted.

"She's been nice to us since we arrived," Tim said. "I guess she moved out because she moved into the Founder's house. That's the big one over on the hill."

In my mind, I thought of the place as "the chateau." The Founder's house had been breathlessly pointed out to me by Felicia and sat in forested grandeur on a little rise away from the rest of the compound. A number of people lived in the chateau. To me, it was the equivalent of getting hotel accommodations versus our wooden tent. The people staying there had electricity and plumbing within the building. When I found out about it, I'd been jealous and annoyed.

I asked, "Do you know if the Founder and Shannon are involved? Something about seeing them together made me think they are."

Mom glanced at Tim. "What do you think? If they are, they certainly haven't spent much time with one another here."

"I dunno. I mean, she was on the stage with him and followed him off, but I couldn't tell you," Tim said.

Riley rested his elbows on the table, leaned forward, and said quietly, "Meg tends to be right about stuff like this because she notices subtle details."

"I couldn't tell you what the specific details are though. It's more like I get a feeling," I added.

"That could explain some of Shannon's comments, I suppose," Mom said.

"Like what?" I asked.

"I didn't think about it at the time, but when she was talking about moving out of the cottage, she was extremely excited. The way she was chattering, it was as if she were a teenager moving in with her boyfriend." Mom pursed her lips. "She never said anything about it again though."

"I'm going to go back to the garden and see what I can learn from Felicia." I said. "She's a blabbermouth and her adulation for the Founder borders on the twisted. I bet she'll know specifically what people are supposed to be doing when they rise up because she'll be first in line."

Riley got up, walked to me, and planted a smoldering kiss on my lips. "Time for me to go chop up large quantities of vegetables."

I wanted to talk to him about my observations about the Founder, but that chat would have to wait. "See you later."

Riley crossed the room to the kitchen, and Tim gave me a goofy grin. "You guys sure seem to be getting along better."

I tugged at my earring. "We had a misunderstanding, but we worked it out."

"I'll say." Tim said with a chuckle.

Mom gave him a stern glare that I suspected was designed to communicate, "Shut up, Tim," but maybe I was imagining it. She said, "We should get back to the lab."

"Well, I'm glad to see you two happy, that's all." Tim got up and gave my shoulder a pat. "I swear that kid thinks too much and makes himself miserable. He's always been like that. Just takes everything so seriously."

After they left, I stayed in my seat and nibbled on the last of my roll, preferring to wait until the last minute to return to the bugs and slugs in the garden.

Riley walked out of the kitchen, grabbed something off the serving table, and crossed the room to my table. "Why are you sitting here all by yourself? Lunch was over a while ago."

"I know. I'm trying to encourage my muscles to get out of the chair, but they hurt and are staging a revolt. I don't want to drag my flabby self back to the garden."

He sat in the chair next to me and set a huge serving spoon on the table. "You're supposed to be interrogating Felicia right now. Did you give up on the idea?"

"No, but you need to know the Founder is green. We were right. He's one of us."

"I was afraid of that. Do you know how he's affected?"

"I don't know. But it could be his hearing, given that he channels or hears voices. Right now, I'm trying to figure out my line of questioning. What am I supposed to ask Felicia? 'Blown up anything lately?' I can't figure out what to say that won't be completely transparent. Shannon already said the Founder knows someone here is leaking information."

Riley grabbed the spoon, stood up, and pulled me up out of the chair. "You'll figure something out. You always do."

"I don't want to."

"Asking people questions is what you're good at." He gave me a kiss. "Go."

I walked as slowly as possible back to the garden, stopping to sniff roses and any other flower that looked appealing.

George was weeding a row near the gate and raised a hand in greeting. "Welcome back."

I returned the wave and walked to where Felicia was busily mulching a row of broccoli. George had told me that my next task was to plant the next generation of brocs, so I figured I could pretend I was interested in the life cycle of cruciferous vegetables.

"Wow, these plants look so happy," I said somewhat over-enthusiastically.

Felicia looked up from her task. "Yes, we're putting on the mulch late this year. It conserves moisture, but we've had so much rain lately, all it did was attract slugs."

I repressed a shudder. The slugs hanging out in the garden were gigantic and came in multiple colors. I'd seen huge black slugs, gray slugs, spotted slugs, and brown slugs. The color didn't matter—they *all* grossed me out. "I'm planting more broccoli, and I wanted to see how this variety is doing."

"It's doing okay. Shannon told me that the Founder likes broccoli, and I think we'll have a few early ones ready to harvest while he's here."

I poked at a crown, hoping I didn't find any slugs or creepy-crawlies. "What did you think of his speech this morning?"

"It was so inspiring!" Felicia set aside her handful of straw so she could clasp her hands together in rapture. "His voice gives me chills."

I didn't want to tell her my response was more along the lines of 'gives me the creeps' versus chills, but smiled warmly. "It's the first time I've heard him speak, and I thought the call to rise up was very moving."

"Yes, it's time to act! I'm hoping to be selected for a mission."

"I didn't hear about any missions."

Felicia brushed her palms together, sweeping off some mulch. "Of course not. It's because you're new. Only true believers are invited on missions."

"Do you know what your mission is going to be?"

"I haven't been selected, so not yet. But no matter where we go, it's an opportunity to spend time with the Founder and learn from him. I have a feeling I'll get to go this time. My intuition is telling me it's the right time for me."

"Where did people go on past missions?"

"They're not allowed to say." Felicia turned her head to verify no one else was nearby. "But I heard that some people went to Portland and Los Angeles not too long ago."

I thought back to the news reports of bombings. Coincidence? Probably not. "That sure would be a big change from being here."

"Don't tell, but the rumor is that Seattle might be the target of the next mission. They're supposed to leave tomorrow. I'm crossing my fingers someone comes to invite me tonight!"

"Target? What does that mean?"

Felicia waved her hand dismissively. "That's what the Founder calls the location. It's not like you're shooting an arrow or something."

The rustling of plants came from behind me. I turned and looked up to find George approaching us down the row. "I see what you mean. I guess I should start in on my next flat of broccoli. Nice chatting with you."

I stood up and met George in the middle of Felicia's row. "I finished the beets this morning. Could you tell me which flat of broccoli seedlings you want me to plant?"

I followed him to the greenhouse and only half listened as he selected a flat for me and talked about the virtues and nuances of the variety. The half of my mind that wasn't listening was occupied with the idea that Riley and I had to find out what the "missionaries" were planning to do in Seattle.

～

At dinner, I huddled with Riley and shared what I'd learned. After silently listening to my information dump, he frowned. "I don't think the fact those people on a mission happened to go to Portland and LA is a coincidence."

I forcefully speared a leaf of lettuce in my salad. "I think your inclination was correct. It's time for us to leave here. I think we've learned what we can, and thanks to Lester the Loser, we know more about Archetypal too. Everything is starting to make a little more sense."

"So now what?"

"We go to Seattle and see what happens on this mission. And get access to the Internet again to dig up dirt on my evil ex, Matt." I grinned. "That could be satisfying."

Riley rested his forehead on his palms. "But Seattle? After our last visit…jeez, I don't want to go back there."

"I know. We're going feel awful." I put my hand on his shoulder. "I have an idea though. We could steal Shannon's crystal."

He raised his head and looked at me with wide eyes. "No! Absolutely not. For one thing, we don't have time. For another, no. Just no. I'm not doing any more breaking and entering."

I pulled my hand away. "All right, fine. Be that way. Shannon told me what the stone is called though. Shug… something or other. I bet we could buy another one somewhere."

"You don't even know that it does anything useful."

"Maybe it would help though." I leaned closer and said more quietly, "If it does anything at all, it's better than nothing. And no matter what it costs, you can afford it."

"When Ryan returns to being a figment of our imagination and Riley goes back on the grid, spending money again, it's going to raise a bunch of flags."

"I know. We need to confront Mel too." I kissed his cheek. "You were the one who said it's time to go."

"I guess the next step is to talk to our parents. Because we're staying with them, people are going to ask them what happened. They're going to need a story."

I took a bite of salad and chewed thoughtfully. "True. What are they going to say?"

"I don't know. I'm the fixer of broken things. You're the one who is the inventor of stories."

I laughed. "How nice that we've got our job roles figured out."

Riley scanned the room. "Our parents never showed up for dinner. That's odd."

"Maybe they decided to hang out at home. They might want some privacy like we did."

"I don't want to dwell too much on that idea."

I poked him in the ribs. "Don't you think it's a little late to get squeamish about our parents doing the deed?"

"I've been choosing not to think about it."

"If you can smell my hormones that means you can smell everyone's right? So you already know what they're up to."

"It's not quite that simple. I have to isolate the scents. But now that we've spent so much time with our parents, yes."

I grinned. "I can't believe I never thought about that before. That's way too much information about Mom and Dad."

"I don't want to talk about it."

"Being you must be extremely complicated."

"You have no idea."

We went back to the cottage and took Zelda out for a stroll. When we returned, our parents were sitting at the table having tea. After Riley unclipped her leash, Zelda ran up to Tim, who gave her some affection.

As he sat down next to his father, Riley said, "We need to talk to you."

"We need to talk to you too," Tim replied. "Our afternoon with the Founder was kind of stressful."

"*Very* stressful!" Mom said.

"I went over all my research with him," Tim said. "I'm not sure how much he understood though."

"You almost put him to sleep," Mom said.

"After I went through the information, I talked about how I'd done some tests with plants to see if radiation might be affecting them as far as maybe the air or their environment or growth changes." Tim exhaled loudly. "But he didn't care about that. He wanted to know if I'd done any tests on people. I said I hadn't done anything like a controlled experiment, but that it was theoretically possible that people could be affected."

Mom said, "He lied, but only a little bit."

"I didn't lie. The test I did on you guys wasn't controlled," Tim said. "There were all kinds of variables and I don't have definitive answers yet."

"The Founder had me go through all my research too." Mom said. "I was terribly nervous and he kept asking health questions. I'm not sure he realizes that I'm not a medical doctor. Maybe he thought I was when I was invited here. There's something about that man that makes my skin itch."

"I can't argue with that," I said and then told her about the Founder's aura and relayed what I'd learned in my conversation with Felicia about the missions.

Mom put her hand on mine. "Shannon mentioned that she asked Lester and Nick to leave. She asked quite a few questions about you and Riley as well. I asked why she was so interested in you two, and she claimed it's because you're new here."

"She made it sound like she was concerned you were adjusting okay," Tim added. "But I felt like she was digging for dirt about you guys. She wanted to know how we became such good friends."

"The whole visit was uncomfortable," Mom said. "At some point, I had to say that if they wanted medical tests done, they should find an MD."

"Yeah, they grilled us about everything. I told her that Riley...I mean Ryan and I became friends because we both liked old cars and that I was helping him fix the Bronco." Tim glanced at my mother. "That part wasn't a lie."

"All those questions can't be good." Riley said, "Which brings us to our next topic. Meg and I have decided to leave here tomorrow morning."

"I had a feeling you were about to go," Tim said, "At least we got those new tires on the Bronco."

Mom put her arm around me. "After today, I understand why you have to leave, but I'll miss you, honey. What should we say when Shannon asks where you went?"

"I've thought of several possible options. The first idea I had was that Ryan isn't feeling well. We're worried his cancer is back so we decided to go back to see his doctors in North Dakota," I said.

"The problem with that one is that they might ask exactly what type of cancer I supposedly have or had," Riley said. "We never said because we were worried someone would know a lot about cancer treatments and chemotherapy drugs and ask hard questions."

"The other option is that Ryan and I got into a huge fight and decided we couldn't stand being around each other anymore and bailed out," I said.

Tim smiled. "Anyone who saw you groping each other this morning wouldn't buy that one."

I folded my hands in front of me, hoping that I wasn't blushing as much as I thought I was. "Okay, how about the reverse? Another option could be that Ryan and I can't stand spending every day apart from one another, so we ran back to North Dakota to get married."

Mom sipped her tea and put down her teacup. "Even more compelling would be that you found out you're pregnant and have decided to move up the date of your wedding and tell your parents back in North Dakota about your impending parenthood."

"Do you think you can sell that story?" I raised my eyebrows and leaned closer. "With the understanding that it's absolutely not true, of course."

"Definitely not," Riley said emphatically.

Mom looked thoughtful for a moment. "Have you considered the possibility that your sensory issues might be genetic?"

I looked down to inspect my cuticles. "Yes, we've talked about it. The only thing I know for sure is that Lars told me his little boy, Nils, wasn't affected."

"So far, anyway," Riley added. "It's possible that Nils could have problems as he gets older. Lars also didn't tell us anything about Nils's mother, so we don't know if she has sensory problems."

"We only know about his second wife, who, unfortunately, we met when she tried to kidnap me. Lars never said anything about his first wife, only that Helen wasn't the mother of his son."

"Who knows how many wives the guy might have had," Riley said with a sly smile at me.

"We know there were at least two, and that Helen is evil. Anyway, that's the long way of saying we don't know. Maybe it takes two mutant sets of genes to make mutant children." I threw up my hands. "The whole thing is too upsetting to think about. Riley and I have enough problems as it is."

Mom put her hand on mine. "I'm sorry, honey."

"It's okay. I've been trying not to think about it, but it's not just us. I've received emails from people who have sensory problems. Some of them have kids and they're worried. I don't know what to say to them." I shook my head. "Let's not talk about this anymore. Thanks for letting us crash with you."

Mom gave me a fierce hug. "You need to be careful out there, honey. Very, very careful."

"I know, Mom. We will."

Chapter 9

On the Road

Early the next morning, Riley and I packed up all our stuff and loaded it into Lurch. I was a little worried about traveling in the junky old heap, but Tim wasn't wrong about the new tires. The tires and wheels were the only clean part of the vehicle, and even in the early morning light, the difference was striking.

All our rustling around and Zelda's running back and forth to the Bronco woke up our parents. Mom made us some coffee, and I gulped it down while I scoured the study for any items we might have overlooked in our packing process. Because I'd been getting up so early recently, I was somewhat more functional than I normally would be at five in the morning.

Finally, we were ready, and I wrapped my arms around Mom for a final hug. I released her and handed her a piece of paper. "This is my email contact information. If you can't email, the answering machine on my phone in my apartment should still work. I'll check on that once we get somewhere with a phone. Please let us know what you find out here whenever you can."

Mom assured me she'd keep in better touch than she had in the past, and after a final round of hugs, Riley, Zelda, and I loaded ourselves into Lurch.

Riley turned the key in the ignition, and the Bronco rumbled to life. Then, much to my surprise, the engine settled into a contented purr. I looked at Riley, aghast. "Oh my God, what did you do?"

He grinned, "I told you I have a few skills."

"I knew that, but this is remarkable. It sounds like a normal car. Better than a normal car." I reached over to put my hand on his. "I have to say that I wasn't convinced Lurch would make it to Seattle."

"It's not that far. Right now, I'm more worried about us." He clasped my palm. "I don't miss having you scream and run into traffic when I'm not paying attention."

"I don't miss you not eating either. And you'd better stay out of the hospital this time." I flipped through the dog-eared Triple A guide for Washington State, dreading even the idea of seeing Harborview Medical Center again. The gate to the retreat opened automatically and we pulled through and turned right onto the highway.

"Welcome to freedom," Riley said. "It will probably be a couple of hours before we start to feel like crap, so enjoy our good health while it lasts."

I turned my head toward the window at the sight of two bedraggled hitchhikers. "I don't think Lester and Nick are having much luck scoring a ride."

"Sayonara guys. Here's hoping we never see you again."

"No kidding." When I returned to my maps and guides, the big yellow blotch of Seattle loomed on the left side of the map, and I wished there were some way around it. We didn't know if or when the big bombing mission might happen. Waiting around in Seattle for someone to do something horrible didn't sound like a lot of fun. "I'm having an idea."

"Uh oh."

"You'll like this one because it's in both of our interests. I think we deserve a reward for successfully infiltrating the retreat and not getting caught. Even better, my mother and I are still speaking to one another."

"Congratulations. I'm guessing this idea is going to be expensive, isn't it?"

"Very funny and not necessarily. I was thinking that you said the Olympic Peninsula is beautiful."

"It is." He glanced away from the road to look at me. "Are you saying you want to go there? What about Seattle?"

"The Olympic Peninsula has the advantage of being close, but not too close. It's still rural, and there's a community college in Port Townsend, which means there's a library where I can do research."

"It's a little town, so the library can't be large."

"It's probably good enough for my purposes." I reached for his hand again and gave it a squeeze. "There are cutesy coffee shops and bed-and-breakfasts. Port Townsend sounds adorable."

"I'm sure it is."

I waved our hands and bounced up and down in my seat. "And the best thing is that if we go there, we get to ride on a ferry! Oh come on, let's live a little. *Please*?"

He laughed, "All right, let go of my hand so I can shift gears. Since you asked nicely, who am I to say no to visiting a cutesy town where I'm *not* going to feel like dirt?"

We cruised down Route 9 to Sedro Woolley and stopped for gas. While Riley poked around under Lurch's hood, I picked up the ferry schedule and lots of brochures about the Olympic Peninsula. We turned onto Route 20 and drove to

Fidalgo Island, which is the gateway to the San Juan Islands. The photos in the brochures were gorgeous, and maybe someday I'd get to see those islands, but today was not that day. We continued southward across the Deception Bridge to Whidbey Island.

We stopped in Coupeville to have lunch and wait for the ferry. The way the ferry works is that you get in line. If there are thousands of cars in front of you, you're unlikely to be on the next ferry, so you wait some more.

Before we got in line for the ferry, we spent some time exploring Fort Casey State Park because Zelda needed some run-around time. The grounds around the old military fort had panoramic views of the Puget Sound and a beautiful old lighthouse. We took a small trail down to a rocky beach area, where Riley threw sticks that Zelda ran after and refused to bring back, as was her custom. Fortunately, the beach had a lot of available driftwood for throwing.

The weather was gloriously sunny, and being completely free of all responsibilities felt unbelievably liberating. No one knew where we were. No one even knew *who* we were. Riley picked up another stick and threw it for Zelda, who ran around like a crazed puppy. I think we were all glad to be back on the road together.

I laughed at the goofy canine antics. "Look at her go! The last time she got to run on a beach like this was when we were in Birch Bay. That feels like a long time ago."

"Time-wise it's not, but a lot has changed." He bent to pick up another piece of driftwood and hurled it down the rocky beach. "We found our parents, for one thing."

"And we found out the illustrious Founder is a loon for another."

Riley threw another stick. "And that you have a disturbing penchant for breaking and entering."

"I also decided I want a crystal like Shannon's. Not only is it stylish, it could be good for my health."

"We also learned that Lester and Nick probably couldn't find their way out of a paper bag."

I pressed my hands to my chest. "I'm proud to say that I overcame my unreasonable fear of slugs. Well, mostly anyway."

Riley laughed and pulled me into his embrace. "Yuck."

I put my arms around his neck. "And then in between the slugs and the breaking and entering, we fell in love."

"Aww, that's much better than slugs." He gave me a kiss. "You're cute when you get all romantic."

"Hey, when I'm not embarking on espionage or criminal activity, I can be as gushy and gooey as the next girl."

"I'm having trouble envisioning you as a schmaltzy bundle of innocence."

"Yeah well, maybe not."

~

After our jaunt on the beach, we were able to get on the ferry for the ride to Port Townsend. Riley drove onto the vessel, and once Lurch was safely parked, we got out and went upstairs to one of the sun decks to enjoy the journey. Dogs on a leash were allowed to enjoy the exterior areas, and Zelda made lots of new friends during the crossing. We sat on the metal benches where Riley answered countless questions about Zelda as people cooed at her and told her she was the most gorgeous dog ever. By the time we reached the other side, it seemed like most of the passengers on the voyage had gotten their fuzzy-dog fix.

We returned to Lurch and drove off the ferry into Port Townsend, which as the guidebook suggested, is a pretty seaport filled with old Victorian buildings complete with ornate gingerbread decor. We passed lots of little shops and galleries as we drove through the downtown area. Tourists were wandering along the sidewalks window-shopping, and a few people were relaxing in the sun at cafes sipping beverages.

From my copious quantities of local advertising materials, I'd targeted a place we could stay that allowed pets and was located a few miles out of town. The complex was secured behind a gate, nestled in tall evergreens, and claimed it had more than a mile of private Puget Sound waterfront.

The entrance was surrounded by massive flowering bushes, and as we drove through the gate, Riley glanced at me. "I'm guessing this might be expensive."

I grinned. "Isn't it great that you're not Ryan anymore? You're loaded again! Time to spend all that money we saved by being volunteer labor. This place has a kitchen, so you can cook fabulous food for me."

"As if I haven't been busy preparing thousands upon thousands of vegetables lately."

"At least you didn't have to grow them."

"All right, I'll give you that."

We parked and Riley went to deal with the check-in process while I read more about the area. When it comes to chamber of commerce marketing materials, I'm like a sponge. I love finding out about all the places to go and things to do. When I looked up, I found Riley approaching Lurch. Sure, I saw him all the time, but part of me was shocked at how good he looked. Eating regularly definitely agreed with him, and somehow he seemed taller and his shoulders broader. When he caught my eye and waved the room key at me like a prize, the amused glint in his eye and the familiar grin melted my heart a little. Holy crap, I *was* being gooey. This whole being in love thing was completely uncharted territory for me.

Riley got in the driver's side and tossed me the room keys. "Two-bedroom condo with a balcony. And yes, it was expensive."

"Excellent!"

We went through the unloading procedure, and once we had everything inside, we ran off to the store to get stuff for dinner and to replenish our stash of road food. The process felt wonderfully familiar, and as I teased Riley about buying food only suitable for herbivores, I felt like I'd returned home after an exhausting, stressful business trip. With cable TV, DVD player, CD player, a telephone, fireplace, dishwasher, and compact washer and dryer in the condo, I'd returned to civilization at last.

After we unloaded our groceries, we unpacked, and Riley fed Zelda. The kitchen opened up to the living room and a row of barstools were arranged in front of a long counter. I parked myself on a stool and set up my laptop so I could watch Riley cook while I typed up some notes. I'm all about multitasking. Zelda was singularly focused, having positioned herself so she could supervise and catch any morsel of food that might fall on the floor.

I typed for a while, and when I paused to think, my gaze strayed to the end of the counter where a beige telephone sat on a phone book. I reached over and held up the handset toward Riley. "Behold, a communications device, the likes of which we have not seen in quite some time."

He paused in his chopping. "I need to call Erin and Mel and find out what's going on at my favorite law firm."

"Are you going to confront him about the money you think he stole?"

"I was thinking I'd call Erin first and find out if she knows what's up with Mel. It might be some kind of misunderstanding."

"I don't see how. You set a trap, and Mel fell for it."

"I suppose." He put down the knife. "I guess I don't want to believe it."

"Well, I'm going to take this opportunity to call my answering machine. I hope it still works."

I dialed my number, listened to myself, and punched in the code to hear my messages. Several people wanted to sell me something. Given that I've been an apartment dweller for a long time, I'm not sure why some smarmy dude spent so much time trying to coerce me into buying something related to septic systems. He got particularly animated when he described the intricacies of clogged drain fields. Eww.

I pressed the code for delete. Poor guy. Selling septic gunk was a job I wouldn't want. My former boss, Leo, left me a message inviting me to a barbecue that had transpired two days earlier. Guess I wasn't RSVPing that one. Oh well.

A smooth voice came on the line and I threw the handset away from me. "Ugh!"

Riley looked up. "What are you doing?"

I reached down to grab the handset, which was dangling from its cord. "Nothing. I was startled, that's all."

I pressed the button to replay the message Matt Eskridge, my ex-boyfriend, had left. "Good morning Meg. I don't know where you are, but I've asked around and I have a good idea. It was gratifying to find that you've kept the greeting cards I sent you. I can't decide if it's sexy or nasty that you keep them in your underwear drawer though. And I saw that you still have that lacy white silk negligee that I bought you at the Plaza too. The reason I'm calling is to let you know that you need to stop writing those articles and putting them on the Internet. If you don't, it will only be a matter of time before I find you and stop you."

I dropped the phone again and shook my hands as if I'd burned myself. "Riley, you need to listen to this."

"What?"

"This message. Get over here."

Riley walked around the counter and leaned down to pick up the phone. "This phone must be slippery."

I pressed the replay button again. "Just listen, okay?"

"Who is this?" He stood motionless for a moment. "Wait, is this Matt, the evil executive?"

I grimaced as I nodded. "He's not happy with me."

Riley handed the phone back to me. "Should I be worried that you saved all that stuff?"

"You're missing the point! He threatened me."

Riley returned to the kitchen. "Why don't you listen to the rest of the messages? Maybe he called back to share more nostalgic moments."

I pressed the handset to my ear and deleted a few more sales calls, and then went back through to find out if I'd missed anything important and to listen to Matt's nasty diatribe again. I hung up and shoved my laptop aside so I could rest my forehead on the cool fake-stone counter.

Riley poked at the top of my head with a carrot. "Why are you making a big deal out of that message?"

I lifted my head. "Why aren't *you*? He broke into my apartment and went through my underwear drawer!"

"You mean you didn't give him a key?"

"No! I never did. It wasn't like we ever were living together. We both worked incredibly long hours. He took me out to fancy restaurants and swanky hotels."

"He never stayed over at your apartment?"

"Now you're being nosy."

Riley raised his palms in a gesture of surrender. "I'm just asking. If he did, he could have grabbed a spare key. Even if he didn't, he could have taken a key from your purse and had it duplicated any time."

"But why would he? Boyfriends don't do that. That's horrible."

"Well, we *have* established that he's evil."

I tried not to roll my eyes. "Did Erin have a key to your place?"

"That's beside the point."

"No it's not! You didn't have that kind of relationship with her, and I didn't have that kind of relationship with Matt either. If you want to get technical, the only man I've lived with is *you*, assuming motels, rentals, and environmental retreats count."

"All right, never mind." He picked up the knife and began chopping up the carrot. "As for the threats, he's thousands of miles away and doesn't know where we are. What's he going to do?"

"I don't know. Nothing good. What if Lester or Nick say something?"

"Why would they? They don't want anything to do with the guy." Riley looked up at me again. "Is there something in particular you're worried Matt might have found in your apartment?"

"I don't know what he'd find." I tried to remember what was there. "A bunch of crummy furniture, knickknacks, and clothes. I've been wearing the same outfits for weeks now, so heaven knows I miss my clothes and my shoes. But he wouldn't care."

"I suppose not. So there's nothing incriminating there?"

"I haven't done anything wrong. Maybe embarrassing." I gestured helplessly. "Like those stupid cards. I don't know why I didn't throw them out."

"People keep stuff for sentimental reasons."

"Why would I be sentimental about him? He slept with half the women in the greater DC area. And he did it while we were supposed to be *together*." I stared down at my shoes and mumbled, "He was so confident, successful, and cosmopolitan. I thought we were perfect for each other, but I was a complete idiot. He treated me like crap."

Riley gave me a rueful smile. "Yeah, well, I learned the hard way that you need to love the whole person, not just what looks good on a resume."

I tried to shake off my memories. "Okay, forgetting how loathsome Matt is as a human being for a second, I can't think of anything he'd want in my apartment. There's nothing there."

"What about notes for articles? Disks full of information about Archetypal? Anything?"

I shoved my hair back from my face with both hands and exhaled heavily. "Um, well, maybe. I'm not sure if I ever mentioned it, but before I was put on medical leave, Leo assigned me to write an article about Online Systems United."

"Which later merged with Archetypal Media."

"To become Archetypal Online Systems. Which is the same company that laid me off and that still employs Matt. And that hired Hector and his creeps to kidnap us. It's possible my notes are lying around somewhere. I was doing a bunch of digging on their CEO, Alan Conway."

"If Matt found that information, would it be a problem?"

"Maybe. Maybe not. Perhaps when we go to the library, I should revisit my research."

"That might be a good idea."

～

With no responsibilities and no parents around, Riley and I ended up staying in bed late the next morning. Sunday is supposed to be the day of rest, after all. We were having all kinds of fun until Zelda apparently decided she wasn't waiting around anymore. She jumped up on the bed and stood over us like a vulture. Having a large furry dog panting over you has a way of killing the mood, so Riley got up and took her outside.

I'd enjoyed the snuggly late-morning warmth and didn't want it to end, so I stayed under the covers and clicked the remote to turn on the television. It had been a while since I'd had any idea what was going on in the world.

For years, I'd been a rabid news hound, but that seemed like a lifetime ago. When I was a reporter, getting the latest information was a major part of my morning routine. The moment I woke up, I turned on the TV. When I got to work, I scoured the latest information from newspapers and the news wires, so I'd be up to speed on what was going on locally, nationally, and internationally. If anyone asked me about current affairs, I was ready. I believed that knowing about all the latest news gave me a competitive advantage. Back then, I was anxious any time I was out of touch and away from the steady, never-ending influx of news.

Now I wasn't interested. With the notable exception of news about Archetypal that could affect my personal well being, I didn't care or want to know about the latest accidents, scandals, drug busts, or idiotic decisions by greedy politicians. And truth be told, it was a relief.

After having been out of the news game for a while, I was shocked to discover I didn't miss being in the know anymore. I missed my job and some of the people I worked with, but most of what I'd read back then was about events and issues I couldn't do anything about. No wonder I'd been so wired all the time. I'd been a walking mass of adrenaline, afraid to slow down and miss something while fretting over stuff that had no direct effect on my life.

Perhaps spending time listening to George's slow, patient instruction in the quiet of the peaceful garden had mellowed me out. At this point, it was difficult for me to listen to the newscaster's melodramatic recitation of a horrific traffic accident outside of Seattle. They showed scary footage, interviewed a few other drivers and witnesses, and made unsubstantiated guesses as to the condition of the accident victims. It was typical news fare, and I was repulsed at the hype. I clicked the remote to change the channel and check the weather on the scrolling local-access channel.

Zelda charged into the room followed by Riley, who stopped short and raised his eyebrows. "Did something happen?"

"I've just been lying here." Zelda hopped up onto the bed next to me and I ruffled her ears.

"You didn't have a vision or some type of panic attack, did you?"

"I turned on the TV. There was a terrible accident on I-5 in Seattle." I sat up and looked around the room, then down at myself. "Is something wrong with me? Do I look funny?"

"Nope." Riley shoved Zelda's furry butt over, so he could curl up next to me. "But you're a cloud of stress hormones."

"The news story was upsetting, and the way the guy presented it made me want to grind my teeth. If lying in bed watching the news stresses me out, how can I ever be a reporter again?" I rested my head on Riley's chest. "What am I going to do with myself? I've been trying to deny it, but my professional life truly is over."

"You can't give up on your reporting skills yet. Today, you have go to the library and research your inquisitive little heart out."

"I can do that, but it bothers me that I have no career and you're still paying for everything. You been funding everything for ages."

Riley sat up and looked down into my face. "I don't know how to respond to that. An extremely complicated road got us to where we are now."

"I wonder what my mother thought about us being together. She's always been so fierce about how she never wanted to depend on anyone." I reached to pet Zelda, who had her muzzle resting on my stomach. "If you look at it objectively, I've been freeloading off you. Now we're even sleeping together. What does that make me? I'm not a reporter anymore, so what's my current career? Hooker? Mistress?"

"I'm not sure what you're getting at, but are you actually *trying* to piss me off? Because if you are, *that* would piss me off."

"No." I slumped down farther into the pillows and pulled the covers up to my chin. "Okay, maybe a little. I'm sorry. It's not you. I think I'm having a massive bout of insecurity. I've never felt this way before. My career was a huge part of who I was. Sometimes I feel completely lost."

Riley leaned down to kiss me. "I do too, and I can't think of anything insightful to say other than it seems to help if I stop myself from dwelling too much on the future."

"Or the past. I think I'm having trouble letting go of who I was."

"You're still you."

"I know, but I was so sure of everything and where my life was going. Now everything's different."

"It's not all terrible, is it?"

I smiled as I ran my fingertip down the front of his shirt. "Well, this morning was pretty great until I turned on the news and realized I can't bear to watch it now."

Riley sprawled out alongside me and clasped my hand. "That was your first mistake."

"There was more than one?"

"You're more than your job, Meg. Everybody is. I didn't even know you when you were a reporter, and you said you couldn't imagine me owning a business, but I did."

I looked into his eyes. "I guess that means neither of us has any illusions. I never got to see all the trappings of your high-powered career to make me all starry-eyed."

He laughed. "That's for sure. Good thing I have a cute dog."

"Zelda is a total chick-magnet." At my comment, Zelda lifted her head off my stomach to look at me. "Yes, you."

Riley brought our joined hands to his lips and kissed my fingertips. "I fell in love with *you*, not what you do for a living. And I don't think you're maliciously taking advantage of the fact that I happen to have a lot of money. But it would be helpful if you got out of bed, since you're the one who wants to go explore Port Townsend."

He let go of my hand and moved to get up, but I pulled him back to me. "I love you too. I wish you'd seen me as a reporter because I was great."

"I've read some of your more recent works and been the victim of countless interrogations, so I believe you."

"Victim?"

"Fine. *Subject*. Whatever you want to call it. You've directed your relentless questions at me and managed to extract information I didn't want to share."

I grinned. "That's true. I *am* good. Okay, tomorrow we research, but today we play."

～

Our day in Port Townsend was fun and all too short. I wished I could play tourist for more than one day, but we packed in as much as we could into our day off. We walked Zelda all over the historic downtown area, window-shopped, and sat at a cute cafe drinking coffee. I also ate a gigantic, decadent pastry that was so sweet and calorie-laden it made even me a little sick. After we got back to the condo and had dinner, we took Zelda on a gorgeous walk on the private beach at the resort and watched the sun set over the sound. The whole day felt like a big, fat, romantic first date, which was ironic because Riley and I had never had any dates at all.

Bright and early Monday morning we cruised over to the community college library. As with my other forays into research, I schmoozed a reference librarian for access to business databases and did a ton of reading. I dug deep into Archetypal Media, Online Systems United, and their merger. For a change, Riley didn't have some other crisis to attend to, so he joined me in reading.

The CEO of Online Systems United had been interviewed many times over the years, and the library had magazine and newspaper articles that had been archived onto microfiche. Although quite a few of the articles were puff pieces, the guy's personality managed to come through in quotations. He sounded like a first-class jerk.

I wanted more first-person accounts, so I dug deeper and found some transcripts of interviews. They were even worse. Reading between the jargon-filled lines, it was clear Alan Conway had no compassion for anyone or anything. He had bitten and clawed his way to the top and was often referred to as "ruthless." Yikes.

I leaned over to see what was on Riley's screen. It was an article I'd already read and I nudged him. "Thoughts?"

"Unprintable. This guy is a real piece of work."

"I know. And to think he could have been signing my paychecks. I'm feeling better about being laid off now."

Riley pointed at the text on the microfiche screen. "Look at this. He's talking about regulations. That any type of oversight is 'obstruction.' Any rules related to safety, health, or the environment are hurting business and the country."

"Here's an outright lie. Apparently he spoke at a college graduation and protesters were there booing him because they didn't like his politics. There's film of this event because all the parents were there. Someone's home video hit the news wires because it was so humiliating. But he describes it as one of the greatest speeches of all time and claims that people loved it and were applauding." I pointed at my screen. "He calls himself brilliant a lot. And great. He's into the word great. I think he's got a Tony the Tiger fixation or something."

Riley grinned. "See what happens when you eat too many Frosted Flakes? Your get a sugar rush and think you're grrrreat."

"The Founder may crank up the crazy, but this guy is just mean to anyone who isn't a billionaire like he is." I leaned over to shut off the microfiche. "I've had enough. Matt will fit right in with this guy in the executive suite. It's sickening to read about these greedy, heartless scumbags."

We returned the microfilm and microfiche to the reference desk and the librarian gave us back our driver's licenses. She was a tiny birdlike woman with frosted light brown hair cut in a short bob. Something about her reminded me of an elf with her delicate fingers skittering across the boxes of microfiche as she refiled them.

It seemed like she was eager for us to leave and as I tucked my driver's license back into my wallet I asked, "Is the library about to close? I thought you were open until five. I'm sorry if we're keeping you here late."

"No, no. We're not closing." The librarian stacked some books. "I'm a little distracted because my daughter works in Seattle near where that bombing took place. It wasn't far from her office."

Riley turned to look at her. "What bombing?"

"Didn't you hear? Some type of radio tower blew up and it fell on another building. There was a fire and they had to evacuate people." She clutched the cover of one of the boxes of microfiche. "I'm worried about my daughter."

I put my hand on the librarian's. "I'm sure she'll be okay. Did you see the news report online? I'd like to read about what happened."

"Go to your home page, and I'm sure you'll find it."

Riley and went to a table and I set up my laptop so we could both see the screen. He put his arm around my shoulders, and I leaned on his chest as we read in silence.

He gave me a squeeze, moved away, and scratched his chin. "Jeez."

"Wow." I looked at him. "I wish we could have warned someone."

"Like who? And no one would have believed us anyway."

"We should go to Seattle and check out other towers. It's possible we might see someone we recognize. Maybe we could stop them."

"That takes the term wild-goose chase to a new level, even for us."

"What else can we do?"

Riley leaned forward and began typing, doing whatever it was he did to get into his server. "Post an article."

"What?"

"A warning. Or something. I don't know." He pointed at the screen. "Write something. Maybe tell people that the bombing wasn't an accident and people should stay away from Seattle."

"What about the people who live here?"

"I don't know." He ran his hand across his closely cropped hair. "You'll think of something. You're the writer, not me."

"Okay, I'll write up what I can, but I don't think it will help. We need to go to Seattle."

"Fine. Let's do this first and then we can figure out what's next."

I got to work typing a new online article, even though I felt sick to my stomach about the bombing. The good thing about having been a reporter is that I can write even when I don't want to or have almost nothing constructive to say. The daily deadlines of a reporter are extremely motivating. When you have an editor breathing down your neck for a story, writer's block becomes nothing more than a quaint concept.

After I finished my missive, Riley downloaded a ton more email from the server and uploaded my replies to the people who had emailed while I was at the retreat. Using my email software, I could compose my replies offline and then whenever I actually had a connection, we could send them. People probably thought I was a crummy correspondent, but hey, my life had been complicated lately so they were lucky to get a response at all.

While we were walking back to Lurch, a question popped into my mind. "I didn't think about it before, but how did so many people find what I wrote so quickly?"

"I haven't had time to search, but my guess is that someone ran across that first post and shared the link in some popular discussion board somewhere."

I gave his shoulder a playful shove. "Wow, you geeks are more social than I would have expected."

"We're only social online, where no one can see us."

When we returned to the condo, we packed up everything, but I moved slowly because I was depressed about having to leave. The worst part about vacations is that they end. I'd hoped for more time before we had to face the unpleasantness of being in the big city again.

Technically, it's only about sixty miles from Port Townsend to Seattle, but that involves taking a ferry. The odds of having to wait were high, so we decided to take the overland route south through Bremerton and Gig Harbor to Tacoma and then head northward on Interstate 5 to Seattle. At almost twice the distance, it wasn't the most direct approach, but it would work. The bombing had taken place near the airport, so it made sense to approach the city from the south and stay somewhere near SeaTac.

After checking us out of the condo, Riley got into Lurch and put his hand on mine. "Ready?"

I gazed out at the darkening clouds. "No. I wish we didn't have to do this, but then I read more emails from other people whose lives are falling apart, and I feel like we have to do something."

"Then we're off to the Emerald City."

"If we found a wizard, it would help."

Chapter 10

Stormy Weather

The trip south felt like it might take forever. The deterioration in the weather, marked by thick, gray, ominous clouds reflected my impatient mood. Riley was equally somber and grumpy. His muttering was a clue that he was becoming annoyed by the increasingly bad behavior of other drivers as the traffic got worse.

I jumped in my seat at a flash of lightning that jolted across the sky. Thunder rumbled, and the clouds opened up with a monster deluge. Water was everywhere, and Lurch's ancient wipers struggled to keep up with the torrential rain. Zelda stood up, and out of the corner of my eye, I noticed Riley's hands tighten on the steering wheel. At least the Bronco had new tires.

The rain fell in thick sheets, as if we were driving through a waterfall. The huge raindrops hammered the windshield, and I reached up to touch the seam where Lurch's roof met the front of the vehicle. Water dribbled down my fingertips, and I held my hand up with my fingers splayed to show Riley. "I'm guessing water isn't supposed to drip down the inside."

"I didn't have time to fix the seal and reseat the top."

I rummaged around in the glove compartment, found some paper napkins, and tried wiping up the water and condensation from the inside of the windshield. I wasn't feeling much love for Lurch at the moment. A removable top sounded like cool idea, but it was less nifty when the roof didn't perform its primary function of keeping bad weather off my head.

The rain was relentless, and the lightning flashes were nerve-racking. The twinge in my head returned, and after my past experiences in lighting storms, I was worried I might have some type of screaming meltdown. Riley must have sensed my distress because somewhere north of Bremerton, he pulled off the road into a Denny's parking lot. "I think it might be a good idea if we stopped."

"Are you okay?" I asked.

"Better than you are, I think. Will you be all right here while I get some coffee?" He turned around and looked at Zelda. "Zee hasn't given any sign that you're about to have a problem."

"Not yet." I reached for my raincoat that was in the back. "But maybe I should go with you."

We got out and ran through the swirling rain to the door. Inside, the restaurant smelled damp from the cranky and soggy-looking patrons huddled on bar stools at the counter. We weren't the only ones waiting out the downpour.

I stood quietly next to Riley while the cashier rang up our coffees. The restaurant was crowded, and I wasn't feeling like being around people, so he got the coffees to go.

The pounding in my head was getting worse. A bolt of lightning lit up the sky as I pushed the door open to return to Lurch. I was glad we weren't on the road because another wave of thunderstorms was descending upon us.

I slowed my pace, took a deep breath, and closed my eyes, trying to envision a tropical white sand beach somewhere far away from this parking lot, but it didn't work. The noise of the thunder made it impossible to sustain any type of fantasy.

I opened my eyes and much to my dismay, I wasn't in the parking lot anymore. *Crap.* I didn't want to deal with a vision right now. The only good thing was that I wasn't standing in the rain. I was inside Lurch, staring through the passenger-side window watching the water stream down in rivers across the glass. Everything was quiet except for the sound of the storm raging outside. Zelda was curled up in the back looking unhappy, probably because the condensation was so heavy on all the windows she couldn't see out and the interior of the vehicle was damp and cold.

I took off my raincoat and huddled under it like it was a tent, with my hands curled around my paper cup of coffee. Riley leaned forward to start the Bronco so he could run the defroster and warm up. The teal blue aura shimmered around him like a radiant mist of color.

The sky was such a dark gray it was as if night were falling. A lightning bolt lit up the sky and then coalesced into a fireball. The huge fiery sphere was falling from the sky toward us, and I shrieked, "We need to get out of here!"

I turned around to look at Riley, who was slumped against the driver's-side door. I reached for him, and tried to shake him awake. I yelled, "Riley, wake up. You can't do this now!"

The sky exploded in light as something huge crashed on the road in front of the restaurant. Zelda was barking, and I could feel heat on my legs. I reached for the door handle. We had to get out of here! I opened the door, ran into the pouring rain, and was immediately drenched. My legs were still burning and my heart was pounding like a jackhammer, but the rest of me instantly froze as the frigid rainwater coursed over me.

Suddenly I was engulfed in a blue haze, and Riley was shaking my shoulders. "Meg, it's not *real*. Wake up!"

We were standing in the parking lot, soaking wet. I turned my head and noticed a couple standing next to a Volkswagen a few spaces away was huddled under an umbrella, looking at me like I was insane. I smiled weakly and lifted my hand in a little wave to indicate I was okay.

Riley pushed my sodden hair back away from my eyes and looked at me intently. "Meg?"

"I'm sorry." Disoriented and embarrassed, I gripped his hand and turned toward Lurch. "I hate it when I do this."

Riley dug out a couple of towels from the back and we attempted to dry ourselves off, which wasn't easy, since the interior of the Bronco wasn't particularly dry either. Zelda poked her nose into the front seat to check on me. "Hi Zee. Sorry I caused an incident."

Riley threw his towel at me. "You need this more than I do. There's coffee all over you. It smells like you've been swimming in Lake Latte."

I looked down at my pants. "There's a stain that's not going away. I think these slacks are doomed."

"Are you ready to tell me what you saw?"

I blew out a breath. "It was horrible. You didn't happen to pass out, did you?"

"No. Would you like to elaborate on that?"

"I thought you were dead and there was this fiery thing about to fall on us from the sky. I couldn't tell if it was a plane or what. I was terrified."

"I figured that out. We were walking back to the Bronco, you started screaming, and ran into the parking lot."

"I thought we were in the car, and there was something wrong with you." I leaned forward and put my face into my palms. I didn't want to cry this time. Not again. But I was so tired of having visions that I didn't understand. I raised my head and looked at Riley. "Why does it always have to involve fire?"

He took my hand from my lap. "I don't know, but the worst part for me is when you run. I wish you wouldn't do that. It scares the crap out of me."

"Having a vision where I think you're dead isn't too enjoyable for me either, you know. I shook you, but you wouldn't wake up!" My heart started beating faster at the memory, and a tear slid down my cheek. Okay, maybe I was going to cry after all. "I didn't know what to do. I felt so helpless."

Riley leaned over, put his hand on my cheek, and kissed me. "I'm fine."

"You scared me!"

"It wasn't real, Meg. I was minding my own business, walking through the parking lot, trying not to spill my coffee. I promise."

I glanced out the window. "Is the rain letting up?"

"A little, I think."

"Let's get out of here. I want to get where we're going and go to sleep for a couple days." I heaved a sigh. "Doing anything heroic isn't going to happen today. I'm done."

"All right. Next stop, Motel 6."

Riley started Lurch, and we left the parking lot heading south. I closed my eyes because hallucination hangover is no fun. The sound of Lurch's engine was soothing, and I fell asleep. The next thing I knew, we were pulling into the motel parking lot. I sat up straight and looked at Riley. "Did I miss anything?"

"Just a lot of bad traffic. I'm going to check in. Be right back."

The sky was clear, and when Riley got out of the Bronco, the sound of an airplane roaring overhead reminded me that the motel was located near SeaTac. I understood why Riley mentioned his remote island fantasy every once in a while. It would be wonderful to forget about fiery visions, get on a plane, and go to Tahiti, never to return. Zelda stood up and watched Riley as he walked to the lobby. How difficult would it be to fly a dog to Tahiti? Were there quarantine rules? Maybe I should look into that.

Riley returned and we went through the unloading routine. I snacked on some leftovers we'd brought with us from the condo, and Riley sprawled out on the bed.

I curled up next to him and snuggled into his chest. He tilted my chin up so he could look into my eyes. "Are you all right? I'm not going to have to tie you to the bed or something, am I?"

"That sounds kinky, and I'm guessing that's not what you mean. If you're wondering if I'm going to run out into traffic, the answer is I hope not."

"Me too."

After we got ready for bed and crawled under the covers, I found I was exhausted, but wide awake because my brain wouldn't shut up. Riley rubbed my back slowly, which was incredibly relaxing, and I finally fell into a fitful sleep.

I had one of those persistent dreams that wake you up, but when you fall back asleep, the dream continues where you left off. Serialized bad dreams are even worse than normal nightmares because it's like watching a crappy TV rerun. I don't understand why if a dream was bad the first time, my brain thinks replaying it is a good idea.

At one thirty-eight, I woke up yet again and found Riley was awake too. In the dark room, the shadows made him seem oddly gaunt, even for him. He gave me a kiss. "You were whimpering in your sleep."

"I keep having a bad dream over and over. It won't stop."

"Do you want to tell me about it?"

"Maybe if I tell you, my mind will stop rerunning it."

"What happened?"

"It was confusing. Like a bad horror movie that makes no sense. I was in a graveyard and there were tombstones everywhere that were old and covered with moss and lichen."

"That's not so bad. You usually find tombstones in graveyards."

"It gets worse." I snuggled up closer. "There's an open grave that someone had dug, so it's all ready for its new occupant. One of those long black hearses drives down the dirt road into the cemetery, followed by a bunch of cars."

He stroked my hair. "So you dreamed about a funeral."

I propped myself up on my elbows so I could see his eyes. "That's when it gets disturbing. You're there, and you disappear down into the grave."

"What am I doing? Digging the grave? What about the hearse and the funeral?"

"It gets confusing after that. First, it's like you fall into the grave, and I run over to see if you're okay. But then I think you're in the coffin. The whole thing is so muddled and horrible. I don't understand it and I want it to stop." I collapsed onto his chest so I could listen to his heartbeat. "I'm exhausted. Dreaming about death repeatedly isn't restful."

"I have to say, I'm not too excited about being the dead guy either."

~

When I woke up the next morning, I still felt cruddy and wanted to pull the covers over my head and give up on the day. But Zelda made it clear that it was time for her to go outside, so Riley and I dragged on clothes and acquiesced to the dog's wishes. Outside, the storm had scrubbed everything clean, and droplets of water sparkled on every surface. Even Lurch looked less filthy, thanks to nature's car wash.

The location was not conducive to a walk, so Zelda had to be content with the narrow strip of grass that ran behind the motel. We stood and waited while she paced around and did what she needed to do. Because it was early, only a few travelers rushing to catch a shuttle to the airport were around.

Riley seemed to be as tired as I was. My tossing and turning, coupled with the loud location near the airport, didn't make for a restful night. I tried to remember if he'd eaten anything when I'd had my big snack attack the night before. His dark eyes had the dulled, slightly glazed cast that happened when he was feeling sick.

Zelda came up to me with an expectant look, and I smiled. "You seem like a dog who wants breakfast."

Zelda turned back toward our room, dragging Riley along behind her. I caught up and took his other hand. "Are you ready to go look at a bombed-out cell tower?"

"If we have to."

We went back into the room, and I dug into the bags of food while Riley fed Zelda. She gobbled up her food and jumped up on the bed for her post-breakfast nap.

I handed Riley an apple. "Eat something."

"You can have it. I'm going to take a shower." He gathered up some clothes and slipped into the infinitesimal bathroom. The sound of the water drowned out some of the noise from the increasing activity in the parking lot. I took a bite of apple and plugged in my laptop.

I worked through the emails we'd downloaded at the library, deleting the spam, salacious innuendo from creepers, and other junk. It was a slow process, but every once in a while I'd run across a real, often heartfelt, email that I carefully saved aside.

After Riley was done with his shower, I washed and then badgered him about eating to the point that he stopped talking to me entirely. He pointed at the door to indicate it was time to depart and visit the site of the bombing.

"I don't believe you. I mean, come on. You are being completely childish about this," I said as I walked through the door. "If you don't eat, we all know what is going to happen."

Riley followed with Zelda and loaded her into the back of Lurch without saying a word. I waited while Riley got in before I resumed my verbal assault. I strapped on my seatbelt and turned to him. "Maybe we can stop somewhere and get something. What do you want to eat?"

He didn't respond, and by this point, I was getting seriously annoyed. "I'm going to make you eat eventually, you know."

Riley shifted Lurch into reverse and glanced at me without saying anything. I wanted to shake him senseless. When he got like this, it made me crazy. The word stubborn didn't even begin to cover it. Mulish? What was more stubborn than stubborn? I folded my arms across my chest. If he wasn't going to talk to me, then I wasn't going to say anything either. He was going to make himself sick again, and I couldn't think of any way to force feed someone who was so much bigger than I was. Grr.

My mind ground through the same repetitive thoughts as we wound our way onto the freeway and sat through tedious Seattle traffic. At the exit, I pulled out the city map and tersely gave Riley directions to the cell tower that had been bombed. Oddly, it seemed like we weren't the only ones heading to the location.

Riley drove around several blocks searching for a parking place, and I folded up the map. "What's going on here?"

Still no response. I turned and put my hand on Riley's arm. "The silent treatment is getting old. I asked you a question. Do you know if there's some event happening here? Why are all these people walking in the same direction toward what's left of the tower?"

Riley shook his head and focused on parallel parking in a questionable space. Maybe a tiny hatchback would fit, but Lurch seemed a little large. Thirty-seven machinations later, Lurch was tucked into the parking spot with about three inches to spare at the front and back.

I said, "Blink four times if we're taking Zelda, okay?"

Riley blinked at me, so I clipped on Zelda's leash and let her out. We followed the crowds walking toward the site of yesterday's disaster. People were crowding around a podium that had been set up near the base of the tower. Yellow tape was crisscrossed in front of the buildings that had caught fire after the bombing. Although nothing was burning, the acrid smell of burnt plastic and debris still permeated the air. I glanced at Riley, who clearly wasn't enjoying the aroma of crispy fried cell tower.

A woman wearing a conservative business suit and holding a small notebook was frantically scribbling. Her actions were reminiscent of my days as a reporter, and she even looked a little like me. I stopped and grabbed Riley's arm. "This is a press conference."

He looked down at me in surprise. "How can you tell?"

"I appreciate your return to audible means of communication. To answer your question, these are my people." I pointed at the woman. "Look at her. I have a suit like that and she's taking notes. And that guy over there has a press pass around his neck. They're reporters."

"I suppose it's newsworthy."

"But the bombing happened yesterday. It's old news now. Why do a press conference today?"

Riley turned to look behind us. "There's a camera crew setting up back there. Maybe old news is more interesting than you thought."

I glanced at the podium, where a group of people was milling around. A man stepped out from behind the group, and I put my hand to my mouth to cover a gasp. I moved behind Riley and yanked on Zelda's leash to pull her around with me.

Riley twisted to look at me. "What are you doing?"

I pointed around his elbow. "That's Matt."

"Evil ex-boyfriend Matt?"

"That's him. This must have been one of the Archetypal towers." I tugged at Riley's t-shirt. "Let's move farther back. I don't want him to see me."

"Do you think he'd recognize you? Your hair is different."

"I don't know. If he knows anything about us, which given his nasty message on my answering machine, we're pretty sure he does, he might recognize you. It's unfortunate that you're so tall and thin. You stand out."

"I can't do much about that."

"Well, eating might help fifty percent of the problem."

"Lay off, Meg."

When Riley lost his sense of humor, he really lost it. "Okay fine, Captain Cranky, then find us a place where we're less conspicuous."

I followed Riley and Zelda to a spot behind a TV news van. We could still see the activities at the podium, but maybe back by the equipment we'd blend into the sea of camera-crew people scurrying around. Of course, reporters and TV news personnel don't usually bring dogs to a press conference, so I tried to shield Zelda's furry body from curious eyes.

Matt strolled to the podium. As usual, he was impeccably dressed in a suit that probably cost more than the annual rent on my apartment. He looked unbelievably handsome, and I remembered why I fell all over myself when he first spoke to me. I felt shallow even thinking that thought, so I pretended he was standing there naked wearing only a pair of tube socks.

I giggled, and Riley nudged me. "What? Are you drooling over there? I see why you went for this guy."

"He's a creep, and tube socks don't make me drool."

◟

In what I thought of as his pontificating voice, Matt proclaimed that Archetypal Online Systems was trying to bring breakthrough technology to Seattle, but it was being thwarted by eco-terrorists that had no regard for safety. He droned on about how the Internet, the Archetypal online communities, and cellular technology would bring us all closer together. And how vital it was for Archetypal to receive support from the great citizens of Seattle to help them track down naysayers and nasty tree huggers.

He said, "There are factions both online and offline that want you to believe that towers like this one pose some type of health risk. We've tested our technology extensively, and there is absolutely no danger to you or your children."

I glanced at Riley, who was scowling. He probably had surly thoughts similar to mine running through his head. What a load a crap they were spewing. I wanted to go back to our disgusting motel room and write a scathing rebuttal. I scanned the crowd to see the reaction. Most of the reporters looked bored, but something was up with a guy who was near the base of the tower. Two burly men that I guessed might be security had grabbed a man wearing a t-shirt with a rainbow-hued peace sign on it.

I poked Riley in the ribs and directed his attention toward the three people. The situation appeared to be deteriorating. Mr. Rainbow Man didn't seem to want to go wherever the other two wanted to take him. The discussion was rapidly turning into a full-on altercation. A yellowish haze surrounded the group, and I rubbed my eyes. I glanced at Riley, who had shifted his focus to the scuffle, but didn't seem worried. Was I having a vision? Or was there truly a glow?

I took Riley's hand and he looked down at me. "This is dull. Your boyfriend sure likes the sound of his own voice."

"He's not my boyfriend. You are, remember?" I squeezed his hand to keep his attention. "This might be an odd question, but I'm not having a vision, am I?"

Riley pulled me closer and stared down into my eyes with concern. "Are you all right?"

"I see a yellow glow around that guy over there wearing the peace sign t-shirt. But Zelda's not barking, and I'm not screaming. So this is real, isn't it?"

"We're just standing here. I don't see a glow, but that guy is creating a disturbance. He's pretty wiry."

"Matt is starting to notice too. He's getting twitchy up there." I inclined my head toward the podium. "See how he's touching his watch and swirling it around his wrist? It's a Rolex, and when he's nervous, he plays with it. Plus, he's rambling. We don't care about your new office in Los Angeles, Matt. Shut up."

"It does look like the press conference is winding down. We should get out of here."

"But I want to talk to Rainbow Man. The thugs let him go and he's leaving. Let's go after him."

Riley sighed, but was willing to follow me as I wound my way through the crowd, hustling to catch up with my glowing rainbow dude. The man had dark blonde long hair pulled back into a curly ponytail, a scruffy blonde beard, and long legs that were striding purposefully away from the press conference.

After Rainbow Man turned a corner and I was sure Matt couldn't see me, I called out, "Excuse me!"

The man kept walking and I shouted, "Hey, you with the peace sign, could you slow down?"

He turned to look, and I waved as nonthreateningly as I could. "Do you have a minute? I'd like to talk to you."

He spread his arms wide. "What do you want? I said I was leaving, okay? Leave me alone!"

I increased my pace. "I'm not with them. I promise I'm not. I don't know who those guys are." Okay, I was lying a little because I had a pretty good idea. But Rainbow Man didn't need to know that at the moment.

He put his hands on his hips. "Then what do you want? Who *are* you?"

I finally caught up to him and tried not to pant audibly. "I'm Meg, and this is Riley."

"My name's Andy. Have we met?"

"No, but I want to ask you a question. It might sound sort of, well, odd though." The golden glow around him was distracting. Even though Riley had an aura, I tuned out the blue around him, probably because we spent so much time together. It's like hanging out with someone with blue eyes. You don't think, "Wow, look at those blue eyes," every moment you're with the person. But when I paid attention, Riley's aura was always there surrounding him.

Riley said, "We don't want anything from you. We'd just like to ask you a couple of questions."

Before Andy could say no, I said quickly, "Do you have some type of problem with one of your senses?"

Andy looked stunned for a moment and opened and closed his mouth, apparently uncertain how to reply. Finally, he said, "Um, are you sure we haven't met? Or did you talk to my friend Kenny? He said he wouldn't tell anyone."

"We've never met, but has something happened to your vision, hearing, touch, taste, or sense of smell?" I said. "Maybe starting about six or eight months ago?"

"How do you know that?" He stepped closer to me. "You need to tell me how you know that. It's private!"

"We know because it happened to us," Riley said quietly. "What happened to *you*, Andy?"

I said, "You can tell us. My vision became, well, strange, for lack of a better word. And Riley has an overdeveloped sense of smell."

"It's not as much fun as it sounds," Riley added.

"No, man, it's awful." Andy's shoulders slumped, "I thought I was some kind of freak, but then I read some stuff online. It's my eyesight. I didn't even wear glasses, but now it's like the world turned into a black-and-white movie. I've had my vision checked every which way, and there's nothing physically wrong with my eyes. But they don't work right anymore."

"Wait, I know about this!" I pointed at him. "You're the artist who wrote to me."

"You wrote those posts? How come you never wrote back?" Andy said. "And how did you know I had this problem anyway? I mean, my eyes look the same."

"That's part of Meg's unusual vision," Riley said.

"I'm sorry about not writing back. It's a long, complicated story. But the email you wrote touched my heart." I put my hand to my chest. "Your paintings are absolutely beautiful."

"Thanks. I've been working as a barista at a coffee shop since I gave up painting," Andy looked down at his sandals. "I had a gallery showing and they were asking for more of my work, but I can't paint anymore. I'm not one of those artists who sees the painting in his head. My process was all about mixing the colors. The way it came together on the canvas was magic. And I can't do that anymore, so it's like I've lost my soul. I can't figure out how to create art now."

I gestured in the direction of the press conference. "How come you came here?"

"I read about it online. I guess you posted a new article after the bombing to warn people away from Seattle. But I live here, and I saw a post about the press conference in the forum."

"What forum?" Riley and I asked simultaneously.

"Like the guy up there was bragging about, the gamer forums and chat rooms on Archetypal get a lot of action. My buddy Kenny is the sysop of one of the big gamer boards."

I glanced at Riley, and he answered my unspoken question, "It stands for systems operator. It means Kenny runs the board."

Andy continued, "After, uh, my problem happened, we started chatting when I mentioned I couldn't see colors in the game. Turns out it's not just me. There are a few us who have been sharing info and kind of commiserating, I guess you'd say." Andy turned to me. "We're big fans of your writing."

"Thanks." I grinned. "I guess you helped spread the word."

Riley smiled at me. "Told ya."

~

While we walked to where Riley had parked Lurch, Andy told us about some of the other people he knew who had sensory problems. Andy's buddy Kenny the sysop lived in Los Angeles and another one of their online friends who had written to me lived in San Francisco.

"Would it be okay for me to let Kenny know we talked to you?" I asked Andy. "I need to reply to his email, and I'd like to let him know we met."

"Fine with me. I've never met Kenny in person." Andy shrugged. "But we've known each other online for a couple years. His username is KenHatesBarbie22."

"I'm Hyrule," Riley said.

I looked at him. "You frequent the Archetypal chat rooms too?"

"I used to, but it's been a while. They were Online Systems United then. I assume my username still works," Riley said. "I guess I should check."

"That's a cool choice for a name. I can't believe you scored it," Andy said. "Zelda rocks."

At the reference to her name, Zelda wagged. I said, "We like her too."

Riley said, "He means the game, Meg. Hyrule is the kingdom where it's set."

"Oh yeah. Legend of Zelda. Got it." My mother would probably love to run a bunch of psych tests on all these gamers. I was completely out of that loop. It was a corner of the Internet I had no experience with at all.

Andy shook my hand. "I'm glad to have met you both. Let's keep in touch online, okay?"

"We'll do the best we can. Sometimes we're not in a position to get a connection, so if we don't reply quickly, it's nothing personal. I promise," I said.

Riley said, "We've been traveling a lot lately."

"It's cool. I'll tell everyone." Andy bent to pet Zelda and gave us a goodbye wave. "See ya online, whenever."

We got into Lurch and Riley drove toward the freeway so we could return to our motel. I pointed at a fast-food sign as we whizzed by. "I'm hungry. We're supposed to stop for lunch, remember?"

"I didn't agree to that, and even if I had, there's no way I'd stop there. There's plenty of food in the room. You can nuke something."

"You need to eat too."

Riley glared at me, but didn't say anything. Apparently, I'd crossed a line again. I folded my arms and stared out the window in silence at the monotonous gray clouds that hovered above us like a heavy wool blanket.

After we returned to the motel room, Riley and Zelda retired to the bed while I began rummaging through our stores of snacks and leftovers. I held up a box of bland crackers. "How about cheese and crackers?"

Riley had one arm over his eyes and his other hand was petting Zelda's head, which was resting on his stomach.

Everyone ignored me and I sat on the bed next to Zelda, who moved her muzzle to my lap. I pulled Riley's arm away from his face. "Hey, wake up. It's food time."

"No it's not. I'm tired. It's nap time."

"You're only tired because you haven't eaten anything." I yanked on his arm to pull him into a sitting position. "Time to eat. I told you I'm not going to let you stop eating again, and I'm not."

Riley moved away from me to lean back on the wall. "Stop it, Meg. I'm tired because your nightmares kept me up. Leave me alone."

"But you need to eat something. You keep doing this to yourself. Hold your breath and choke something down." I extended my arms in exasperation. "You have to, or you'll end up so sick we'll have to dump you in the hospital again."

"Do you honestly think I want to feel this bad?" He leaned forward. "Here's the thing. It's not only food smelling terrible. It's like every aroma in the area is assaulting me, which makes me feel terrible in general. When I feel like this and I force myself to eat, I throw up. I hate that, so I don't eat."

"You never said that before."

"I figured it was more information than you needed to know."

"You could have said something. How about drinking some juice?"

"Maybe later. How about if you let me sleep for a while?"

"I guess I could reply to my email. Then maybe you could have some juice, okay?"

"Fine." Riley sprawled out on the bed, rolled over toward the wall away from me, and Zelda placed her muzzle on his waist.

Okay, maybe the dog was a better nurse than I was, but I didn't want my bad dreams about Riley to come true. When I get anxious or worried, my typical response is to do something to fix whatever is bothering me. Because you can't fix someone else, I'd turned into a nagging shrew.

After mentally beating myself up a little, I returned to the desk and focused my attention on going through email. Now I knew more about some of the people behind the email addresses, so I wanted to find out more about their experiences.

I queued up a bunch of replies and looked over at Riley and Zelda. They hadn't moved, and it wasn't like I'd gotten much sleep last night either. I went over to the bed, shoved Zelda aside, and stretched out alongside Riley's back. I put my cheek on his shoulder and wrapped an arm around him, putting my palm on his chest. When he clasped my hand with his, I whispered, "I'm sorry."

"Me too."

"What do you think about leaving here? Even for a cheap airport hotel, this room is disgusting. The noise from the parking lot is driving me nuts. We could be out of the city in a couple of hours."

He turned to look over his shoulder at me. "And go where?"

"I don't care. Someplace with less radiation where we're not falling apart."

"All right, although I'm not sure what to do next or where to go."

"Me neither." I sat up and looked down into his eyes. "But I think I got spoiled seeing you healthy. This is too hard."

"Agreed. Let's get out of here."

Riley got up and we started packing. He logged into the server so I could send my email off into the great cyber-beyond, and I did some snacking before putting the food away.

When I looked back at the laptop, I found I'd already received a reply from Kenny. "Hey, check it out. I'm guessing Kenny doesn't get out of his gamer dungeon much."

Riley looked over my shoulder at the screen. "He claims he has information."

I sat down and began typing. "I love information! C'mon, Kenny, you know you want to share. Tell me what you know."

"You might want to tell him you'll be offline for a while because we're on the move."

"Yeah, I don't want to hurt his feelings again. Andy was pretty miffed about not hearing back from me."

Riley gave me kiss on the cheek. "You're a slave to your geeky fans."

Chapter 11

Good and Bad Ideas

After checking out, we got on Interstate 5 and headed south, away from the city. It was a relief to be away from the noisy motel, and I flipped through our Triple-A guide, looking for a place with a low population density that we could get to before dark. Big expanses of green on the map indicated forests or parks, and I figured the presence of lots of trees might be a good option for those of us who were desperate to get away from civilization.

I narrowed my search to an area around Mount Rainier National Park and targeted potential places to stay in the little towns of Packwood and Ashford, which were located off US Highway 12 right outside the park.

After we left the interstate, I immediately felt better. The twinge at the side of my head that had been my constant companion in Seattle went away, and I felt like I could think more clearly again. And Riley agreed to consume a few crackers from the food stash that I kept tucked into my tote bag. I wanted to shout with joy when he agreed to eat, but I controlled myself and gave a piece of cracker to Zelda instead.

We stopped at a roadside motel called the Elk Creek Lodge, which proudly proclaimed on their sign that they would accept pets. It had a quaint Western rustic look with a timber-frame design and a river-rock facade around the bottom of the building. Even better was the setting. The lodge was situated far back from the road in a lush green meadow with a backdrop of massive evergreens.

Riley parked in front of the office, and Zelda stood up in the back, staring out the back window with her ears pointed at attention.

I followed her gaze. "Check out those deer. They're huge! Since when are deer so casual about lying around like that?"

"I think they're elk having an afternoon siesta." Riley grabbed the keys and leaned over to give me a kiss. "Keep an eye on Zee. She seems a little too interested in the ungulates."

"Way to use a big Latin word to throw her off."

He grinned. "I'll be right back."

Zelda sat and stared at the elk but seemed to realize that she'd get in huge trouble if she tried to break out of the Bronco. I certainly wasn't going to help, and it was relaxing watching the elk sleep. They were considerably quieter than the people wandering around and shouting at each other in the parking lot at the airport motel. I was looking forward to getting a decent night's sleep.

We had a peaceful evening. After settling in, we microwaved some dinner and I chowed down on some curry and rice while sitting at my laptop. I determined we could get a dial-up connection, so Riley logged into the server, and I checked for email from my new buddy Kenny.

I scrolled past a plethora of spam and let out a little cheer. "Kenny replied. And wow, he has a lot to say."

Riley looked up from his dinner. "So did he share this fabulous intel you're so excited about?"

"He sure did." I pointed my fork at Riley. "He says he knows where Hector's been taking people. Kenny called it a bunker. It's in LA in the warehouse district. It used to be a toy factory. Hmm."

"No."

"What? I didn't ask a question."

Riley set his food aside. "You want to go to Los Angeles, don't you?"

"We don't have any other leads." I waved my fork for emphasis. "There could be people there. People like *us*. We need to help them."

"It's fifteen hundred miles away. And the last time we went to LA was almost as awful as our last trip to Seattle."

"Well, that's a toss-up."

"This is a bad idea, Meg."

"You need to find out what's going on with Mel anyway. Maybe you should talk to him in person."

"I'm fine with calling him on the telephone, thanks."

"I suppose." I turned back to the laptop and resumed scrolling through email messages. "Hey, I don't believe it! Your dad sent us an email."

Riley got up from the bed, set his plate on the desk away from Zelda, and looked over my shoulder. "I was hoping he would."

"Way to be sneaky, Tim. I wonder if he broke into the office."

"I left my laptop with him because we agreed that ancient piece-of-crap computer was too unreliable."

I hadn't noticed the absence of Riley's laptop because he'd always been the one carrying it in and out of motel rooms. In one of those tacit agreements, he never carried my laptop and I never carried his.

We scanned the email in silence. Tim had a lot to say. I looked up at Riley. "He and Mom have been busy."

"I'm impressed he's communicating with the outside world again. They found an MD who is interested in their research."

"Mom is probably thrilled." I pressed my fists to my heart in a gesture of adulation. "She's probably writing some long-winded thesis even now. What's he mean by candy corn? Like Halloween candy?"

"It's a code name for a prototype of an idea we talked about," Riley grabbed his plate and returned to the bed. "Dad has all my notes on the laptop."

"You named it candy corn? What does candy have to do with anything?"

"Nothing. It came from a girl in my first-grade class. Her name was Joanie Kornitzky, but somehow Joanie got turned to Candy and she was Candy Corn forever."

"What does this have to do with a prototype?"

"Joanie gave me a valentine in first grade, but I didn't like her because she was a blabbermouth."

"I don't see how this relates to a prototype."

"After I got the valentine, I wasn't impressed enough to suit her and we got into a fight. During the argument, I said she never shut up and that she needed a muffler, like a car. My teacher wasn't amused, so Dad had to come in and get a lecture. Since then, we've referred to a person who never shuts up as a candy corn."

"I'm not liking where this is going."

Riley grinned. "If you're wondering, yes, he called you a candy corn."

"Are you saying you named the prototype after me?" I crossed my arms. "I can't decide if I'm insulted or flattered."

"It's not about you. The idea of the prototype is that it muffles the radiation that affects us. Like a muffler quiets the noise from a car's exhaust."

"I don't get it."

"A car muffler is designed to reflect sound waves from the engine so they cancel themselves out. My idea was to do the same thing with radio waves."

"Okay, that's kind of cool."

"Only if it works. The trick would be having it affect only the frequencies that cause problems for us, as opposed to something like a Faraday cage that blocks everything." He shrugged. "If it actually worked, it would be a cheap add-on that could be easily attached to cellular towers. The towers would still work and people would still have their cell phones."

I leaped off the chair and jumped onto the bed, kneeling in front of him. "But we wouldn't feel like crap! Oh my God, have you actually figured out how to fix this?"

"Maybe. It's just an idea. The problem is that Dad thinks what affects us isn't only radiation. Some type of interaction is happening that we haven't isolated."

I threw my arms around him and squeezed as hard as I could. "I can't believe you didn't say anything."

"I don't know if it will work. You shouldn't get your hopes up, Meg. We still don't know exactly what we're dealing with, and I've had a lot of ideas that were complete failures."

"But what if it *did* work?" I gave him a kiss. "We could live normally."

"We'll see. Dad and I talked through a bunch of ideas."

I went back to the desk and tried to concentrate, but my mind was whirling at the possibility that I might be able to enjoy a life free of screaming hallucinations. I read over the email again. "Hey, Tim says the Founder went to Seattle and is heading to Los Angeles next."

"Is this the Founder's world tour or something?"

I leaned back in the chair. "I doubt it, and I doubt it's a coincidence that the Founder and the EF entourage and Matt and his Archetypal entourage are in these places at the same time."

"It could be."

"No it's not. I think it's another sign that we have to go to LA."

Riley set his plate aside. "I really hate this idea, Meg."

"I know, but we have to go."

～

The next morning we checked out and I waved goodbye to the elk that were still dozing on the lawn. They had to be quite well rested by now. I had to admit the place was relaxing, and I was in a far better state of mind than when we'd arrived.

Although I was dreading seeing Los Angeles again, the idea that Tim was busy developing a prototype that might help me buoyed my mood. Plus, it was easy to be cheerful when we were still thirteen hundred miles away from LA. Because we were taking the inland route away from the coast and its many large cities, I had some time before I'd feel lousy again.

Our route would take us through Yakima, then south through a corner of Oregon and east to Boise, Idaho. Then we'd pick up Route 93 and go south through Ely, Nevada, to Las Vegas, and then over to Los Angeles. I wasn't too excited about seeing the bright lights of Vegas again, which was another place that I'd had strange and unpleasant visions. But we didn't have much choice because there aren't a whole lot of roads that go through Nevada. If we hauled on through and didn't get out of the vehicle, it might be fine.

Once we left the green of western Washington, we returned to the land of blazing sunlight and wide expanses of farmland. I thought wistfully of the convertible Mustang and the feel of the wind and sun on my face. Lurch was a poor substitute, but at least the old clunker was running, and it had the whole Faraday cage thing going for it. Whatever Riley had done to fix Lurch was holding up to his need to exceed the speed limit.

Even at high speed it was a long day of driving, and by three in the afternoon, I was fried and ready for it to be over. We stopped for gas outside of Boise and afterward pulled into a spot on the other side of the parking lot next to a field so Zelda could get a little time out of the vehicle and I could snack.

Riley was obviously tired but still willing to make sandwiches. Boise was a decent-sized city, so our plan was to blaze through as quickly as possible to avert any potentially nasty experiences.

I took the sandwich Riley handed to me and paused before taking a bite. "I could drive, you know. Lurch is hardly a precision automobile like your precious Mustang. What could I possible do to it?"

"The mind reels."

"I'm serious. Aren't you sick of driving yet? I've never driven Lurch and it could be fun."

"Not for me." He bit into the sandwich and looked at it.

"What's wrong?"

He looked around, then up. "Crap. Those things are everywhere."

Behind a row of trees, a cellular tower loomed above us like a steel vulture. I sighed. "Well, that explains my headache. I used to get headaches because I'd stayed out too late having fun. Now I don't get to enjoy the fun part, just the cruddy aftermath."

A booming noise filled the air, and we both dropped to all fours onto the ground next to Lurch. Riley had his arm over Zelda's back, and as I turned to look up at the tower, a ball of yellow flame billowed out from its base.

Smoke boiled up from where the bomb had gone off, and one of the trees caught on fire. An alarm went off at the gas station, and Riley shoved me. "Get into the Bronco!"

I leapt up and opened the passenger door, letting Zelda shoot into the back. Debris was raining down all around us, and I wasn't sure if it was pieces of the tower or something else. The bits and pieces clattered on the hood of the Bronco as Riley started the engine.

Dust and the sound of metal tearing and grating against itself filled the air. I rolled up my window as Riley gunned the engine and roared out of the parking lot and onto the highway. I could feel the vibration through the floorboards as the tower crashed to the ground almost exactly where we'd been parked.

I grabbed Riley's bicep and turned to look between the seats at the view behind us. People were running toward the parts of the tower that were scattered across the parking lot. Someone with a hose was heading for the tree that was now completely engulfed in flames.

Riley pulled my hand off his arm. "You're cutting off my circulation."

"Have you noticed anyone following us?" I demanded.

"No, but we've been on a long stretch of Interstate 84 with no exits to other highways. It's pretty obvious we were heading to Boise."

"But how would they know we'd stop for gas there?"

"No idea, other than that we haven't stopped for gas in a while."

I wrapped my arms around my body. "I'm completely freaked out. How could someone be keeping such close tabs on us?"

"I don't know."

"How long does it take to set up a bomb? Did they do it while I was eating my sandwich? How is that possible?"

"I have no idea." He reached over to put his hand on my leg. "I know you're upset, but I don't have any answers. Setting bombs doesn't happen to be one of those life skills I've ever needed."

"What are we going to do? We can't drive forever. Where are we going to stop?"

"Not here. Look for a place away from populated areas."

I flipped through the Triple-A guide. "Okay, I vote for Jackpot. It's about three hours away on the Nevada border after the turn onto Route 93 going south. After that, there's a whole lot of nothing for a while, and I don't think it would be a good idea to drive all night."

Riley focused on driving and left me alone to my fretting. With the exception of a request for me to pour him some more coffee from the thermos, it was a quiet ride.

According to my travel information, the town of Jackpot was founded after Idaho outlawed all forms of casino gaming in 1954. An enterprising fellow relocated his slot machines from Idaho to what is now the town of Jackpot. He didn't go far from Idaho though because Jackpot is less than a mile from the Idaho-Nevada border. The Cactus Pete casino is the largest one in Jackpot and was named after its founder.

By the time we arrived in Jackpot, it was getting dark and it seemed like we were the only people on the road. If we were being followed, they were certainly sneaky about it. Although Cactus Pete's had a great neon sign, the casino didn't allow pets, but another place across the street did, so we checked in. We parked in the back and unloaded as quickly as possible.

Once we were settled in the room, I flopped back on the bed, spread-eagled. Zelda jumped up to join me and Riley sat at the desk chair. "I know you'll hate this idea, but I think we should roll out of here as early as possible."

I sat up. "I know. There isn't a cellular tower in sight, but after the other things that have happened, I'm worried about Lurch getting sabotaged or you getting attacked on the way to the ice machine."

"That didn't happen."

"But it could! I feel like we're about to be killed." I put my hand on Zelda's head for comfort. "I hate this sensation of being watched all the time. I'm totally paranoid and it stinks."

"It's not paranoia if they really are out to get you."

"This isn't funny!"

"I know, but there's nothing we can do about it right now, so maybe you should try and get some sleep." He wrapped me in his arms and gave me a bone-melting kiss. "Have some chocolate. You'll feel better."

"Probably." I flopped back on the bed, grabbed his arms, and pulled him down on top of me. "If I'm going to die, at least I should die happy."

A slow smile crossed Riley's lips and his dark eyes had the smoldering cast I was getting to know well. He whispered, "*Carpe diem,*" and kissed me again, provoking all sorts of exciting tinglies throughout my body.

Although jumping Riley was a nice diversion, it was temporary. In the category of things I never thought I'd know, I've discovered that worrying about being blown up is all-consuming and makes it difficult to get a good night's sleep. I tossed and turned, throwing off the covers and then pulling them back over me, which Riley made clear he didn't appreciate.

The next morning, we woke up at the crack of dawn, packed, and blew out of town. It was seven hundred sixteen miles to Los Angeles, and Riley was determined to make it in one day.

One very, very long day.

~

The ride to Los Angeles was so long that Riley actually let me drive Lurch. Maybe it was because we were in the middle of nowhere Nevada, which was more or less where we'd been the last time he'd let me drive. Areas with a population density nearing zero seemed to be the only places he'd ever been willing to let me behind the wheel. His reticence may be because I'm not particularly good at driving a manual transmission. Shifting gears is a lot of work, and I don't always do it when Riley thinks I should. Picky, picky.

By the time we stopped at a motel outside of Los Angeles, our tempers were running short and we'd achieved total exhaustion. Even Zelda seemed grumpy. We made it to Rancho Cucamonga, which is in the foothills of the San Gabriel Mountains in San Bernardino County, about an hour east of downtown LA. It's one of the umpteen suburban communities near Los Angeles filled with strip malls, grocery stores, mechanics, hair salons, restaurants, motels, and every chain store imaginable. On our long, strange journeys throughout the West, we'd been through everything from virtually invisible towns to gigantic cities, and learned that the utter sameness of suburban American is striking.

Once we found a pet-friendly motel, we unloaded as quickly as possible so we could collapse. I've always found it odd that sitting in a car on a road trip can be so exhausting. As a passenger, you're not doing much except watching the scenery, but it still wipes you out.

The next morning, Riley logged into the server, and I went through email. Kenny had sent me six emails with subject lines in all upper-case letters. I looked at Riley, who was lying on the bed. "I think Kenny is getting agitated about my lack of response."

Riley looked up from his book. "We were busy. It takes a while to get to SoCal from Seattle. He's going to have to get over it."

"Wow."

"Wow, what? It's rarely good when you say 'wow.'"

"I see why Kenny is agitated. The bunker was blown up yesterday."

"*What?*" Riley got off the bed and stood behind the desk chair, so he could see the email over my shoulder. "Is he all right?"

"I think he's fine." I pointed at the screen. "This was in the *Los Angeles Times*. Kenny scanned the article. According to fire officials, a blast injured a number of people at the site of a former toy factory in downtown Los Angeles."

"Jeez." Riley stood up straight and rubbed his eyes with his palms. "Someone blew up a machine, so people got hit with metal parts that acted like shrapnel. That's gruesome."

"It blew out all the windows of the building, so glass and metal rained down everywhere. There were paramedics, and the fire department showed up too. The whole nine yards." I looked up at Riley. "If we'd driven faster, we might have been there."

"I don't think it would have been possible to drive any faster, but I see your point."

"It says no one was actually inside the building at the time, but there was evidence of transients. I'm betting that building wasn't full of teenage runaways or homeless people." I scrolled through more email. "Come on, Kenny. Don't leave me hanging here. Where did they put all the people Hector abducted?"

Riley returned to the bed. "Email Kenny and ask. We've already established that the guy spends a lot of time at his computer."

I got to work typing a reply that was full of more questions than Kenny was probably prepared to answer, but I was going to throw them out there anyway. I sent the email and resumed scrolling through my typical complement of spam and other Internet flotsam.

"Hey, your dad replied." I opened the email. "Uh, I think you need to look at this. It's got an image attachment that's incomprehensible to me."

I relinquished the chair, and Riley sat in front of the laptop. He rubbed the scruffy stubble on his chin. "Hmm."

I peered at the screen. "Wait! Is that the hieroglyphics code? Like the note you got at the house?"

"It is, and I'm a little alarmed that Dad is worried enough to be using code."

"What does it say?"

"Dad says the scuttlebutt around the retreat is that the Founder was faking the whole channeling thing."

I chuckled. "Gosh, there's a shock. That must have rocked Felicia's world. She probably chastised everyone for their lack of faith."

"She's not there. A number of people left right after we did, including the Founder, Shannon, Felicia, and a couple others."

"Why does this not surprise me?" I put my hands on his shoulders. "Someone had to go on these important missions to blow stuff up. Felicia was desperate to be one of the chosen ones."

"Dad also said that initial tests on candy corn are going well, but he needs more tests to find out what element x is."

"I don't know what element x is." I leaned down to kiss his cheek. "But at least there's a tiny bit of good news, thanks to you."

"Well, Dad mostly. Even if he figures out what the unknown interaction is and can get a prototype working, what are the odds that anyone would use it? It would cost money to retrofit all the towers."

"You were brilliant enough to come up with a cool idea in the first place, so I'm sure you'll figure something out."

"Thanks for the vote of confidence, but I'm not quite so optimistic. I need to send him a reply because I'm not sure about one of the variables in the equation we were working on."

"Don't be a downer. I'm sure your equation is fine. It's not like you've had time to deal with it."

"I've had a lot of time to think. I keep going through the data in my head, and I'm sure there's something I overlooked."

"Okay, but first check to see if Kenny wrote back to me yet."

Riley turned back to the computer and found a new email from Kenny. "He replied, but it's confusing."

I peered at the screen. According to Kenny, the people had been moved. "How does he know this stuff?"

"Good question."

"So he thinks Archetypal moved the people. Why? Did they know the place was going to be bombed?"

"He doesn't say."

"I'm thinking I need to visit Matt's swanky new office in LA."

Riley turned around in the chair and reached for my hand. "I don't think that's the safest idea you've ever had. He's evil, remember?"

"So what? We can't spend our whole lives running away from bombers. I'm betting Matt knows what's going on, and I intend to find out."

"Assuming he does know, why would he tell you?"

"Because he's an egotistical prick." I put my other hand on Riley's. "That man knows every way to push my buttons and make me so incredibly angry that I can barely see straight."

"I don't see how that's useful."

"Because I do the same thing to him. If I can royally piss him off, I bet he'll blab."

"I think you've come up with yet another idea I don't like." Riley kissed my knuckles and let go of my hand. "If we have to go downtown, I should pay a visit to Mel."

"We both should. My headache is back and before I start hallucinating again, I want to get a look at this guy who is ripping you off."

"You want to yell at him, don't you?"

"Maybe a little."

~

After dealing with the morning routine, we ventured out to the deepest, darkest depths of Los Angeles. The law office was in a gigantic high-rise building with outrageously expensive underground parking. Riley pulled Lurch into a spot between a Lamborghini and a BMW. Poor Lurch. The filthy old Bronco looked like the country bumpkin who'd rolled down off the mountain into town and didn't know how to dress appropriately for the occasion.

Riley suggested that Zelda take a nap, and we took the elevator up to the law offices.

I rubbed my temple with my fingertips, and Riley raised his eyebrows at me. "Are you all right?"

"I think so, but you probably know as much or more than I do."

"I'll try to pay attention, but it's hard to filter out the rest of LA. Why does everyone in the metropolitan area feel compelled to wear perfume and aftershave? It's like wading through a toxic chemical spill."

"You're worried we might run into Erin, aren't you?"

Riley didn't say anything, but he snagged my hand as the elevator doors opened into the Law Offices of Stratten and Boggs. The vast space was a sea of chrome, glass, and leather.

I squeezed Riley's palm. "This place is huge. How many people work here?"

"There are more than a hundred lawyers, and the firm occupies multiple floors. Mel's office is in the back. It's kind of a maze."

I followed Riley to the reception desk, where an older woman wearing a headset was writing something on a legal pad. She glanced at us and her bouncy brown curls bobbed as she ripped off her headset, leaped out of her chair, and ran around the counter.

She threw herself at Riley and cried, "I thought you were dead."

I tried to retain a straight face as Riley attempted to peel the woman off and step away from her. "Hi, Cheryl. It's good to see you again. I'm sorry for the confusion. This is my friend, Meg." He pointed at Cheryl, who looked like she was about to burst into tears. "Meg, Cheryl was my assistant, and after I sold my company she came here."

"Riley got me this job, but I miss the old gang something awful." She turned to Riley. "Have you talked to Mike, Susan, or Eddie lately?"

"I haven't talked to anyone. I've been traveling for a while," Riley said.

Cheryl studied Riley. "I hate to ask this, but are you okay? Have you been ill?"

I could practically feel Riley's sigh. He hated getting this question all the time. I volunteered, "It's a long story. We're only in LA for a short visit, and Riley was hoping to see Mel. Is he around?"

The expression on Cheryl's face clouded. "Mel is in a meeting and can't be disturbed."

"Can you tell us who's he talking to?" Riley asked.

"I don't see why not. I don't know why Mel would meet with that man. He's loathsome. Absolutely loathsome. You should have heard how he talked to me when he arrived," Cheryl said.

I suspected I might know, but asked anyway. "What's his name?"

Cheryl made a sneering face and said, "Alan Conway. The CEO of Archetypal Online Systems. Frankly, I didn't know this firm had any dealings with that company. There isn't a file for them anywhere that I could find."

I glanced at Riley and could tell he was thinking the same thing I was. Our timing couldn't have possibly been worse. Unless, of course, we opted to be nosy and learn something. "We could come back later. But before we go, could you point me toward your ladies room?"

Riley said quickly, "I'll show you." He turned to Cheryl. "Meg's not good with taking direction *at all*."

I shot him a glare and smiled at Cheryl. "It was so nice to meet you. We'll let you get back to work. It sounds like Riley knows where everything is around here."

Riley grabbed my hand and bent down to whisper in my ear. "What are you doing? You have no idea where Mel's office is."

"That's why you're going to take me there. I want to know what they're saying."

"Jeez, Meg. What's wrong with you?"

"I seek the truth. And also the ladies room. I wasn't lying about that part. Lead on."

Riley walked purposefully, as if he knew where he was going, which he probably did. I tried to look equally officious, like I belonged and was about to have an important legal discussion instead of a potty run.

After my pit stop, Riley led me to Mel's corner of the labyrinth. He stopped by a tiny office kitchen and wordlessly handed me a glass. We went down a long empty hallway and then Riley looked around, opened a door, and shoved me through it.

He closed the door behind me and pulled a cord to turn on an overhead light.

I looked up at him and fingered a gray stapler that was sitting on a shelf along with a row full of other staplers. "I'm assuming Mel doesn't work in the office-supply closet."

Riley put his finger up to his lips and held his glass up to the wall. He whispered, "Shut up and listen."

I held my glass up and jumped at the jarring animosity from the next room.

A deep voice said, "I warned you about this, Flood."

A second voice, presumably Mel's, replied, "I did what you asked! There were rumors, but I knew it wasn't true because I heard from him. But after they went to Bellingham, I didn't hear anything. He just disappeared."

"No one disappears."

"Unless they're dead. When I told you I thought Riley had been killed, I was telling the truth. You have to believe me."

"Unless you believe in resurrection, he wasn't killed. In fact, he was seen yesterday."

"Well, there has been some credit-card activity over the last couple of days. But I swear to you, until then I didn't know he was still alive."

I moved my glass and silently mouthed "Oh my God!" at Riley who looked equally alarmed and pointed at the wall. I put my glass back, and Alan Conway boomed, "You'd better fix this!"

A door slammed and I could hear footsteps stomping by the closet. Apparently, Mr. Loathsome had said his piece and was moving on. I nudged Riley. "Do you still want to talk to Mel?"

"I think I found out what I need to know," Riley said with a frown. "I trusted him with everything. I need to think about what I'm going to do."

"Well, I'd suggest getting a new lawyer, for one thing."

"No kidding. Since we're here, I think it's time to talk to Erin."

"Oh boy. This should be fun."

Riley led me back the way we'd come, past several glassed-in conference rooms to another long string of offices. He peered around a door, yanked me into the office, and shut the door.

"What are you doing here?" Erin stood up with a horrified look on her face, as if she'd seen a ghost, which from her standpoint probably wasn't too far off the mark. "Mel told me you were really dead this time."

Riley dropped my hand and said, "My demise seems to be a work in progress. I need to talk to you."

"Well, thank heavens you finally took my advice and cut your hair. You might consider getting a new barber though. That's quite a hatchet job." She sat down heavily at the desk and gestured for us to take seats in the guest chairs across from her.

As he sat down, Riley rubbed the extremely short hair on his scalp. "We had to hide for a while and shaving my head was a necessary part of going undercover."

I sat down, feeling awkward. I'd only met Erin once before, back when she and Riley were technically still a couple. We hadn't exactly hit it off. "It's nice to see you again."

Ignoring my comment, Erin flipped her long blonde hair over her shoulder and leaned toward Riley. "What could you possibly want to talk to me about? I think we said everything that needed to said in Seattle, the locus delicti of our most recent breakup. And yet another time I thought you were dead or dying."

"I'm pretty sure that was the last breakup," I said.

Riley turned his head to give me the stink eye, and I offered a weak smile. "Well, it *was*."

Riley cleared his throat. "Remember when I called you and you told me how you found that odd name, Fred Loolem, on the payroll."

"Yes. I talked to accounting, and they said they'd look into it."

"They don't look very quickly, do they? Here's a hint. It's Mel. He's stealing from the firm and from me."

Erin said, "What? That's impossible. I asked discreetly, and as I said, accounting is looking into it. How can you be sure it's Mel?"

"After he talked to you, Riley determined that Fred Loolem is an anagram of Elmer Flood," I said. "I'm guessing you've never played Scrabble with Riley, have you?"

Erin ignored me again and gestured in exasperation. "This is a nightmare, if it's true."

"I need your help." Riley leaned forward. "You probably have a form for representation, right? I'll sign it, so you can help me get my money away from Mel."

"Riley set a trap, and Mel took the bait. But being right stinks financially," I said.

Erin said, "I can't represent you. It would be a conflict of interest."

"Not anymore," I said, leaning forward. "I'm *very* sure that ship has sailed."

Erin seemed to understand my not-so-subtle comment this time. She pursed her lips. "I'm not comfortable with this idea at all."

Riley said, "In addition to stealing, I believe that Mel is working with Archetypal to have me and Meg killed."

"Mel? That's far-fetched." Erin folded her arms across her chest. "So you're honestly telling me you might die this time? Why am I not believing you?"

Riley went through a synopsis of what we'd overheard, and Erin knew enough about the rest of our story to understand what was happening. As Riley had pointed out in the past, the woman wasn't stupid.

She reached down and pulled a piece of paper out of her desk drawer. "I'll help you, but only because I want to see Mel fry for this."

I smiled. "Thank you. I feel that way about quite a few people."

Chapter 12

Duct Tape & Reunions

We managed to leave the law firm without being spotted by Mel. After finding out what he'd been up to lately, I wasn't particularly eager to meet him. We took the elevator down to the parking garage and walked back to Lurch. Inside the Bronco, Zelda was jumping around, barking her head off. Exuberance was one thing, but sheesh, what a nut.

Riley unlocked the vehicle, and I laughed as I opened the passenger-side door. "This is a little over the top, isn't it, Zee? We weren't even gone that long."

Zelda growled and Riley yelled, "Meg!" I turned to look at him as a pair of hands grabbed my shoulders from behind, ripping me from the Bronco onto the pavement and rolling me over onto my stomach. I tried to move away from the man's grip, but his fingers dug into my forearm, wrenching my arm behind me. He splayed his other hand across my cheek, his rough calloused fingers holding my head against the pavement. I couldn't see his face, but the putrid scent of his breath made my stomach turn as he leaned down close to me and hissed, "Not so fast, sweetheart." He jerked my hands together behind me and wrapped tape around my wrists. Above me, Zelda was growling and Riley yelled, "Zelda, no! Get out of here. Zee, *go!*" Although I couldn't see what was going on, I heard my captor say, "Do something about that damn dog!"

I struggled to see what was happening, but was unable to move because of the way my attacker had pinned me to the concrete. Zelda's barking and growling grew more distant, and then Riley's shouting was abruptly silenced. My captor whispered in my ear, "So you like to fight, do you? Well, we'll have to do something about that." I felt a stinging pain in my arm and then everything went black.

When I opened my eyes, I was lying on my side on the floor of an empty room. Riley was lying about three feet away from me with his eyes closed. He was breathing, but he had a cut above his eyebrow and blood smeared across his face. Like me, his arms were bound behind him, his ankles were taped together, and he had duct tape over his mouth.

I evaluated our environment and did a mental inventory of my physical state. We were alone, and aside from a wicked headache, I was basically okay. I moved my fingers and toes and found that everything still worked. How long had we been lying here? And where was Zelda? My stomach clenched at the idea of her wandering the streets of downtown Los Angeles. Had these people done something to her? Even if she'd gotten away, what if she'd been hit by a car?

I shook off those thoughts and focused on getting closer to Riley, which entailed an inchworm-like maneuver to slide myself along the linoleum floor. I was able to push with my feet and propel myself toward Riley, but it was a slow process.

When I was finally right in front of him, I kicked at him with my feet. He groaned and opened his eyes, which registered disorientation, then alarm, and then relief at seeing me.

I raised my eyebrows, and he widened his eyes at me in response. I closed my eyes and opened them slowly to indicate how relieved I was to see him too. I blinked four times to inquire if he knew what happened to Zelda. He shook his head, and I closed my eyes slowly and fought back the urge to cry. Poor Zee.

I opened my eyes and Riley and I stared at each other for a long moment. He moved a shoulder in a quasi-shrug that I took to mean, "Now what?"

Relieved that he still had a functioning mind, I shook my head slightly, which is difficult to do when you're lying on your side. But he got the idea and inclined his head to indicate something lower down on me.

I wiggled my legs, and he shook his head. I moved one of my arms, and he nodded, then titled his head. I widened my eyes and raised my eyebrows to let him know I had no clue what he wanted.

Riley moved and head-butted me to indicate I should roll over on my back. Then he head-butted me again to get me to roll to my other side. I wasn't seeing the point of this activity until his fingers touched mine, and I felt him fingering the duct tape on my wrists. We were lying back-to-back, and I inched closer so he could get a better grip on the tape.

Duct tape is tough stuff, but Riley was determined and given all our time on the road, he probably hadn't cut his fingernails in a while. I helped by clenching my fists tightly and pushing my wrists out as much as I could to increase the tension on the tape. The tape finally tore, and I shook my hands free. I rolled over, pulled the tape off my mouth, and tried not to shriek. It was like ripping off the biggest, baddest Band-Aid ever.

I kissed Riley's cheek, whispered, "Thank you," and set to work on the duct tape on his wrists. Once I'd freed his hands, he pulled the tape off his mouth, cringed, and silently mouthed an extremely bad word.

We busied ourselves getting the duct tape off our ankles. While I worked at the tape, I looked around the room, trying to get a better feel for where we were. There wasn't much to see. The room had nothing in it and no windows. Only a door. It was undoubtedly locked, which was okay because I had no interest in opening it. Finding out what was behind door number one wasn't high on my list of fun things to do.

When we were both free, Riley pulled me into a fierce hug. "I was so afraid something had happened to you."

"At the risk of sounding like a broken record, for a minute there I thought you were dead again." I touched the blood that had congealed above his eyebrow. "You have a nasty cut."

"I have the mother of all headaches too, but I think that's because they drugged us. How long have we been here?"

I took a shaky, shallow breath as the reality of our situation sank in. "I don't know. Or what happened to Zelda. I couldn't see anything, but I heard you yelling for her to go. Did she?"

"I hope so." He took both of my hands in his. "We'll find her. But first we need to find a way out of here."

"Yeah, about that. I don't suppose you have any ideas, do you?"

"None."

I leaned closer and kissed Riley's warm lips. As we pulled apart, he stared into my eyes as if he were looking for answers. Unfortunately, I didn't have any.

I rubbed my thumb against his cheek, pulled it away, and looked down at the blood. "What are we going to do?"

Riley collected all our pieces of duct tape, glanced at it, then at the door. "I don't know. That's the only way out."

"I'll bet you all the money I have that it's locked. It's not much, but winning the bet would double my current asset portfolio."

Riley stifled a laugh and stretched out his leg so he could jam the tape into a pocket of his jeans. "Not taking that bet, and there's probably someone right outside anyway."

"This is like one of those David Copperfield magic conundrums. How does he get out of those locked cages anyway?"

"I wish I knew." Riley looked up at the ceiling. "How do you feel about crawling through air ducts?"

"Air ducts are filthy. I've seen that in movies and wondered how people stay so clean. So while normally I'm not a fan of crawling around dirty and potentially spider-filled spaces, today I'm willing to make an exception."

"Good. Because I think it's our only option."

We stood up and stared at the ceiling. Riley was tall, but getting up to the air vent without anything to stand on was going to be tricky.

Before we had figured out a plan of action, the door burst open and we spun around.

My jaw dropped at the sight of Matt, the evil ultra-prick. I sputtered, "What are you doing here?"

Matt smoothed back his hair from his face. "Wondering why those morons didn't tie you up like they were supposed to."

"Good help is hard to find," I said. "Maybe they figured the drugs were enough. I've got a raging headache now, so thanks for that."

"Oh, you'll have more than that," Matt said, stepping closer to me. "Once we've finished with you, you'll be rotting in jail for your role in plotting a series of bombings."

"*What?*" I put my hands on my hips. "Are you insane? We were almost killed by a tower that was blown up yesterday. Even you have to realize I'm not stupid enough to blow *myself* up."

Matt said, "Alan thought you had the decency to get yourself killed, but when that didn't happen, we had to move to Plan B."

I glanced at Riley, who I could tell was silently seething with anger. He didn't appear to have anything to add to the conversation, so I smirked at Matt and opted to run with my own plan. "And what's this ever-so-brilliant idea? Better than hauling people off and forcing them to join the circus. Because that was a real winner."

"It worked quite nicely actually." He stepped closer and looked down his nose with disdain. "You always were inquisitive, weren't you?"

"It served me well when I investigated all your extra-curricular activities. Being a lying, cheating, scumbag is more difficult when you're involved with a reporter. And not so great when she tells everyone what a low-life you truly are." I spread my arms. "Guess you had to move to an entirely new city to get away from your reputation."

"That's not why I left, as I'm sure you know." Matt stood up straighter. "I moved to Los Angeles because I was promoted. Alan Conway thinks I'm a rising star. In fact, he thinks so highly of me that I'm now heading up the entire media division."

"So is this the new HQ? Wow. I'm impressed." I waved my hands as if I were throwing confetti. "You've got some fine office space here."

"You idiot. My office isn't down here. I'm on the top floor with an office right next to Alan's because he wants my input. I've got a view of the entire city, and it's like being on top of the world. You used to love my office back in DC. As I recall, you had a thing for the desk in particular."

"Right next to the boss, huh? You think you're a rising star? I hate to break it to you, but that's so he can keep an eye on you. It's obvious you're a flunky. And *you* were the one obsessed with that stupid desk," I snapped.

Matt twisted his Rolex around his wrist. "Yeah, right. Are you trying to pretend you didn't like it? What a laugh. You know you did. You always say things like that to piss me off. In fact, that's one of your great skills. You've always known exactly how to get on people's nerves. No wonder you're impossible to get along with. Who would ever put up with you?"

"Far better people than you, I'm happy to say," I replied. "So how do you think you can frame me for bombings I didn't commit?"

Matt dropped his hand from his wrist and gave me a smug smile. "While you're enjoying the hospitality here, it will be easy enough to write a few articles online that appear to be you confessing to your crimes."

"No one will believe it's me," I said, perhaps not quite as convincingly as I could have.

As if he sensed my distress, Matt pounced. "Why wouldn't they? You've been anonymous, so all we have to do is write something implicating you, then magically track you down, so you can be arrested. All your sob stories about people having health problems go away. The world agrees with me that you're insane and everything you wrote before is discredited as the ravings of a lunatic. Problem solved."

"Yeah, good luck with that. Too many people know what you're up to. You're hurting innocent people," I said. "And too many people already believe me."

"But not enough people know who you are, so I'll tell them," Matt said as he turned toward the door. "Oh, and since you both enjoyed the drugs so much, I think it might be time for another little cocktail. Nighty night."

Matt slammed the door on his way out, and I turned to Riley, who was standing completely still with his hands in his pockets. "Are you okay? You didn't add much to that conversation."

"I didn't want to interrupt. You were right about getting under his skin." He shook his head. "I hope you never speak to me like that. You were nasty."

"As you can tell, Matt brings out the worst aspects of my personality. You don't." I gave him a quick kiss for emphasis. "Before they come to drug us again, let's think about what we learned. We now know we're in the Archetypal headquarters, so we're still in LA."

"We're about to be implicated in bombings we didn't commit."

"Matt admitted Hector abducted people."

"Even though we were right, he's going to discredit everything you wrote." Riley rubbed the back of his neck. "Jeez, we have to get out of here."

"I know."

We both turned as a gigantic bald man dressed in black walked through the door carrying needles. Riley reached to clasp my hand, and we backed away toward the wall.

As the man approached us, I looked up at Riley and then down at my foot, which I wiggled as I stepped backward. He inclined his head slightly as we took another step back.

My back touched the wall, and as Mr. Huge drew closer, he said, "Where do ya think you're gonna go?"

I kicked out with my left foot and nailed him squarely in the nuts. He dropped the needles and crumpled over onto himself, groaning in agony. Riley pulled the duct tape out of his pocket, knocked the man to the floor, and sat on the guy's back.

After slapping a strip of duct tape over Mr. Huge's mouth, Riley turned to hand me the wad of tape so I could bind his feet. The giant flailed his arms and legs around, and Riley grabbed one arm, then the other, so he was pulling them behind the man.

The mass of duct tape Riley handed me wasn't in the greatest shape after being stuffed in his pocket. I held it up. "I can't do anything with this. It's a mess. Now what?"

As he struggled to keep the huge man immobile, Riley rearranged his hold and put out his foot toward me. "Pull out the shoelaces."

I bent to untie his shoe, pulled out the shoelace, and handed it to Riley, who wrapped it around the man's wrists. The giant man was wriggling, but didn't seem to be able to do much. Riley removed the shoelace from his other sneaker and tied it around the guy's ankles.

I picked up the needles, wrapped some duct tape around them, and slid my prize into a back pocket of my jeans. I looked up at Riley. "I have no idea where to go."

"I don't either." He pulled me into his embrace. "But if we survive this, I'm buying your self-defense class teacher one heck of a thank-you gift."

I stood on my tiptoes to kiss him. "I'm sure Diane would appreciate that."

"Let's get out of here."

~

I peeked around the doorway and saw nothing. It was a long hallway with a lot of doors, but no one was around.

Riley peered around me and pointed at an exit sign over a door. "Head for the stairs."

We went to the sign and through the fire door into the stairwell. I stopped to look around. "Crap. We're on the twenty-fifth floor."

"At least your shoes aren't falling off because they have no laces." Riley took my hand and we ran down the stairs to the parking garage.

By the time we hit bottom, my legs were burning and I let go of his hand. I bent over, waved my index finger at him, and gasped, "Give me one second."

"Come on, Meg. We need to move."

"Okay, okay." I followed him out into the parking garage. "Now what? Lurch isn't here. Our ride is in another parking garage...somewhere."

Riley walked away from me down the row of cars, and I hustled to catch up. "What are you doing?"

"Looking."

"Looking for what?"

He pointed at a convertible BMW. "I'm dying of thirst, but I need your help."

I walked up to the car and looked at the interior. A bottle of water was sitting in the center console. "You want to steal this guy's water?"

"Yes, but if we touch this car, I'm willing to bet an alarm will go off. I can't reach in far enough." He grabbed me around my waist and lifted me up over the car. "Grab it."

I reached down and plucked the water bottle out of the cup holder. Riley set me back down, and I handed the bottle to him. "I thought you weren't up for committing crimes."

"These are desperate times." He opened the water, took a long drink, and handed it to me as he continued walking down the row of cars.

I sucked down some water and instantly felt better. Drugs are evil. "Now what are you looking for?"

Riley stopped in front of a dirty, ancient-looking small motorcycle. He gestured toward the machine. "Transportation."

"Are you thinking what I think you're thinking?" I grabbed his arm. "You'd better not be stealing that thing."

"I don't want to keep it, so it's more like borrowing." He crouched down and yanked me down with him. "Keep an eye out for people."

"What are you doing? You can't seriously expect both of us to ride on that."

"Shh." He ran his hands down some wires and glared at me. "This will only take a minute. I need to connect a couple of wires to bypass the ignition switch."

"Do you even know how to ride a motorcycle? They scare the crap out of me, and this one looks particularly old and unsafe."

"Yes, I do. I've been riding bikes since I was fourteen."

"I've written too many articles about crashes. People die in motorcycle wrecks all the time. You hit the pavement and it's all over."

"Shh. It will be fine." He stood up swung his leg over, fiddled with something, pressed a button on the handlebars, and did something with his foot to the nasty machine.

The motorcycle roared to life, and I stepped back away from it. "No way, Riley. I'm serious. There's not enough room for my butt on that seat."

Riley revved the motor and handed me the helmet. "Get on."

"No!"

The stairway door clanged open and Riley grabbed my hand, jerking me toward the motorcycle. "Meg, you're going to have to trust me. Get on this bike now!"

I put the helmet on and threw my leg over the seat. Riley turned, grabbed my arm, and pulled it around his waist. "Hold onto me tight. We're leaving."

I wrapped my other hand around and fisted his t-shirt in my fingers. The soft cotton wasn't much of a seatbelt, but it was all I had. Riley had the nerve to say *my* ideas were bad, but this was a new low.

Riley hit the gas and I continued to clutch the water bottle and his t-shirt, squeezing my eyes shut and making a valiant effort not to scream and cry like a baby. I peeked to look as he roared through the parking garage and leaned to bypass the gate on the way out.

Because of the helmet I couldn't hear much of anything, but the rush of the wind and the roar of the engine seemed to vibrate through my entire body. My heart pounded, but the warmth of Riley's back against my chest was comforting somehow. He weaved in and out through traffic, and I leaned into his back, trying to go with the flow of the turns. Apparently, he really *did* know how to ride this stupid thing.

We screamed through downtown Los Angeles, and the experience was both terrifying and thrilling. Along with weaving through traffic instead of sitting in it, the sense of freedom of being outside and soaring away from the horrors of our abduction was exhilarating. I understood why people risked their lives riding motorcycles. It was a rush.

Riley pulled into the garage at the building where the law firm was located and pulled a ticket from the dispenser. He more slowly motored down to where we'd left Lurch and parked next to the Bronco. Although almost all the parking spots were filled, spaces remained on either side of Lurch. Maybe those snooty lawyers didn't want to be seen parking next to a dirty old rust bucket.

I finally released the death grip I'd had on Riley's stomach and got off the motorcycle while he shut off the engine and put the kickstand down. My legs felt rubbery and strange, and I was relieved to take off the helmet.

A low growl echoed from somewhere below us. "What was that?"

Riley crouched and peered under Lurch. "It's okay, Zee. You can come out now."

Zelda crawled out and wiggled and wagged with unadulterated joy.

I leaned over her so I could wrap my arms around her furry body. Although I didn't burst into ugly sobs, tears were streaming down my face and my voice was thick as I told her how much I'd missed her. "You're such a good girl! The best dog, ever."

Riley opened the driver's side door. "We need to get out of here, but she's probably as thirsty as we were. Give her some water."

Zelda and I got in and I pulled our makeshift doggie water dish from the glove compartment. I filled the old plastic margarine container and passed it back to Zelda, who lapped up the water happily.

"Wait!" I said. "Did you check the car? How long have we been gone? Someone could have tampered with Lurch like they did the Mustang."

"Would you touch a car that had a vicious dog hanging out under it?"

"Oh yeah. Good point. Thanks for guarding Lurch, Zee."

Riley pulled out and got on the freeway, headed for our motel in Rancho Cucamonga. Now that the drugs and adrenaline had worn off, I was starting to worry about the possibilities of screaming hallucinations.

Riley looked at me. "Are you all right?"

"I think so. This feels so tame after being on a motorcycle. You've really been riding since you were fourteen?"

"That's when I finally talked Dad into letting me get a dirt bike. I did motocross and that type of thing for a while when I was a teenager."

"That's difficult for me to imagine." I stared at his blood-streaked face. "Every once in a while, I realize there's still a lot I don't know about you."

"It's not particularly mysterious. Lots of people have motorcycles." He glanced at me with a grin. "But I guess I never mentioned the airplane, either, did I?"

"You can fly airplanes too?"

"Well, I sold the Cessna, but I still have my pilot's license."

I looked back at Zee. "Did you know this?"

"Sure she did. She likes plane rides almost as much as car rides."

"That's scary. I've read about way too many crashes with tiny private planes."

Riley tapped his fingertips on my leg. "You've spent too much time reading the news. Statistically, planes are safer than automobiles."

"I suppose anything would be safer than that old motorcycle. I can't believe you convinced me to get on that thing."

"Lighten up. It wasn't so bad."

"That's not what I meant. You said I had to trust you." I put my palm on top of the back of his hand on the gearshift. "And I did. It wasn't even a question. That's so unlike me. I don't trust anyone."

"It looks like you do now."

⁓

Back at the motel, we collected our stuff from the room. We figured we'd been drugged for about twelve hours, which meant someone might come check on us when they thought our second dose had worn off. So we had a maximum of twelve hours before someone would realize we were missing and go after us. Odds were good we had much less time than that because sooner or later someone might notice that their giant man in black was missing.

Riley checked out of the motel and we hit the road. I picked up my stack of maps. "I have no idea what we should do now. It seems like everyone is after us."

"I'm not sure what to do either, other than drive away from where we were."

I unfolded a map. "We need to get online and see where the Founder is. And find out how your father is doing with the prototype."

"If we stay at a motel, I think we're practically asking to get caught again, particularly if we start feeling bad again. We need to keep moving."

"You're right about the ugly problem of Los Angeles itself. My headache is returning."

"I have an idea, but I'm pretty sure you won't like what I'm thinking."

I set the map down and looked at him. "Is it worse than the motorcycle?"

"No, but the road is popular with bikers."

"What road?"

"The Angeles Crest Highway, which goes into the Angeles National Forest. I'm thinking we can drive up into the hills in the evenings to recuperate, then go back down to the city during the daytime and do things like go to the library. I also think we should avoid parking garages from now on."

"I agree about the garages. Never again." I had a bad feeling about where he was going with this forest idea. "I don't suppose there's any place to stay in the forest, is there?"

"There's a roadhouse with lots of junk food you'd like. It's kind of a biker hangout. And a general store and gas station are up there too."

"Are there cabins?"

"This is the part you won't like. There are several campgrounds in the national forest and a bunch of picnic areas. I was thinking we could camp in the car." Riley gestured toward the back of the Bronco. "If we move our stuff to the front, we could probably sleep back there."

I turned to look through the seats behind me. "You want to sleep in Lurch? Yuck." Zelda wagged from her spot among our suitcases and bags. She didn't have a problem with the concept because she slept there all the time.

"It's either sleep in the Bronco or in a tent on the ground outside."

"At least Lurch doesn't have fabric walls. But what about bathrooms? You know how I feel about indoor plumbing."

"We'll figure something out. I'm hoping we can find out what we need to know quickly and then get out of here. I hate LA."

"I *so* wish I had a better idea, but I don't." I ran my fingers through my hair. "As it is, I'd kill for a shower. Lying in a drug-induced coma on the floor doesn't leave a girl feeling pretty."

Riley didn't say anything and I closed my eyes, suddenly exhausted. The ache in my temple was getting worse, and Technicolor rainbows flashed on the back of my eyelids. I found myself in one of those dreams where you're aware that you're dreaming. I saw myself slumped on the ugly old sofa in my apartment, being a couch potato and watching the marketing video from Archetypal Online Systems. A lilac halo surrounded me, and beautiful images of the Grand Canyon at sunset and a family eating dinner flashed on the TV screen. The audio track featured a smarmy guy doing the voice-over about how the environment was important.

My eyes popped open and I sat up straight in the seat.

Riley glanced at me. "That was a short nap. Is everything all right?"

"It wasn't a nap. I found out I've seen the Archetypal video before."

"What video?"

I waved my hands in excitement. "You know! The one I had a vision about back in my apartment. But in my vision, it turned into fire. It's the video that I was convinced had subliminal images and I went back home to my apartment to check it."

"That idea led to nothing, as I recall."

"But now I know that I'd seen it before! Some of the images were from an environmental documentary I saw years ago. The pretty sunsets and happy people were footage that I saw long before I had that vision."

"I guess that company you almost worked for must have grabbed it from somewhere."

"Yeah, Centerfield Technologies. I wonder what that means." I rubbed my temples with my fingertips. "Are we getting close to this forest yet?"

"Working on it." He gestured toward the crowded highway. "Have I mentioned lately how much I hate Southern California freeways?"

"I need to call the woman who interviewed me for the Centerfield job and ask why they used that particular sequence of images. Maybe it's stock footage that has been used a million times, but the environmental connection seems like an odd coincidence. I'm sure Christina will know."

"Do you think it ties Enviro Freedom to Archetypal somehow?"

"I have no idea. But it's one of the only visions I've had that seemed prophetic because I saw the video after the vision. The reason it was in my vision is because I'd seen it before."

"You keep saying you're not a prophet."

"Thank goodness for that too. I've got enough problems without that thrown into the mix."

We exited the clogged freeway and headed away from the Los Angeles freeway system to a winding road that led into the forest. The temperature dropped as we gained elevation, and as the ache in my temple subsided, I saw the wisdom in Riley's idea. If we could find a campground with a shower, I'd literally be a happy camper.

By the time we encountered a campground that had a space for us to park in, it was almost dark. After rearranging our stuff, I managed to convince Riley to eat something. We staggered off to the public showers and afterword collapsed in a heap in the back of Lurch. To say it was cozy was an understatement. We were all crowded together in a tangle of arms, legs, and paws, but having Zelda and Riley inches from me was comforting after the trials of captivity and escape.

We woke up with the sun the next morning. It streamed in the windows of the Bronco, and I groaned as I attempted to disentangle myself from my car-camping cohorts.

Zelda stood up and stepped on my arm. "Hey, Zee, easy with the claws."

Riley sat, pulled his legs up, and wrapped his arms around them. "Did you get any sleep?"

"Like the dead. Maybe the drugs were still wearing off." I stroked Zelda's head. "I feel better, but I think Zee needs to go out."

I went to take another shower because I could. By the time I got back, Riley had walked and fed Zelda and rearranged all our stuff inside Lurch, so we were ready for travel again.

We stopped at the roadhouse for breakfast, and I made a pig of myself with coffee, eggs, hash browns, and a big stack of pancakes. I went for the whole greasy deal, and it was fantastic. Riley negotiated with the chef about something to do with vegetables, but I didn't pay attention because I was too busy stuffing my face.

Our next stop was at a library, to find out what had happened in the world. I still didn't know where the Founder was in Los Angeles, and I was anxious to reconnect with Kenny to see if he knew anything more about the toy-factory bombing and where the people had gone. My new-found gamer buddy might be irritated that we'd disappeared from the cyber world for longer than expected again, but hey, it hadn't been my idea.

It took more than an hour to get to the Pasadena public library, which was an enormous and gorgeous old Mediterranean-style building that was listed on the National Register of Historic places. I grabbed my laptop, and we left Zelda to guard the Bronco.

The library had a courtyard with a fountain, and the carved stone and columns on the stone facade above the three doors made me feel like I was heading into some Italian palace of learning instead of a big city library. Over the last few years, the old building had gone high tech with access to some of my favorite databases, a computerized magazine and newspaper index, and public access to the Internet. I was thrilled.

Inside, the library had high ceilings and beautiful dark wood trim and bookcases. There was a sea of tables, comfy chairs, and nooks where we could curl up and do our research.

We settled into a spot and I turned on my laptop. I shoved it toward Riley so he could do his geeky logging into the server thing. While he typed his mysterious codes and passwords, I stared up at the ceiling, which was made of the same dark wood as the bookcases.

He mumbled something that sounded suspiciously filthy, and I looked at the screen, then at his face. "What's wrong?"

"Someone took the server down."

"Down? Down where?"

"Offline. I can't get to it."

"So everything I wrote out there is gone?"

"Probably not gone forever, but I can't access it." He shrugged. "So much for email."

"*Do* something!"

"Shh, Meg. There's nothing to do. Normally, I'd call Mel. It's possible he didn't pay the server company and they took the site down. But given the current situation, I'm reluctant to chat with him."

"Call Erin then." I put my hand on his arm. "How about if you find a pay phone and call her while I read the news. At least I can do that. When you're done, I'll call Christine at Centerfield about the video."

Riley agreed that seemed like a decent idea and wandered off, leaving me alone with a copy of the *Los Angeles Times*. I started reading to get caught up. The first thing I learned was that Archetypal's CEO Alan Conway had given a speech about the bombings. Apparently, Matt's little PR show in Seattle wasn't good enough, and Conway wanted to expound on their technological greatness too. Ugh.

Riley returned from the pay phone and reported that he'd left a message asking Erin to look into the server payments. He pointed me in the direction of the phones, and I stopped by the reception desk to get some change.

I'd almost taken a job with Centerfield as a documentary researcher, and even though I hadn't accepted the position, Christine and I had hit it off, probably because we had a mutual intense dislike of Matt Eskridge, the evil prick. Matt had dated Christine's sister, and Christine had made no bones about the fact that she loathed him as much as I did.

I looked through my address book, found the number, and deposited the required amount of coins into the phone. I only had so much change, but fortunately the Centerfield receptionist didn't make me wait too long before I was connected to Christine, who was understandably a little surprised to hear from me.

I said, "I know it's been a while, but I have an odd question. Where did the footage for the Archetypal video come from? Recently, I remembered that I've seen it before. I think it was on an environmental documentary I saw a long time ago."

I could hear Christine sigh through the phone, "Well, I'm glad *someone* noticed. I probably shouldn't be telling you this, but I used it as a message to my sister."

"I don't understand."

"My sister thinks she has a sensitivity to electronics. I've always been skeptical, but I wanted to give her a message that

Archetypal was about to dramatically increase the amount of electronics in our lives."

"That seems like an odd way to go about it."

"The original footage was about an environmental group that she'd been involved with a while ago. We had been estranged because I didn't approve of the man she was seeing. Then something happened with them, and she got involved with that piece of pond scum Matt Eskridge. I told her what I thought of him too, and we got into a huge fight. We stopped talking again, so I used the earlier video footage because I knew she'd see it."

Christine went on to describe how she felt about her sister's poor choice in men. Even though I had a feeling I already knew, I asked the question anyway. "What's your sister's name?"

"Shannon Soloman."

"And the environmental group was Enviro Freedom, wasn't it?"

"Yes! You've got a good memory."

"Are you in touch with your sister now?"

"After she broke up with Matt, we mended fences. She went back to her work with the environmental group. She's been a little vague about whether or not she's involved with Ralston again or not."

"Do you know where she is right now?"

"I talked to her yesterday and she was at LAX, heading back to Seattle with Ral."

I thanked Christine for the information and returned to the table where Riley was typing on my laptop. I sat next to him and leaned my head on his shoulder. "I have much to report."

Riley patted my hand. "Kenny says 'hi' and that he's sad your articles are gone."

I straightened. "How did you get in touch with him?"

"My old gamer forum username still works, and I found KenHatesBarbie22 in a chat room."

"I think we should go back to the retreat."

Riley jerked his attention away from the screen. "You can't be serious. You want to go *back*? We just got here."

"Shannon and the Founder are headed back to the retreat. We have no way to get in touch with Mom and your dad. I'm worried about them because of some of the things Christine said. She shares my opinion of the Founder."

"How do you know they're going back to the retreat?"

"Christine told me." At his incredulous look, I went over what Christine had told me about her sister and the Founder.

"All right." Riley typed furiously. "I gave Kenny my father's email address and told him to tell Dad we're coming back."

"Ryan and Mandy return!"

Chapter 13

Winding Down

After we decided to return to Washington, the next question was how. I said, "We need to get back there as soon as possible. Christine said that the Founder was like a cult leader and that Shannon had fallen under his spell, as if she couldn't tear herself away from him. After hearing the Founder's speech, I thought the whole thing did seem cult-like."

"Come on. You honestly think that Ralston Landecker is going to get everyone to drink poisoned Kool-aid like the Jonestown massacre?"

"I don't know. Remember when he spoke and everyone was yelling 'Rise up' and cheering? That level of religious fervor is cult-like. I'm sure Felicia would follow the Founder anywhere."

"Our parents aren't that stupid."

"How do you know for sure? They were completely snowed by these people. Did you read about the Heaven's Gate suicide pact in San Diego a few months ago?"

"They believed in UFOs, Meg. Our parents are research geeks who wanted cool lab equipment."

"Still, Heaven's Gate was like a religion. They willingly committed suicide to ascend, or *rise up* to some other celestial plane."

"I think you're pushing the analogy. Both of our parents are into science, not religion. The Founder has one of those personalities that draws people to him. Our parents would never buy into something like a suicide pact, no matter how persuasive he is. Your mom called the Founder a lunatic."

"Maybe not, but I'm worried about what the Founder is up to. If we get on a plane, we could be at the retreat tomorrow."

Riley shook his head. "I know it's faster to fly, but what about Zelda?"

"You said she likes planes. Or I could go alone."

"I don't think Zee would be thrilled about the cargo hold of a 737. And for all we know, you'd have a hallucination and run screaming onto the runway."

"Then you go."

"I'm not leaving you and Zelda to drive fifteen hundred miles alone. We're going together. If we leave now, we can be in Washington in three days."

"Okay, but you need to drive fast."

Riley smiled. "I always do."

We left the library and made our way to Interstate 15 so we could head north toward Las Vegas. The plan was to more or less take the same route we'd taken south, but in reverse. It had the advantage of avoiding most cities, except for Las Vegas. Once again, we were going to see a whole lot of the state of Nevada. Riley also suggested avoiding motels, which I wasn't too excited about, but sleeping in Lurch was better than being captured again.

After a long day of driving, we stopped for the night somewhere along route 93 in nowhere Nevada. Before it was completely dark, Riley found a dirt road that went off into the desert. He was excited about trying out Lurch's four-wheel drive capabilities.

I was significantly less excited about going off-road, but Riley found a patch of desert that he deemed acceptable and we managed to make some sandwiches before the blackness of night descended on us.

Riley crawled up onto the hood of the car and encouraged me to join him, reaching out his hand to me. "You should check out the stars. The night sky in the desert is amazing."

I scrambled onto the Bronco and lounged next to him, looking up at the sky and chewing my sandwich slowly. I leaned over to toss Zelda a chip and returned to my prone position. "I'm starting to see why people go camping. I mean, I'm not gonna lie—I'd really like a shower. But this is cool."

"You showered this morning."

"So sue me. I like showers. And toilets. I really, *really* like toilets. What if there are snakes out there?"

"Be cautious."

"Why am I not feeling reassured here?"

Riley took my hand in his and gave it a squeeze. "Life is full of risks. I'd like to tell you that we're in an area that has fewer snakes per-capita than elsewhere, but I don't know."

"Okay, you get extra-credit points for being honest."

"When have I lied to you?"

"You've withheld information regularly, but I don't think you've lied outright. Which places you in a unique category among the men I've known."

"Speaking of honesty, did you think about the fact that your ex confessed? You were right. He blabbed about everything."

I sat up and looked down at Riley's face. "Thanks to the recent traumas, I didn't think about that before, but you're right. We can nail him to the wall."

Riley grinned. "Yup. He can kiss the executive suite goodbye. You even have the hypodermic needles to prove it."

I returned to my horizontal state and stared up at the sky, digesting the information. "I guess we should have called the police while we were in LA."

"Maybe it's just as well we didn't. I'd like to read your articles from the server again. They've got a ton of details we should go through before we lay it all out there. I hope we can get them back." He looked at me. "I don't suppose you backed up what you wrote to your laptop, did you?"

"Not exactly."

"You mean not at all, right?"

"I do have notes and some early drafts of some of the stuff."

"That's better than nothing, I suppose." Riley leaned over, looked deep into my eyes, and put his palm on my cheek. "If you learn nothing else about computers, learn to back up your work."

I gave him a kiss. "Spoken like a true geek."

We held hands and gazed up at the sky as the moon rose over the mountains. Even though I was worried about our parents, I knew in my heart that Riley was right. They were both far too independent to behave like sheep, blindly following some insane directive. I wasn't so sure about some of the other people at the retreat though.

As I lay there in the moonlight, I recalled the Creedence Clearwater Revival song "Bad Moon Rising." What made a moon bad? Whether John Fogarty was talking about

Vietnam, Nixon, the Apocalypse, or a bad acid trip, the lyrics I remembered were a downer. A sense of melancholy swept over me, and in the silence of the night, I wondered what would happen next. What would I do with my life? When Riley and I weren't on this bizarre journey anymore, would we stay together? Or would we realize that we were so different that we'd never be able to stand being with each other long-term?

Riley pointed at the sky, "Hey, it's a shooting star. Make a wish!"

Startled, my mind went blank and I blurted out, "World peace!"

"Unlikely, but always a good standby in a pinch."

"I was thinking about something else. The stars don't give you much warning when they do that."

"Meteors are unpredictable that way." He massaged the back of his neck, and looked at me. "What are you fretting about?"

"I'm not fretting."

Riley stared at me without saying anything and I said, "Okay, I might be fretting a little. I feel like the story is winding down."

"What story?"

"The story we've figured out. Our story. Or more accurately, the story I'm going to write that explains everything we've learned. Like you said, we have proof that Archetypal knew they were harming people with their technology."

"Does your story have a happy ending?"

"I don't know. I already put a lot of it out there, and only nerds and other people with sensory problems noticed."

"Those were theories. Now we have a confession because your evil boyfriend at Archetypal noticed too. That's why they abducted us."

"I suppose. And he's not my boyfriend. I mean he's as much my boyfriend as Erin is your girlfriend."

"Very funny. Although it turns out she wants to talk to me about that."

I sat up straight and glared down at him. "*What*? When did that happen? I assume you said there's nothing to discuss, didn't you?"

"You were stomping off down the hall and I had a limited amount of time, so I ignored it."

"The word 'no' wouldn't have taken much time either."

"Sorry, but I had to run and catch up with you before you ended up in Mel's office or started screaming. We were in downtown LA, and I figured it was only a matter of time before you had a meltdown."

I waved off the comment. "Okay, so you want to know what I was thinking about? *That's* what I was thinking about."

"What? Hallucinating? Erin?"

"Not exactly. More like what happens to us when this story ends? Are you interested in staying together, or are you still hung up on Erin?"

Riley narrowed his eyes. "Why are you bringing that up? I think we had this conversation, and you were the one who told Erin 'that ship has sailed.' Are you trying to pick a fight for some reason?"

"No." *Was I?* "I was thinking about the future again."

"I love you, and you know I do. The future is going to take care of itself."

I curled up on Riley's chest. "I love you too, and intellectually I know I can't do anything about the future, but I worry anyway. I blame Creedence and their bad moon for my sense of foreboding."

"More upbeat music would help. I need to put a decent stereo system into this vehicle."

~

Day two of driving was interminable and we'd seen so few people anywhere that I was successful in badgering Riley into staying at a roadside motel overnight. I wanted a shower in the worst way and didn't want to greet my mother smelling like Lurch. We left early the next morning, and by the time we got to the retreat all of us were incredibly sick of being in the Bronco.

At the gate, I got out and used the intercom to announce our return. The device hadn't been fixed in our absence, and the same unintelligible garbled voice that I'd heard the last time came from the speaker. Figuring that if it worked once, it might work again, I said, "My name is mumphegic. I want to come in."

The speaker squawked off an angry tirade that I couldn't decipher, and I said more forcefully, "My name is mumphegic! I'm here to see olesmurf. Let me in!"

The gate opened, and I grinned at Riley as I walked back to the Bronco. This time we knew where we were going, so we wound through the compound to our parents' cottage.

I got out and Riley let Zelda out of the vehicle. She leaped around like a dog possessed, but she'd been so good about the many hours in the car, who could blame her?

Riley walked to the door and tried the handle. "It's locked. They're probably at the lab."

"I still have the key, I think." I went back to Lurch and began rummaging through my bag. As is so often the case, I had to dump everything out of it on the passenger seat to find the elusive item I sought. Finally, I held up the key and waved it. "Got it!"

Riley was sitting on the front step hunched over with his elbows resting on his knees. He looked tired, which wasn't unreasonable. Although he'd let me drive in a couple remote areas, for the most part he'd driven more than three thousand miles in less than a week.

We unloaded and had something to eat. Mom would be annoyed that we were eating her food uninvited again, but I was so sick of sandwiches that I could barely stand it. Riley was even amenable to cooking, probably for the same reason.

After we ate, Riley and I set up the cot in the office again, unpacked some of our things, and then took Zelda for a walk over to the lab, where our parents were undoubtedly happily working on their projects.

As we walked through the retreat hand-in-hand, a few people seemed to recognize us. I nodded at Jane, who gave me a funny look from under her straw hat. When Veronica offered Riley a flirtatious smile, I squeezed his hand more tightly. He glanced down at me and chuckled softly.

When we got to the lab, we opened the door and Riley unclipped Zelda's leash from her collar so she could run over to Tim. Apart from Riley, I think Zelda loved Tim best. I wasn't sure where I fell in the canine view of humanity, but if Zelda's behavior was any indication, Tim definitely outranked me.

At the commotion, my mother and her research assistant, Sid, emerged from her office. Tim's assistant, Patrick, stood in the doorway of the office that housed the antique computer, smiling as Zelda expressed her enthusiasm. Tim was laughing as she leaped around him. "I guess Ri…uh, Ryan is back, huh?"

I walked to my mother and gave her a hug. "I'm so glad to see you, Mom."

"I'm glad you're here! Tim is ready to run some tests," she replied.

I tamped down my irritation that Mom was more excited to have a lab rat available than she was about the return of her daughter and said evenly, "Isn't Shannon around? I told you she has a sensory issue. You could have run tests on her."

"That wouldn't make sense, honey. We don't know what her reaction was before. We need to replicate the test on Tim's invention with the same subjects to isolate the variables."

"I suppose this subject is ready." I glanced at Riley, who was on the other side of the lab, deep in conversation with his father. I opted not to point out to Mom that the radiation-canceling idea was actually Riley's, not Tim's. Instead, I asked, "What do you want us to do?"

"Tim will explain it." My mother strode purposefully across the lab and interrupted the nerdy confab.

Tim said, "I want to do the test, but only if you're okay with it. The last time you both ended up on the floor. I could do some more preliminary testing if you want to hold off."

"I told you that what happened to me was unrelated." Riley pointed at me. "But Meg had a hallucination, so her reaction was valid."

"I understand that I'm the guinea pig, and it's fine. Riley told me about his idea and I want to know if it works. I like the idea of waves canceling themselves out *before* they give me a hallucination. Can we get the test over with?"

As we did before, Riley and I stood near Tim's miniature cell towers and waited while he got all his monitoring devices set up.

Tim turned away from the electronics and clapped his hands. "All set! Let's do this."

Riley reached for my hand and gave it a reassuring squeeze.

I smiled up at him. "So hey, how about we sit on the floor this time? And do me a favor and don't hold your breath, okay? *Breathe!*"

"I'll work on it."

We sat holding hands while behind us Tim fiddled with dials. Sid and Patrick were staring at us, probably waiting for us to turn into turnips or something. They'd missed the first experiment, so there were at least two people who hadn't seen me transform into a screaming lunatic. I gave them a nervous smile.

We waited for what seemed an excruciatingly long time. I glanced at Riley, who shrugged. I finally turned around and saw that Tim was just standing there, staring at his monitors. Riley stood up and leaned around his father to take a look. "I think...Dad, did you see this? It looks like you isolated the interaction with those magnetic fields."

Tim nodded. "Yeah, I think so. And then the device cancels it out when the transmission hits that problematic frequency. It tells it to hop to the next one. Since you're standing, I guess you didn't feel anything."

"Nope. So you're saying it actually works?"

"Yup!" Tim clapped Riley on the back. "I knew it would! That last change to the equation you sent me was the key."

Riley bent down to look at Tim's notepad. "Interesting."

"That's all you have to say?" I stood up and launched myself at Riley, wrapping my arms around him in a massive hug. "Don't you know what this means? No more hallucinations!" I let go and started dancing around the room. Zelda joined me in my celebratory happy dance, and I bent down to ruffle her ears.

Riley said, "I hate to rain on your parade here, but you're missing an important detail. Just like cars need mufflers to run more quietly, every cell tower will need one of these."

"That's great. You could make millions…*again*!" I said and resumed my dance around the lab with Zelda.

"It's a nice idea, but we have to convince Archetypal to spend money on a device to solve a problem they don't believe is a problem in the first place." Riley turned up his palms. "You do see the little marketing problem there, don't you?"

Tim nodded. "I didn't think about that. A company like Archetypal isn't going to add this out of the goodness of its greedy heart."

I stopped dancing. "Riley, you mentioned before that they might not be enthusiastic about listening to us. But now we have proof that people are affected and that Archetypal knew it. We need to get my articles from your server. I'll expose all of their greedy little hearts. They'll have to use the device, and you'll make millions. Yay!"

"I know you think the power of the press will convince people, but they'll weasel out, whining about the expense.

Think about how long it took the tobacco companies to admit that smoking causes cancer," Riley said. "They'll throw lots of lawyers at the problem, and it could take decades to resolve."

"I could do without decades of hallucinations. Does Archetypal have any incentive to do the right thing?" I asked.

Riley said. "Dad and I came up with the design, so we could put it out into the public domain so that anyone can use it."

Mom said, "It would be for the public good, like pollution abatement for clean air, which benefits everyone."

"If you gave Archetypal the design, would they use it, though?" I said.

"I think this is where your PR campaign comes into play. If we explain the risks, show the proof, and provide a solution, they'll look pretty bad if they don't use it," Riley said. "Even worse, if their competitors do include it, they get a marketing advantage because they look like heroes providing safe communications, as opposed to evil corporate scum who knowingly make people sick."

"Okay, I like this idea. We could get the entire gamer community to boycott Archetypal until they fix their towers." I raised my fist to the sky. "Geeks rise up and be heard!"

"Anonymously from your parents' basement." Riley added.

~

On our walk back to the cottage, I was still riding high on the successful results of the experiment. Before we'd left the lab, Riley had conferred with his father about communication with the outside world. We knew Tim had connected the laptop, but it turned out he wasn't emailing us from the lab. He'd found an old phone line in the cottage and done something or other to make it work. I was thrilled because we had calls to make, and chatting with people from the cottage would be a lot more private than using the phone line in the lab.

Riley called Erin, and they talked for quite a while. I tried not to eavesdrop, but the kitchen was right next to the living room where the phone was, so what was I supposed to do? Not eat? Yeah, right. This is me we're talking about.

When Riley finally hung up, I sat on the sofa next to him and proffered the bag of pretzels I'd been carrying around. He reached in and took one. "So you obviously heard all of that."

"The server is back?"

"It's online again. As I suspected, Mel didn't pay the bill. Erin gave them money and they yelled at her for not cleaning out the email often enough. They're threatening to charge for more storage space."

"Hey, we've been kind of busy." I chomped on a pretzel. "While you were talking, I had time to think."

"If you say we have to drive back to LA, you won't like my response."

"As far as I'm concerned, we're done with that place. I don't care if I never see the city of angels again. But I do think we need to suck it up and confront the Founder." I chomped another pretzel, grabbed one from the bag, and handed it to Riley. "If we tell the Founder we have a solution, maybe they'll lay off blowing up towers."

"That would be nice."

"Erin seemed to want to talk about more than your server. It sounded like money matters were discussed. Also Mel and me. Do tell."

"She talked to Mel and demanded that he explain why he was stealing. As we found out, he has a few skeletons in his closet. Apparently, someone else found out a few of his secrets and was blackmailing him. He took a little vacation, and the stealing was so he could take a longer vacation. But it didn't work out."

"Is he giving the money back?"

"Erin says the money I used as bait is back in my account, but the law firm isn't too pleased with Mel. It sounds like he's looking for a new job now."

"Cry me a river, dude. Who was blackmailing him?"

"He wasn't specific, but it was someone from Archetypal."

"I'm not surprised. I bet it was Matt. But I don't want to talk about Matt or Mel. What about me?"

"Erin wanted to know more specifically what my status with you is. I think she finds me more interesting now that she has a better idea how much money I have."

"How could she not know?" I waved a pretzel in a 'hurry up' motion, "And you said…"

"Attached."

"That's an odd word. I thought you were talking about Lurch or Velcro. Then you said 'it's been a bumpy ride, but I chose it willingly' or something."

"Well, it's true."

"Maybe. But bumpy? Pardon me while I swoon over all this gushy romantic poetry." I tapped my chest. "My little heart is going pitter-pat over here."

Riley put his arms around me, "I think you're missing the point. I said I chose you willingly, and I want to be with you, even when the crap is hitting the fan. Which it has been, almost since the day we met."

I gave him a kiss. "Well, you're right about that. The ride hasn't been smooth. I'm tired of people trying to beat me up, blow me up, and imprison me in small spaces."

"Me too. I can't imagine what I would have done if you hadn't been there."

I looked into his dark eyes. "I know. All the things you've done to help me, encourage me, settle me down, care for me, and keep me happy and mostly sane through some incredibly strange experiences are beyond what any other person has ever done for me."

Riley gave me an electrifying kiss, and right when I was seriously getting into it, as was typical, the door opened and our parents walked in. It doesn't matter how old we are. It's like parents have a sixth sense about their kids making out on the living room sofa. Zelda leaped up from her prone position on the rug in front of us and gave them her traditional canine welcome.

We had an enjoyable evening sharing the highlights and quite a few low lights of our trip to Los Angeles. Not surprisingly, our parents were horrified by our capture and drugging. Before Riley and I retired to our cot in the office, I enjoyed a reassuring, if belated, hug from Mom as a reward for escaping.

Because Riley and I were not at the retreat in any official capacity anymore, I didn't see any reason to embark on volunteer activities like gardening. The charade was over, and after days of intensive driving, we were exhausted, so we slept in the next morning. When Riley got up to walk Zelda, I ignored him and went back to sleep. Later, he dragged me out of bed for coffee.

Our parents had already left for the lab, and I was pleased to have some time to relax and snuggle up with my coffee. Not having to go anywhere or talk to anyone except Riley seemed like an unbelievable luxury after so much running around.

Before they left, Riley asked our parents to set up a meeting in the afternoon with Shannon and the Founder so we could talk to them. That gave us several hours to get on the server and access my articles.

Riley logged on and I was relieved to find that everything was exactly as I'd left it. All my articles documenting everything we'd learned on our many journeys were still there. I sipped my coffee while Riley typed some code that would automatically back up everything to the laptop.

He stopped typing and pointed at an icon. "I backed up everything, but the next time you write anything new, click that and it will copy anything that has changed to the laptop."

"Just click it?"

"The icon runs a script on the server. So you need to be online for it to work."

At noon, Mom returned to the cottage and reported that Shannon and the Founder would be stopping by the lab at two o'clock that afternoon. Mom said, "We told them that we'd run some tests and wanted to share our results."

"They'll have the opportunity to chat with the test subjects too," I said.

"I hope you'll be pleasant to them, Meg," Mom admonished.

"If they've been trying to blow me up, I'm not going to be a nice, well-behaved little girl. Think what you want of me, but that's not going to happen." I said.

Riley put his hand on mine and turned to my mother. "Ellen, I was making lunch. Do you want some too, or are you going over to the dining hall?"

"I should get back to the lab, so if you have extra, that would be lovely."

While Riley and Mom chit-chatted about food in the kitchen, I returned to my articles and took notes on where and when bombings had occurred.

It was possible that I knew about only a small percentage of the bombing events, so I did some low-key online searching to see if there was anything I'd missed. I didn't find anything new, but the information I had was plenty. Apparently, being an eco-terrorist kept you pretty busy.

$\sim$

Riley and I went over to the lab a little early for our meeting with Founder and Shannon so we'd have time to chat with Tim beforehand. He had his equipment set up and was ready to explain the experiment he'd performed with us the day before.

I pointed at one of the mysterious monitors. "You could run the test again on the Founder and Shannon to be sure."

"I guess I could ask their permission," Tim said. "You knew what to expect and were pretty motivated, but I don't know how they'd feel about it. Shannon might be annoyed that I was running tests after she asked me not to."

When the Founder and Shannon walked in, they seemed imposing to the point that I was intimidated. I'd forgotten what a massive, burly man the Founder was, and as usual, Shannon was impeccably dressed, looking sleek and put together. I tried not to think about how many miles my beat-up old jeans had traveled.

Shannon stopped short at the sight of me. "Mandy! I thought you and Ryan had left to get married."

"I'm not pregnant, and we didn't get married," I said.

"Oh no!" Shannon said. "I'm terribly sorry."

"No, it's not what you think." I waved my hands to emphasize that she was way off. "I never was pregnant. I'm also not Mandy, and he's not Ryan. My name is Meg Jennings, and this is Riley O'Shea. Tim and Ellen are our parents."

The Founder broke his silence and his deep voice resonated through the lab. "*You* are the leak! It's all your fault."

"Do you have any idea what you've done?" Shannon asked.

I stood up straighter. "Actually, I'd like to ask what *you've* done lately. As I understand it, your missions involve blowing things up. Eco-terrorism is a serious offense, and I intend to expose your activities."

"We haven't done anything except provide a safe haven for people who are looking for a simpler life," the Founder said.

"You mean when you're not out bombing cellular towers, I assume," I said.

Shannon put her hand on her hip. "I think you've made a tremendous amount of assumptions. And now that loathsome Matt Eskridge has gotten on board, making speeches accusing us of blowing up their towers. We've done no such thing."

The Founder said, "And we never would."

"Then why is everyone out here in a forest in rural Washington?" I asked, and pointed to my mother. "And why did you drag these two from their sabbatical in Alpine Grove out here?"

"We were interested in their research. Tim and Ellen came with us quite willingly," Shannon said.

"We did," Mom said.

I narrowed my eyes at her. "I know, Mom. You've pointed that out before."

Riley glanced at me and said in an overly reasonable tone, "Why were you interested in their research?"

Shannon took the Founder's hand. "We heard about a man living near Alpine Grove who had a problem that sounded similar to Ralston's."

"Do you mean Dean Wolfe?" I asked. "You *know* him?" Riley and I had spent quite a lot of time with Dean, so this was a surprise.

Shannon said, "I have a cousin who works at a restaurant in Alpine Grove, and she gave me Dean's number. I talked to him on the phone and he explained that something had happened to his hearing. He also told me about Ellen and Tim and their expertise, so we invited them here to continue researching the environmental and health effects of radiation."

Riley glanced at me and then at the Founder. "Do you have an issue with your hearing?"

The Founder's shoulders slumped and he nodded. "I hear voices."

"More than just Dwayne's," I said, not entirely facetiously.

"I hear multiple voices, like a running chatter that won't stop. Saying that I'm channeling helps explain my sometimes odd behavior and keeps up appearances. The problem is better when I'm here," the Founder said, gesturing toward the room. "I get some peace here, but when I go to cities I feel like I've lost my mind. We've seen specialists in Seattle, Portland, Los Angeles, and no one can find anything wrong. I've visited doctors, mental-health professionals, and taken dozens of medications."

"The person who started the rumors about us, which I now know is you, thinks the problem is electromagnetic radiation," Shannon said. "We had speculated that it might be technology-related. You say cellular towers are the problem, which led to the rumors about our involvement."

"The part about radiation is true, although it's a little more involved than that," Tim said. "We did some tests, and I think we might have a solution."

Shannon and the Founder both started talking at once and I waved my arms. "Tim can run the test again on you, if you're willing. It will show that we're not making this up. And, um, you might want to sit down."

Tim got his equipment ready and Shannon handed me her necklace. "This crystal is supposed to help me, but I don't know that it does much of anything. Could you hold it for me?"

The stone was warm, and I held it out in front of Riley. "If you're looking for gift ideas, just so you know, I still want one of these."

He smiled. "I'll see what I can do."

Tim said, "Here's what I'd like to do. I'd like to run the test without the device and then again with it attached. Is that okay?"

I nodded and settled into a spot on the floor. With a glance at Riley, I took his hand and silently mouthed, "Uh-oh." He squeezed my hand in solidarity, and I said out loud, "Please breathe."

The last thing I heard was Riley saying, "This is likely to be unpleasant." Then lights flashed, and my head exploded in excruciating pain.

I opened my eyes and found myself cradled in Riley's arms on the floor. He ran his thumb across my cheek. "I breathed, but I don't think you did."

"It was so fast and horrible, I have no idea what I did." I looked around, and Shannon and the Founder were sprawled on the floor looking shell-shocked. Shannon reached out to collect her necklace, which I apparently had dropped.

I offered a watery smile. "I guess it worked."

Tim said, "This was an extremely concentrated example because I isolated and focused the frequency."

"You get the idea though." I stood up and Riley clasped my hand again. "The next test should be a lot better."

Tim fiddled with the devices and then turned around. "Ready when you are."

We all assented, and Tim flipped some switches. I returned to my spot on the floor next to Riley, who raised his eyebrows at me.

The Founder, who was seated on the other side of me, said, "Did you turn it on? Nothing is happening."

"That's the point," I said.

The Founder looked around me at Riley, "Wait, are you the Riley O'Shea who spoke at the MIT symposium a few years ago?"

"I hate public speaking, but they talked me into it," Riley said.

"*MIT* talked you into it?" I said.

He shrugged, "They're really convincing."

The Founder said, "Your presentation was brilliant. You look different now. No wonder I didn't recognize you."

Riley smiled. "I knew I remembered your name from somewhere. You were on a panel about the environmental impacts of emerging technology, as I recall."

It was turning into geek old-home week, and I felt wildly out of place. "Okay, so you believe us now. But I'm not sure I believe you didn't bomb those towers. You had good reason to."

"Even if I did, I cherish all life. People could be hurt unintentionally, and I would never put innocent lives at risk," the Founder said.

Shannon added, "Ral would never hurt anyone. He may have stretched the truth about Dwayne to explain his debilitating issues and retain our followers' attention, but he certainly didn't hurt them or blow anything up."

"Okay, if you guys didn't set all those bombs, who did?" I said.

"That's a very good question," Riley replied.

Chapter 14

Clarification

After the big experiment, I had a hallucination hangover, which, coupled with my confusion about the bombings, made me want to take an extremely long nap. Riley and I walked back to the cottage with Zelda, who seemed equally subdued. Seeing humans suddenly collapse into a heap was probably stressful for her too.

Riley said, "If it wasn't EF doing the bombings, could it be Hector? I mean, Archetypal isn't going to bomb their *own* towers. That doesn't make any sense."

"I guess it's possible, but why would Hector do that? He was working for Archetypal, capturing people like us and even enlisting the likes of Lester, Nick, and Helen to help. We spent so much time avoiding Hector and those losers that we've never talked to him, even after all this time. I guess I can scope out a few of the Kiss fan boards online and see where the Specter of Hector is playing these days."

"If you say we have to go to Los Angeles, I'm never speaking to you again."

I shoved his shoulder. "Yeah, yeah. You've made your position clear on that. I get it. We'll figure something out. I need to check the server email again. Maybe Kenny or one of his buddies can give us a lead, since they're scattered all over the country."

"True."

"But only after I take a nap. I'm exhausted."

Riley smiled. "You nap. I'll check around some of the gamer boards and see if I can find Kenny and Andy hanging around there."

When we reached the cottage, Zelda and I retired to the cot. After I woke up, I was able to face dealing with email again, and I walked out into the living room where Riley was tapping away at my laptop.

He looked up from the screen. "Feel better?"

"Much. How's life in cyberspace?"

"Action-packed. The gamer community in Oakland is going to attend the Specter of Hector show tonight and get some answers."

"You did all that while I was napping?"

"Your fans are pretty hard core. I think these guys are all half in love with you." He stood up and gestured toward the chair. "Read your email."

I clicked and found the list. "You deleted all the spam for me! Now that's *true* love."

He bent to kiss my cheek. "Love to the tune of two hundred and twenty-five pieces of junk mail."

I read a few emails and placed my palm flat on my chest. "These are so sweet. Did you see the one from Craig? He said his girlfriend has been sick, and what I wrote gave them hope."

"I told you. Maybe you're right about the power of the pen."

"The last piece of the puzzle is the bombings. Once we figure that out, I think I need to pull my notes together and create one large, comprehensive article to send out to the press."

"You'd better get busy. That byline in the *Washington Post* awaits."

I spent the rest of the afternoon writing. Riley pulled out the unbelievably nerdy book he'd been reading since I'd met him and promptly fell asleep on the sofa.

Later, Zelda emerged from the office and poked her nose in his face to indicate that it was dinnertime. She wasn't wrong. I was hungry too, so Riley fed the canine and the humans.

Our parents returned, and we had a peaceful evening. My mother was particularly quiet, giving me a little more latitude than usual. She flashed me a number of worried glances when she thought I wasn't looking. I suspect she and Tim knew that Riley and I were still decompressing from our travels, tests, drugs, and other recent stresses.

The next morning after Riley handed me my coffee, we got online to see if the gamers had anything to report.

Riley logged on while he sipped his coffee. "Meg! You need to see this."

I pulled up a chair so I could see the screen. "Look at all these emails. Wow, we should have enlisted help from these guys a long time ago."

Riley laughed, "No kidding. Think of all the gas we could have saved."

"Here's an email from Kenny. He says that Archetypal didn't pay Hector the money they owed him for capturing people, and he was pissed. The first circus fire was an accident when one of the guys he'd captured ran into the fire-eating dude." I glanced at Riley. "Ouch. That had to hurt."

Riley scrolled down, "This guy says the fire gave Hector the idea to blow up the circus trailers. The animals were already safe, and the circus was going bankrupt. When Archetypal screwed him out of his payment, Hector was broke."

"He went for insurance fraud! Oh Hector, you slime."

"Jeez, look at all of these reports. They all heard what Hector said because he left the microphone on." Riley took a sip of coffee. "Talk about a lot of witnesses. This one says that after bombing his circus, Hector moved on to blowing up Archetypal cell towers, and when you thought it was Enviro Freedom, it was great for him. He could get back at Archetypal, and everyone would blame it on eco-terrorism."

"What a troll." I pointed at another email. "Open this one. I can't believe what incredible interrogators these gamers are. When you take them out of the basement, they get rugged."

"That's for sure. Check this out: There was a riot at the Specter of Hector show, and someone called the police. Hector's in jail."

I leaned forward. "Holy crap. This guy says that because so many people heard him confess to his misdeeds at the concert, Hector told the police too. Leaving the microphone on was a bad mistake. It sounds like Hector confessed to *everything.*"

Riley gestured toward the screen with his mug. "Here's a warning from the system administrator. There was so much email and traffic late last night that it brought the server to its knees. They want to charge more money for the spike in usage."

"You can afford it." I pointed at the screen. "Wait, what about the toy factory? Did Hector bomb that too?"

Riley scanned through some more emails. "Here's one that mentions it. I guess that's one of the things Hector blabbed about to the police. It makes sense that Hector did it. I'm not sure anyone else knew where the holding facility was located."

"Where did the people being held at the factory go?"

"It doesn't say. I'm sure the police will investigate. Apparently, Hector said he was 'making a statement' to Archetypal by blowing up the factory."

"The moral of that story is don't rip off a whacko who has a failing family circus. Archetypal is so screwed."

Riley put his arm around me. "I think you have everything you need for your story now."

I kissed his cheek, then reached out my arms and splayed my fingers. "Okay, all you swanky big-city newspaper editors, get ready for one heck of a story. I want my byline!"

Chapter 15

Epilogue

A few weeks later, I was sitting at the kitchen table in my mother's house in Alpine Grove, riffling through a stack of papers.

Riley sat down next to me. "Are you going to do it?"

"It still strikes me as odd that they want a book when most of the story is already online."

"As you pointed out, until recently, no one except for a bunch of gamers and your evil ex-boyfriend read what you wrote."

I flipped through the pages. "Yeah, but I didn't put anything personal in the articles, and they want the whole saga. That includes you, you know."

"I was there."

"You played an integral part." I leaned down to stroke the fur between Zelda's ears. "You too, Zee."

"What did the intellectual-property lawyer say?"

"She thinks the contract is fair, although she's negotiating for a bigger advance." I shook my head. "I've never written a book before."

"You're a journalist, Meg. I've seen you write anywhere, anytime."

"Are you sure you're okay with letting me divulge all your ugly secrets?"

"Only if you let me read the draft." He took my hand. "And let me take you on vacation first."

"Being here has been like a vacation!" I stroked the table. "Except that Mom's table is with me on vacation. I feel so much better knowing that Helen is the one who took the table and the photograph. She knew I'd find the business card in the frame and try to find Lars. We were lucky she didn't catch me again or track down Lars and his son."

"Disguising herself as a man was sneaky."

"She sure hated Lars, and I don't think that the kid who helped move the table was the sharpest tool in the shed."

"Don't mess with a woman scorned."

"That woman was pure evil. If she tucked her hair under a hat and wore baggy clothes, it wouldn't be too hard for her to pass for a guy. Now she's probably making new friends in jail." I grinned, "But finding out Matt was indicted along with Alan Conway is even better. Even though the people the two of them captured are okay, the Archetypal board of directors wasn't too keen on their activities. If those two ever get out of the pokey, they might have some trouble finding a job."

"Law enforcement and prospective employers tend to frown on kidnapping and attempted murder, no matter how rich you may be."

"At least the company has agreed to retrofit the towers."

"Yeah, although it sounds like you still get to see colors forever. If the doctor is right, the radiation penetrated the blood-brain barrier, so we're permanently altered."

"It's not all bad. You'll remain the best cook in the known universe. And your ability to sniff hormones benefits me in sexy ways too numerous to mention."

Riley laughed. "I suppose so."

"Have you heard from your dad?"

"Yeah, he and the Founder are buddies now, so I think I've been replaced. Some of the gamer dudes have arrived at the retreat to learn more about how to adapt to living with their sensory problems."

"It's like a dream come true for my mother. Research subjects walking right up and saying 'pick me!' She's probably in heaven."

Riley clasped my hand in both of his. "Getting back to the vacation, there's a remote island I found that I think you ought to see."

"I always thought you were kidding about the island."

"You mean you don't want to stroll along white sand beaches and lie around drinking mai tais?"

"When do we leave?" I looked down at Zelda's muzzle on my thigh. "Sorry Zee, but we can't drive to an island. I heard there's a dog-boarding kennel somewhere near Alpine Grove though."

"I've got a pilot's license, remember? Zelda can go with us."

I laughed. "So you're saying you want to fly off into the sunset?"

"We have our whole lives in front of us, Meg, and I'm ready to get started. I'm not worried about the future anymore. Life is short, and I want to spend it with you."

"I'm not anxious about what happens next either. Little did I know when you drove up to this house that I'd be meeting the person I'd want to spend my life with."

Riley pulled my hand to his lips and kissed my knuckles. "Here's to lots more adventures, together."

Thanks for Reading

Thank you for dedicating some of your reading time to *Sensing Truth*. I hope you enjoyed Meg, Riley, and Zelda's adventures. If you would like to be notified by e-mail when I release a new book, you can sign up for my New Releases e-mail list at SusanDaffron.com.

I know that not everyone likes to write book reviews, but if you are willing write a sentence or two about what you thought of *Sensing Truth*, I encourage you to post a review at your favorite book vendor site or share a message with your social networking friends.

If you would like to share your thoughts about the book with me privately, you can reach me through the contact page on the SusanDaffron.com web site.

I look forward to hearing from you!

~ Susan C. Daffron

Acknowledgements

Writing a novel is never easy and I'd like to thank my husband James Byrd for his support and encouragement throughout the publishing process.

I'd also like to thank my alpha and beta readers for their eagle-eyed reading and great feedback. I couldn't do it without you!

About the Author

Susan Daffron is the author of the Jennings & O'Shea series and the Alpine Grove romantic comedies, a series of novels that feature residents of the small town of Alpine Grove and their various quirky dogs and cats. She is also an award-winning author of many nonfiction books, including several about pets and animal rescue. She lives in a small town in northern Idaho and shares her life with her husband and three really cute dogs.

www.ingramcontent.com/pod-product-compliance
Lightning Source LLC
Chambersburg PA
CBHW020334120726
47904CB00002B/417